The True Ruler

WORLDS APART SERIES: BOOK FIVE

Evelyn Lederman

Cover Design by Fiona Jayde Media
Interior Design by The Deliberate Page
Editing by Tina's Editing Services and Lori Garside Editing

Titles by Evelyn Lederman

Worlds Apart Series

The Chameleon Soul Mate: Book One
The Crystal Telepath: Book Two
The Warrior Woman: Book Three
The Mind Control Telepath: Book Four
The True Ruler: Book Five

Nightshade Saga

Nightshade: Book One
Feral Nightshade: Book Two
Lethal Nightshade: Book Three

Magic New Mexico Kindle World

A Touch of Patience (Novella)

Zaratan Trilogy (YA Sci-Fi Adventure)

Selected: Book One

Once again I dedicate one of my books to my father, Ralph Lederman.

My father taught me many things, including the importance of finishing what I started. When I began the Worlds Apart series, I had a starry-eyed intention of finishing all five books. Since 'The Chameleon Soul Mate' was the first book I ever wrote, that was a significant commitment I made to myself. His teaching and the wonderful readers I met along the way made 'The True Ruler' a reality.

When Cassie calls her father 'Daddy', I channeled myself calling my dad that same name. A day does not go by that my father does not enter my thoughts. He has been gone thirty years, but he still has a major impact on my life.

Chapter 1

THE TROYK PENAL COLONY WORLD

Cassie Jarlyn scoured the lakeshore for flat stones she could skip across the water. Darden kept telling her it was all in the wrist. She hated the inane games he invented to distract her from what she really wanted. Sex.

The water was calm compared to what brewed inside her. Since entering this parallel dimension, she felt like one festering wound opened after another. She could not control the men in her life.

"How is this one?" her friend Beatrice asked.

The girl was from the Nightshade universe. A parallel dimension populated by vampires. The blonde sixteen-year-old had escaped a breeding farm with her sister Miranda. For some inexplicable reason, Miranda chose to stay in the Nightshade universe. Taking care of Beatrice became Cassie's recent mission in life.

"It's perfect," Cassie responded. She praised the girl as often as possible. It was important to build her self-esteem, something sorely lacking.

Cassie knew firsthand how self-confidence could erode based on one's surroundings. She was a mind control telepath who grew up in a non-telepathic world. Her father Benko Jarlyn was a political refugee after failing to overthrow the Troyk government led by his father. It was not a stretch to believe her dad would have been happier if she had not inherited his gifts.

"And what is the purpose of skipping stones?" Beatrice asked.

"I have no idea," Cassie mumbled to herself, loud enough for Beatrice to hear. "It's Darden's way of distracting me from what's important."

"And what's important?" the quizzical teenager parroted Cassie's words.

Cassie was not discussing her sex life, or the lack there of, with a sixteen-year-old. Especially one petrified of men. They had finally gotten to a point where Beatrice didn't flinch when Darden approached.

"We should get back to camp before Chartail comes after us," Cassie said. Using her father's soul mate as a diversion seemed the easiest way to escape a discussion she felt ill-prepared to have with Beatrice.

"Yes, we would not want the evil stepmother to complain to your father," Beatrice replied.

Cassie winced at the reference. She told Beatrice as many fairy-tales as she could remember when the girl first arrived. It was Cassie who first brought up the comparison. To be fair, she was no Cinderella. Chartail was the one who worked from sunup to sundown, even while pregnant.

They walked to camp and were immediately set upon by Chartail. Cassie did not miss the sideways glance Beatrice shot her once the teen saw the topic of their conversation. She knew the young girl was trying not to break into laughter. That reaction would only further aggravate her father's soul mate.

Cassie had to admit her instant dislike for Chartail Adholm was due to the other woman's beauty and the position she held in her father's life. For as long as she could remember, it had just been Cassie and her dad. Now, he had Chartail and eagerly awaited the birth of a son.

The tall blonde was stunning with her perfect complexion and china blue eyes. She always wore outfits that accentuated her full breasts. How she managed to scrape up the alluring clothing in a penal world was beyond Cassie's comprehension. Cassie's own negative body image only helped to fuel her initial loathing of the other woman. The more Chartail pushed their relationship, the further Cassie pulled away.

"How come you girls steal away every time there is work to do?" Chartail asked.

Cassie found it amusing that her father's soul mate instigated a plot to kill *his* father. She was ultimately sentenced to the penal colony world because of her failed attempt to assassinate the Prime Ruler of the Troyk universe. Due to the ramifications of that experience, Chartail felt hard work was the best means to help Beatrice recover from her own trauma.

"I'm sorry, Chartail," Cassie answered. "We were looking for stones for my next match with Darden. I need to have a better showing since I represent all womankind."

If the widening of Chartail's eyes was any indication, Cassie had surprised Chartail with her response. She was trying to be nicer, not the spoiled brat Cassie generally presented to the world. She had even embarrassed herself with some of her behavior toward her father's mate. The juvenile antics she was guilty of was beyond what one should expect from an eighteen-year-old woman.

Before Chartail could react, a portal opened and two women entered the penal colony world. They were immediately followed by their soul mates. Without hesitation, Cassie ran into the tall blonde's arms and embraced her. Her old friend, Shirl, was a regular visitor to the world with her soul mate Starc. The crystal telepath was not scheduled for a visit today.

Shirl's beauty could easily rival Chartail's. They had the same shade of blond hair, a honey-golden yellow rather than a white hue. Their eyes were both blue, but Shirl's were closer to a blue-gray. The big difference between them was that Shirl never seemed to realize how attractive she truly was, nor did she use her looks to get what she wanted.

Starc was Darden's fraternal twin, but there was only a slight resemblance between the two brothers. Shirl never traveled through portals without Starc providing her companionship and additional power. Something had happened on one of Shirl's portal trips the crystal telepath had yet to share with Cassie. She did not want to press her friend for the particulars. Shirl would share what occurred when she was ready. Cassie knew she was still troubled by whatever happened.

Cassie lifted the aquamarine that hung around the crystal telepath's neck. She'd given the necklace to Shirl for her birthday years ago. "You still have it."

"It's one of my prized possessions," Shirl responded. "Your gifts always made my birthday special. I always looked forward to what crystal I would be adding to my collection."

The other woman who arrived with Shirl was JoAnna Carlson. Like Cassie, she was a mind control telepath. Unlike Cassie, twenty-three-year-old JoAnna had mated with her soul mate Koel and started the evolutionary process enhancing her telepathic abilities.

JoAnna was stunning. She wore her long black hair loose and it shimmered in the sun. Shirl was a little taller than JoAnna, but the mind control telepath's regal bearing made her appear taller. Confidence in herself and her abilities seeped from her. Rather than wearing the usual tunic and leggings the Troyk people wore, JoAnna had on a short skirt and a beautiful fuchsia top. She could have stepped off the cover of Vogue.

"What has happened?" her father asked. Cassie's father and Darden had to hide when other crystal telepaths arrived in case they were accompanied by Chartail's father, Prime Adholm, and members of his security force. Benko was a wanted man, so was Darden by his absence from his duties to the Prime Ruler.

Benko left working on the construction of additional housing when he saw the party arrive. Her dad always seemed to have one eye on the area containing the inter-dimensional gateway. They were safer here than on Earth, but her dad never let down his guard.

"Somehow, your father knows Cassie Clark is his granddaughter and is demanding to see her," JoAnna relayed. On Earth, Gingko Terra, they were known as Ben and Cassandra Clark. "He is becoming unstable, abusing the power of crystals. Shirl, Candy, and I may be in danger. His warped mind may use us as a means to get his granddaughter into the Troyk universe. Fortunately, he doesn't know who Alex really is. She is safe for the time being."

"Where is Candy?" Benko asked

"Off world collecting crystals," Shirl answered.

The Warrior Woman of legend would go on missions when not guarding Shirl. Very few people knew of Candy's additional gifts made possible once she mated Tolfer. Cassie wished her father had taught her how to physically defend herself rather than focusing solely on telepathic defenses.

"I should join my grandfather in the Troyk universe," Cassie said.

As expected, her declaration was met with shocked silence. Cassie had kept quiet too long. She was no longer going to hide who and what she was. It was time she started to live up to her future destiny.

"It is too dangerous," Chartail cried. "You are an innocent and Jeryl Jarlyn is a monster."

Cassie had not expected Chartail to be the first to voice her opposition. She was dumbfounded when Chartail ran to her, taking Cassie into her arms. Pregnancy must have stimulated her maternal instincts.

"Chartail is right," Benko added. "My father is a dangerous man. He will not hesitate to manipulate you or your powers for personal gain. JoAnna has witnessed firsthand his growing madness because he is abusing the power of crystals."

Cassie was not sure how crystals could be used to enhance telepathic powers, but she did not doubt what JoAnna and Shirl had shared. Her father had once tried to teach her how to use them to enhance her abilities if she was attacked.

Both women were suspiciously quiet. Each of them had returned to the universe of their birth and faced her grandfather. It was their counsel she most sought.

"What do you two think?" Cassie asked.

The two women exchanged glances, daring the other to answer first. From what Cassie witnessed watching the two, Shirl generally conceded and always spoke first.

"Although you were not orphaned, you are one of us," Shirl said. "We each returned to the Troyk universe to meet our destinies. It's your time now."

Cassie knew Shirl was right. Her father's world continued to call to her. She somehow knew whoever she ended up being, she was incomplete until she faced her grandfather and evolved her powers. However, she wanted to hear from JoAnna. She was the outsider who left the orphanage by using her abilities to get adopted. JoAnna shared the gift of telepathic mind control. Ironically, she was also Chartail's cousin.

"You cannot evolve into what you will one day be without learning to use the powers you currently possess," JoAnna said. "As I keep telling you, you are ill-prepared for further powers if you cannot control what you are capable of now. I know Benko wishes to protect you, but not teaching you to use and control your telepathic gift was a terrible mistake. With all his faults, Jeryl has taught me a lot. Besides, you won't be alone."

"Before you make any decision," Starc advised, "you should discuss it with Darden."

Starc had not inherited the crystal telepathic gift as his twin Darden had. Now mated with Shirl, he could hear the frequencies in his head and navigate inter-dimensional portals beside his soul mate. He was one of the few beings who knew what Shirl was capable of, but he kept the knowledge hidden.

"If Darden treated me like a soul mate instead of a demonstrative older brother, I would eagerly seek his guidance. Besides, he's off on a quest for my father searching worlds for more dissidents."

Cassie had literally run into her soul mate when she was ten years old. For the next eight years, her father had given Darden a say in how she was raised. Their relationship had evolved over time, but paled in comparison to what her friends had with the men in their lives. Darden was truly like an older brother in his behavior and actions. It was not the type of relationship she had longed for.

"Cassie, that is not fair," her father said. "He has spent years respecting your age."

She was tired of being treated like a child. Sure, she spent most of her time acting like one, but things had to change. Suddenly, she viewed journeying to the Troyk universe as a new beginning. Maybe some distance between her and Darden was a good idea.

Cassie had been thrilled when Darden came to take her to the penal colony. She thought they would finally take their relationship to the next level. Instead, she was housed with older women who monitored every breath she took. Originally, she thought it would be fun to sneak away with Darden, but he would have none of it. His rejection only fueled her immature behavior.

"Maybe it's not a bad idea to have someone in the enemy camp," Cassie said. "If I am in any danger, Shirl can whisk me away through a portal. If Grandfather has me, he may call off the relentless search for you. It's only a matter of time before he figures out where you are and then the whole settlement is in jeopardy. Haven't these people suffered enough?"

Her father was at least considering her argument. It was a good sign he would not immediately say no. From Chartail's body language, she must have been arguing telepathically with her father through their soul mate channel.

"It is out of the question," her father finally said. "JoAnna is right about one thing. You need to be trained how to use and control your gift. I did you a disservice in not properly training you."

Cassie took in her father's words. She knew his intentions were good, but he would unconsciously hold back teaching her about the darker aspects of her telepathic powers. Nature had a balance for everything in creation. The people in this settlement would not have fought the mind control government if there were not aspects of the gift that could be manipulated.

She reached into the telepathic channel opened in the orphanage all those years ago. Cassie often heard the girls conversing in the link and pretended not to hear what was being shared.

"Can my grandfather be trusted to safeguard me or has his abuse of the crystals made him untrustworthy?"

Both Shirl and JoAnna tried to hide their surprise at Cassie's telepathic question in a pathway they were unaware she had access to. Their reaction would easily be misinterpreted to be in response to her father's words, although Cassie knew better. Fortunately, Chartail who also had access to the channel, remained quiet.

"Your grandfather feels threatened by my abilities," JoAnna replied through their closed channel. *"Maybe if he focuses on you, he will feel more confident in his own abilities and reduce enhancing his own gift with the power generated from the crystals. It may also buy your father more time to hone his plans to take over the government."*

"I have not shared anything about our relationship with Jeryl," Shirl said. *"We can exaggerate our closeness while you were growing up. It would not be unreasonable for Benko to have found ways for his daughter to interact with the orphaned children of his followers. The Prime Ruler does not know what I am capable of. He will not dare separate us."*

Cassie was frustrated at yet another tease about Shirl's unknown telepathic capabilities. She hoped her relationship with her old friend would continue to grow until Shirl was comfortable enough to share her secrets. Although, to be honest, Cassie had secrets of her own.

"I will be returning to the Troyk universe with Shirl and JoAnna," Cassie announced.

Cassie had weighed her options. Beatrice had been adopted by a family who had recently lost their daughter. Her new friend would be taken care of in her absence. This dimension frowned on the use of telepathic powers. If she was going to learn what she was capable of, Cassie needed to enter the Troyk universe.

She raised her left hand to forestall any objections from either her father or Chartail. There was no one she respected more than her dad, but Cassie was now an adult and needed to step out of his shadow. She was scared to death, but knew she had to take this next step. It was time she started down a new path and embrace, rather than run, from her destiny.

Chapter 2

THE TROYK UNIVERSE

The one inter-dimensional gateway outside Aster Province, the gem of the Troyk universe, was constantly monitored for unplanned activity. Anything foreign, regardless of size, was investigated by the Crystal Telepathic Guards. Shirl and her companions had entered the Troyk penal colony world from a portal Shirl had opened from the home of Zane and Leenea Childers. The female crystal telepath did not need a natural portal and created her own gateways.

Cassie had heard stories about the Troyk universe for as long as she could remember. However, seeing the purple sky and the city of stone below took her breath away. They were probably twelve hundred feet from the valley, and the vista was amazing. This was the world of her parents and her future home. A sense of belonging embraced her like nothing she had ever experienced. Tears welled in her eyes, but were not shed.

She knew armed C.T. Guards would meet them as they made their way down the mountain trail. However, it still alarmed her when weapons were raised at her party when they were halfway down the path. Phaser-like weapons were holstered as soon as members of her party were recognized. Cassie witnessed the relief wash over the two men's faces. She thought it must be a difficult job investigating an unexpected opening of the portal.

"Why the unscheduled trip, Shirl?" one of the guards inquired.

He was Darden's height, but was bulkier than her soul mate. She figured other women would find the guard's dark brown, wavy hair and light brown eyes attractive, but he paled in comparison to her soul mate. Starc moved past Cassie and stood beside Shirl, not liking the way the guard's eyes were caressing the crystal telepath's body. His positioning also hid Cassie from the guards' sight for the time being.

Before they left the penal colony, the small party concocted a story to explain why Shirl left through a portal she created, but returned through the naturally occurring gateway. It appeared Shirl told more lies than truths since she started living in the Troyk universe. Lying seemed to become second nature to her.

"I knew the Prime Ruler wanted to meet his granddaughter," Shirl admitted. "As soon as she was identified, I knew where to find Cassandra. However, I did not want to advertise I was bringing her home and disappoint Jeryl Jarlyn in case I returned empty handed."

Her traveling companions shifted slightly on the narrow path, allowing the C.T. Guards to see Cassie clearly. She wondered what they thought as their expressions changed. Cassie knew she needed to get used to being the center of attention. When the guards first arrived, they only had eyes for the exquisite Shirl.

The guard who initially spoke to Shirl approached, apprehension on his face. "Are you feeling all right, Cassandra?"

Cassie felt great, but wondered if there was something wrong with her outer appearance that led to the question. She turned to Shirl in a panic. Her old friend was the one most likely to level with her.

"You look fine, Cassie," Shirl assured her. "Barash was one of three guards who found me when I first exited the gateway. I did not know how to navigate the portal and had a brutally rough ride. By the time they found me, I was bleeding from my nose, ears, and eyes. I was a bloody mess. Candy also had a reaction during her first inter-dimensional trip, but JoAnna did not. Since you are a mind control telepath, like JoAnna, I think your brain has an inherent ability to withstand the forces within the wormhole or whatever the portal is."

What Shirl shared made sense. Cassie had suffered no ill effects after her first portal ride when she arrived in the penal world. As far as the guards knew this was her maiden journey and she wanted to keep it that way.

"Well, I, for one, am thrilled I will not have to carry you down the mountain trail," Barash added. "Although it would have been an honor to assist such a beautiful woman."

Cassie couldn't help the blush that now graced her cheeks. It was obvious his comment had to do more with her appearance than the fact she was Jeryl Jarlyn's granddaughter. She watched as Barash consumed her with his eyes. Darden never looked at her with the same hunger Barash's stare contained.

"Down boy," Starc said. Her soul mate's twin brother obviously did not like the way Barash looked at her. "The Prime Ruler will be anxious to meet his granddaughter."

The second guard had not uttered a word. Truly non-descript, everything about him was average. Medium brown hair, average height, and no distinguishing characteristics about his face made him utterly forgettable. No one introduced him and the guard did not bother to correct the oversight.

Starc grabbed Cassie's hand and started down the trail, leaving the love-struck C.T. Guard behind. After weeks of being ignored by Darden, Cassie enjoyed the bit of harmless fun at the man's expense. Besides, it held off the inevitable meeting with her grandfather.

It was not long before they were in the valley and at the outskirts of Aster Province. The stone buildings she saw from the trail were not as purple as they appeared from a distance, nor was the air. Cassie would have liked more time to explore her new surroundings, but Starc set a rapid pace.

The streets were crowded with people all dressed in colorful tunics and leggings. She stood out, wearing a pair of jeans and a T-shirt, but no one seemed to notice she was different.

Numerous telepathic conversations assaulted her mind, but she was able to quiet down the chatter. What little time she spent in the penal colony had trained her how to reduce the volume of the noise in her head. Although there was more telepathic activity than she was used to, it did not negatively affect her ability to control the myriad of links she was connected to.

Her eyes soaked in the storefronts and street vendors selling their wares. Purple trees, shrubs, and flowers were in full bloom. They passed a large park with children playing and restaurants flanking the green lawns. This place was something out of a dream.

There was no pollution in the air. Troyk's citizens walked everywhere and environment friendly trams connected the cities within this dimension. She was surprised electric cars had not been introduced. The Troyk people leveraged technology from other worlds they believed would enhance their standard of living.

Cassie pulled back on Starc's grip when a massive building came into sight. Crystals were embedded into the marble and the structure sparkled as the sun's rays bounced off the stones. It was absolutely gorgeous.

"That's the Aster Province's palace," JoAnna informed her. "I stopped and stared the first time I saw it, too. People from other provinces travel here just to see it."

"Wait until you see inside The Palace," Shirl said. "The place is amazing."

JoAnna swatted at Starc's hand and he released his vice-like grip on Cassie. His hand was immediately replaced with JoAnna's. Cassie had not met JoAnna until she intercepted a phone call meant for her father. Since arriving in the penal world, JoAnna visited her and Chartail often. Sharing the same telepathic gift brought them together. They were both fifth-generation mind control telepaths.

"We will return to Crystal Telepathic Headquarters," Barash said.

Barash gave Cassie one last heated look before he and his silent partner strode away. Cassie imagined she'd see Barash again and his interest would die as soon as Darden eventually returned to the Troyk universe.

Before they headed into The Palace, Cassie hazarded a glance in Barash's direction. At that very instant, his silent partner turned his head in her direction and nodded once before continuing on his way. Cassie was not sure what to make of the silent communication. She did not have time to consider his actions, it was time to meet her grandfather.

They entered The Palace through the front entrance with the rest of the tourists. Everywhere she looked were paintings, sculptures, and crystals on display. A magnificent marble staircase dominated the space.

Considering the number of people present, the hall was relatively quiet. It was not surprising since the Troyk were telepathic people.

Only conversations people did not want to share in the communal pathways were expressed aloud. Family members were able to communicate through their familial links.

"The Prime Council is in session on the second floor," Starc shared. "Prime offices and the province's government are housed on the third floor. Your grandfather lives on the fourth."

With JoAnna still holding her hand, they started to ascend the stairs. Koel situated himself on her other side. Cassie imagined JoAnna requested her soul mate journey next to her via their soul mate channel. How she wished Darden were here.

When they reached the top floor, Shirl skirted around them and talked to one of the guards on duty. The man Shirl addressed looked surprised, directing his attention to Cassie and then walked down a long hallway. It did not take a rocket scientist to figure out he was heading to see Jeryl Jarlyn.

"We are to wait for the Prime Ruler in his greeting room," Shirl informed them when she rejoined the group. "I don't think it will be long before Jeryl joins us."

Cassie and JoAnna dutifully followed Shirl with Starc and Koel lagging behind. They entered a comfortable looking room with numerous crystals on display. Shirl stopped to examine the stones while JoAnna and Cassie headed to the seating area. Crystals were like catnip to her old friend.

She sat on a chair rather than one of the enormous sofas. For some reason, Cassie did not want to be physically close to her grandfather. At this point, she wanted her own space. Without having to mention anything, her friends sat near Cassie, which would force her grandfather to ultimately sit across the table from her when he joined them.

Two older men entered the room. Cassie did not immediately know which was her grandfather. She once asked her father which of his parents he resembled. Benko told her he looked like his mother. He had never known the woman who had given birth to him, but assumed he took after her. Jeryl Jarlyn had taken his mistress's son and dismissed her from their lives.

JoAnna rose and embraced the heavier of the two men. "Hello, Uncle," her friend said. It was clear that Chartail took after her mother. Cassie did not see any resemblance between this man and her father's soul mate.

From a process of elimination, Cassie knew the other man was her grandfather. He was tall and looked to be amazingly fit for a man in his mid-sixties. She was paralyzed in her chair, unable to move. Jeryl Jarlyn seemed as affected as she was.

Jeryl Jarlyn's nose was covered with gin blossoms. She never knew what those red blotches were called until a rock band named their group after the skin condition. Cassie imagined they were caused by her grandfather's abuse of crystals, not alcohol.

Her grandfather stood staring at her. It seemed like an eternity before he finally spoke. "You look like your grandmother," her grandfather said. "I would have known you, even if they had not told me you were here. Come here and give me a hug."

Cassie somehow made it to her feet and mechanically walked to her grandfather. Her legs shook as she made the short journey around the table. When she saw the tears in her grandfather's eyes, Cassie's heart warmed. This man had been devastated when his son betrayed him and escaped from this world.

"Grandfather," Cassie said as Jeryl Jarlyn embraced her. She struggled to hold back her own tears.

For nearly Cassie's whole life, it had just been her and her dad. Even when Darden entered their world, it was primarily still the two of them since Darden was rarely around. Now that her grandfather was holding her, Cassie was surprised by the overwhelming emotions threatening to pull her under.

"I'm sorry for the tears," Cassie said. "I feel so stupid not being able to stop crying. Only babies cry and you must be disappointed." She imagined her speech was garbled by the rate she spoke and the sobs fighting to escape.

"My beautiful girl," her grandfather said, "nothing could be further from the truth."

He cradled her head and kissed her wet cheeks. Love she was not expecting to feel for this man engulfed her. Jeryl Jarlyn was the enemy, after all.

The reunion was interrupted when a small army of servants paraded in with a tea service, mountains of sandwiches, and delectable pastries. Serving food must be customary when the Prime Ruler entertained guests.

"My favorite part," she heard JoAnna mutter. Cassie turned to see her friend bite into a pastry. JoAnna held up half of the treat she had not yet consumed. "Try one of these. It has a sweet, nutty flavor."

Cassie could not remember the last time she had eaten, but all of a sudden realized she was famished. Her traitorous stomach confirmed her hunger when it growled loudly. She hoped the others in the room had not heard the rumble.

"Let us sit and have something to eat, child," her grandfather said.

Instead of returning to her chair, Cassie joined her grandfather on one of the sofas. JoAnna was gleefully enjoying her second pastry. The poised, beautiful ebony-haired woman had quite a metabolism considering how slim she was. Cassie always struggled with her weight and the new delectables in front of her would go straight to her hips. She could already hear her fat cells crying out with joy.

She closely examined the sandwiches and selected what she believed was minced chicken salad on some kind of dark bread. Cassie bit into the sandwich and tried not to moan. Flavor exploded in her mouth, quickly slaking her hunger. Between the taste of tarragon and the tender chicken, she was delighted with her choice.

Cassie noticed her grandfather staring at her. "That was your father's favorite. I adored that boy. Nothing will ever hurt more than his betrayal."

Unwarranted guilt choked Cassie, making it difficult for her to swallow her third mouthful of food and she struggled to not cough it up.

How was she to respond to her grandfather? No force in existence would ever cause her to tell her grandfather where he could find his son. Before she ever stepped foot in the Troyk universe, Cassie knew her grandfather would ultimately request that information. As Jeryl knew the existence of Cassandra Clark, she was certain he knew Ben Clark still lived.

"Daddy always made his famous chicken salad on pumpernickel bread," Cassie said intentionally referring to the past. "Whenever I had friends over for lunch or dinner, they always demanded his chicken salad. Every block party we attended, Daddy was assigned chicken salad sandwiches rather than allowing him to select what he wanted to bring."

"All these years, he kept you from me," Jeryl complained. It was not hard to miss the anger in his voice.

Feeling this inquiry was safe, Cassie responded to her grandfather's statement. "By the time I came along, they lost their crystal telepath, Shirl's mom. They were stranded, and one by one, he lost all his friends. The chlorofluorocarbons in Earth's air caused the adult telepathic brain to disintegrate in their mid-twenties. It was only his mind control telepathic brain chemistry that saved him from the same fate as his followers."

"Ben brought Cassie to the orphanage to play with me and Candy," Shirl said. She noticed Shirl had referred to her father using his Earth name. "I had no idea Cassie Clark was your granddaughter when we first met. She was just a friend who gave me a new crystal every year for my birthday."

Shirl held up the aquamarine gem Cassie had given her all those years ago. Purchased on the trip to Sedona that would forever change her life because it brought her Darden. Fortunately, her grandfather did not react badly to Shirl's news.

Cassie took a cautious bite of her sandwich, hoping the lump in her throat was gone. She relaxed when she swallowed with ease. Her grandfather poured her a cup of hot tea. After several cooling blows across the cup's rim, she took a sip.

"I have a lovely room all ready for you," her grandfather said. "You cannot imagine how long I have been waiting for a member of my family to occupy it."

Shirl and JoAnna shared a look. The blonde had once again lost the battle of who would speak up. Shirl knew Cassie when they were children, so it would be more realistic for the crystal telepath to suggest where Cassie should reside.

"Jeryl," Shirl said, "we thought Cassie could stay with the Childers."

Before Shirl could continue her argument, Jeryl Jarlyn spoke up. "I am her family. Cassie will stay with me."

"Your granddaughter complained about having a headache shortly after she arrived," JoAnna lied. "You are such a busy man with a government to run and Leenea has all the time in the world to pamper Cassie. Besides, Candy and Tolfer also live there. I understand Candy and Cassie are childhood friends. Tolfer also has the ability to teach Cassie how to manage the communal telepathic pathways. She is a young woman and needs to be with other people her own age to properly assimilate into this world."

In response to JoAnna's compelling argument, Cassie saw her grandfather struggle to come up with counterarguments. Jeryl's glance bounced between Shirl and JoAnna. If Cassie was not mistaken, she saw glimpses of fear in Jeryl's gaze from time to time. She knew they were home free when the Prime Ruler sighed in exasperation.

"Fine," her grandfather acquiesced, "but Cassie will spend her afternoons with me as, well as dinners. There are a number of state functions she will attend as my hostess. She must take her rightful place in Troyk society. I will make sure one of our finest designers is here tomorrow afternoon to see to her outfits. Eventually, Cassandra, I want you living with me."

Cassie had to suppress the laughter that arose when she noticed her grandfather's distaste at her clothing. He no longer saw his granddaughter, but the young woman who would soon represent the future of the Troyk government. She was surprised he had not asked her about what telepathic gifts she possessed.

"We should head out and help prepare dinner," Shirl said. "Leenea is a warm, loving person, but an atrocious cook. Thank goodness Tolfer is in residence. Besides his talent for teaching children how to manage their telepathic gifts, he is an outstanding chef."

Cassie rose and was once again in her grandfather's embrace. "Make sure you bring my granddaughter back after the mid-day meal. I have many questions that must be answered."

She had an evening for the group to come up with believable answers to questions she was certain her grandfather would ask. There were so many stories provided to Jeryl Jarlyn with Shirl, Candy, and JoAnna's arrivals. Cassie was not sure which questions she was dreading more: the ones about her father or those about her mind control telepathic powers.

Unlike the trip to The Palace, their walk to the Childers's residence was made at a leisurely pace. The park they had passed earlier was called a gathering place. It was where Troyk citizens, young and old, came to socialize. Her friends were already hatching plans to get her excused from official dinners in order for Cassie and Darden to join the couples and enjoy the second seating at a number of the restaurants. She was not sure what a second seating involved, but she was game.

Things would change once Darden arrived. Cassie imagined her soul mate would be furious when he returned to the Troyk penal colony to find her gone. For far too long, Darden had heeded her father's concerns about the additional powers Cassie would develop when they finally made love. Darden's caving to her father's wishes and not her inherent goodness to control her abilities had driven a wedge between them. If she were honest, Cassie made the decision to come to the Troyk universe partly to spite her soul mate. She knew it was juvenile to think that way, but she was hurt and needed to lash out.

Cassie was startled back to reality when she found herself in front of a wooden door and Koel knocking on it. Lost in her own thoughts, she had not realized they had arrived at their destination. The door suddenly opened and a tall, handsome older woman stood before her.

Leenea Childers brought Cassie into her arms, welcoming her. "Finally, the last of the girls is finally home. Come in. I know another of your friends has been anxious to see you once news of your arrival started to seep through the communal channels."

Cassie followed Leenea into a giant room dominated by a huge dining table and a large sitting area with numerous sofas and chairs. If possible, the space was larger than her grandfather's greeting room. Everything in the room from the colors to the furnishings emitted a welcoming ambiance.

A woman with light auburn hair sat on one of the sofas with her back turned to her. She was talking with two men, both with hair as black as coal but one's was longer. Aware they had company, the woman and the man with the short black hair turned in Cassie's direction. Cassie stared into the green eyes of Alexandra Mann.

Although Cassie tried not to have favorites between the girls at the orphanage, Alex was always like a sister in the early years. Cassie had begged her father to adopt Alex so they could be true sisters. Benko felt the girls were safer where they were and the visits ceased for their safety.

Alex maneuvered out of the man's embrace and headed toward Cassie with tears in her eyes. "I'm so glad to see you again, Cassie," Alex cried. "I just can't believe you left the safety of the Troyk penal colony."

Cassie was not sure how to answer her old friend. Perhaps if they were alone she would have confided in Alex, but they were in a room full of people.

Somehow Alex must have sensed her discomfort because she continued talking, filling what might otherwise have been an awkward silence.

"Candy will be back shortly from wherever she was sent," Alex said. "Then we'll all be back together again. I know your father must have had his reasons for stopping your visits, but I missed seeing you. First we lost JoJo and then you."

Her friends had long since stopped calling JoAnna by her childhood name. Cassie had remembered how upset Alex had been about her absent friend. She knew she would cause her the same pain when her father pulled Cassie from the girls' lives.

"Alex took both your departures badly," Shirl added. "She became more withdrawn and started to blend into the shadows. It was about that time our telepathic channel opened, but we didn't know it at the time. We just started finishing each other's sentences and somehow knew what the other two were thinking."

Alex initially nodded her agreement to what Shirl said, but then got a strange look on her face. Cassie felt like she was under a magnifying glass based on how Alex was studying her. Her friend's expression went from confusion to wonderment in a matter of moments.

"Our pathway opened during one of Cassie's visitations," Alex claimed. The communication came through a channel that had been long dormant in Cassie's brain until earlier that afternoon. The small woman with the light auburn hair used a pathway neither Shirl or JoAnna bothered to try before today.

It would be senseless to deny Alex's words. The girls did not know what had transpired on their first visit together. Cassie knew the pathway opened and that she was responsible. However, she was not ready to divulge the significance of the channel, even if she knew what it was. Her suspicions were negated when Chartail entered their channel when she arrived in the penal world. Cassie later discovered her father's soul mate had entered the channel while she was still in the Troyk universe.

"Dad did not want the three of you to know you had telepathic abilities," Cassie admitted. *"JoAnna had already used her gift to get adopted. There was too much at risk to reveal any more. What you experienced could easily be explained away as three friends who were as close as any family. People would believe you were so devoted to each other you could almost read each other's thoughts."*

"You girls can catch-up later," Leenea said. "Let me show Cassie her room."

Cassie felt guilty she had been communicating telepathically with her friends and left the rest of the people in the room standing around waiting for them to finish. She had not been introduced to the two black haired men. She assumed the older one, built like a linebacker, was Alex's soul mate Tarsea. The other had to be Candy's Tolfer.

Leenea led her down a small hallway. The rest of the group remained in the common room. They entered a small bedroom where several bags sat on the bed. The room was decorated with warm and inviting colors. Several decorative pillows graced the bed. She felt the tension in her shoulders weaken. Cassie had not realized how stressed she was.

"JoAnna was staying here," Leenea informed her. "When she returned from Gingko Terra with Koel they moved into his apartment. So little time has elapsed, she has not been around to pick up her things. When Shirl communicated through the warrior channel they were bringing you here, I quickly collected JoAnna's possessions. I am sure the girls will want to go shopping with you, particularly JoAnna and Shirl."

Leenea did not have to explain to her what the warrior channel was. It was a closed channel for those who were loyal to the True Ruler of the Troyk universe. The telepathic link opened shortly after the soul mate channel opened when she and her father met Darden. Once again, Cassie kept quiet about having access to the pathway.

"Alexandra and Candy do not like shopping?" Cassie asked.

"Sweetheart, you need to call Alexandra either Alex or Alexia," Leenea corrected her. "For the time being, she is posing as a young woman who was raised in the Starling province by her aunt Norrie.

Tarsea and his friends have done a fine job of keeping Alexia from Jeryl Jarlyn's attention. Alexia's cousin Solfa is in charge of the Prime Ruler's intelligence division. It has made things very interesting, particularly since Solfa is one of us."

Cassie had been made aware of all the fictional stories and relationships when she arrived in the penal colony world. It was totally different keeping the narratives straight now that it was critical she did so. One slip and Cassie could endanger her friends.

Chapter 3

THE TROYK PENAL COLONY WORLD

D arden stepped through the portal into the parallel dimension in which he currently resided. He was returning to Cassie and was anxious and excited to see her. She remained unaware of how difficult it was waiting for his soul mate to grow up. The friction that currently existed between them since he took her to the penal colony world was weighing him down. Her face no longer brightened when she saw him as it once had.

He could still remember the electrical shock to his system when he bumped into the little girl. His life had changed that day, as had his allegiances. The most wanted fugitive in the Troyk universe was before him and he selected to protect his soul mate and her father. Cassie had become his world, his reason for living.

They were soul mates, destined to be together. The fear of what she would evolve into had kept him from consummating their relationship. As soon as they made love, their brains would excrete a hormone that would start the evolutionary change of their telepathic abilities. Darden knew how much he hurt Cassie restraining his ever-growing lust for her.

Cassie had been a promising youth. She developed into a beauty beyond his expectations. Darden knew he was biased, but he did not miss the looks other men gave her. She had no clue how extremely attractive she was. Fortunately, Cassie seemed oblivious to the attention she got from other men.

The mission to find Troyk dissidents in other dimensions kept him away from Cassie too long. There was an emptiness in his soul only she could fill. He was now incomplete without her.

His eyes roamed the crowd that came to meet him. The one face he sought was not present. Cassie must be off sulking. His abstinence brought out the worst in her. It would be wrong of him to blame her dark moods on anyone other than himself.

Darden's pulse raced once he saw the look on Chartail's face. The once spoiled beauty had been a pillar of strength and optimism since meeting her soul mate, Benko Jarlyn. Something was terribly wrong.

"What has happened?" Darden asked. "Where is Cassie?"

He held his breath awaiting a response. His mind whirled at all the terrible things that could have occurred to his soul mate. There were still lone insane fugitives who prowled the jungles outside the settlement. Had one of them attacked and harmed his love?

"Cassie is in the Troyk universe," Benko Jarlyn responded. "Shirl and JoAnna came with news that my father discovered that the identities of Ben and Cassandra Clark were a ruse. The girls believed they were in danger now that part of the truth had been exposed. My daughter voluntarily accompanied them back. They spouted some nonsense of her needing to learn to use her telepathic gift in order for her to grow into the woman she was meant to be."

"You did not try to stop her?" Darden asked in a condemning tone. Although they were soul mates, Benko Jarlyn had placed numerous obstacles around their ability to be together. He painted frightening scenarios of what a fifth-generation mind control telepath might be able to do. After watching JoAnna evolve her telepathic powers, Darden was no longer as concerned as Benko.

"Obviously, my daughter no longer heeds my advice," Benko replied. "The girl is now taking her direction from Shirl and JoAnna. I seem to only drive her away."

Darden knew what Benko said was partially true. To be fair, he was as much to blame for Cassie leaving as her father. Their relationship did not give Cassie the foundation to withstand her need to discover for herself who she was. Shirl and JoAnna had matured and become powerful telepathic beings once they left Gingko Terra.

How could his soul mate resist the opportunity? As much as they painted the Troyk universe as being a dangerous temptation, it was also a place her friends had thrived.

"I am going after her," Darden declared.

He walked in the direction he came and stood before the gateway as his telepathic ability and crystal opened the natural portal. Before he stepped into the event horizon, a hand landed on his shoulder. He shifted his head to see Chartail by his side.

"You cannot re-enter the Troyk universe through the mountain pass," Chartail warned him. "As soon as you are detected, C.T. Guards will be dispatched to take you in. Jeryl Jarlyn will blame you for keeping his granddaughter away from him. Upon your arrest, you will be put in a cell, never to be seen again. Crystal telepaths were never sent to the penal colony. No one knows what happened after they were convicted of whatever crime they were supposedly guilty of."

"She is right," Kelog Potts said. The former C.T. Guard probably had accompanied a convicted crystal telepath to whatever fate was determined by the Prime Ruler. "Although no public trial for desertion will be held, Jeryl Jarlyn will see to your quick conviction and sentencing. It is rumored he has his own private facility where people disappear, particularly if their crime was not visible to the population."

"Worse," Chartail continued, "if he discovers you are Cassie's soul mate, the Prime Ruler will force a mating and take control of molding his granddaughter's powers. You would be kept alive solely as leverage so Cassie will be afraid to thwart Jeryl's plans."

"We know my father is capable of such behavior," Benko said "He forced Koel and JoAnna to have sex, while holding Koel's sister hostage. Fortunately, JoAnna was able to control the additional powers she developed and my father slid further into madness."

"Wait until your crystal has enough power to open a portal into the Childers's common room or until Shirl returns to this world," Chartail recommended. "Shirl, JoAnna, and Candy will protect Cassie. Jeryl Jarlyn has been waiting so long for his family to return to the Troyk universe, the last person he will intentionally hurt is his own granddaughter."

Darden considered everything the people around him had to say. There was nothing he wanted more than to be a hero where his soul mate was concerned. He had to admit everything they said was correct. At this point, following Cassie's trail would only put her in harm's way.

He headed for his hut without saying another word. What could he say? His soul mate's life was in the hands of the four women he brought to the Troyk universe. Each had a telepathic gift to help protect Cassie. It never dawned on him that Cassandra Jarlyn could protect herself.

The stone skipped five times across the lake's moonlit surface before it fell into its depths. He kept telling Cassie the proper technique was all in the wrist to properly launch a stone across a body of water. Her impatient nature made her want to master the act immediately.

Darden sat on a nearby boulder and watched the light shimmer across the water. It was a beautiful sight and he wished Cassie were there to share it with him, but an impulsive act temporarily took her away from him.

Cassie was not impulsive. She was frustrated. He knew his soul mate better than she knew herself. He should have seen this coming.

He would be lying to himself if he did not acknowledge he was worried sick for her. Jeryl Jarlyn became more unstable with each passing day. Candy, Shirl, and JoAnna would protect her, but it was of little comfort. It was his responsibility to safeguard his soul mate.

"She will be all right," Benko Jarlyn informed him. The future leader of the Troyk universe stepped off the path leading to the lake and joined him on the large weathered rock. A chill in the air caused the older man to pull his sweater across his chest.

"I should be with her," Darden murmured.

"In a perfect world, you would be," Benko replied. "Your presence would only complicate matters. My father will not harm Cassie. She is what he's waited for his whole life — a fifth-generation mind control telepath. Fortunately, my daughter is too stubborn to be manipulated by him."

Darden could not help but laugh at that comment. Cassie was a true Leo, as she pointed out numerous times. He knew little about Gingko Terra's astrological signs, other than what Cassie shared with him. "Leos are stubborn," she often declared when he commented on her bull doggedness.

"That she is," Darden said. Then he sighed. "But she is defenseless. We should have trained her how to defend herself. I know Candy will look out for her, but she cannot be with her constantly."

Darden turned and looked at Benko, only to note the look of surprise on his face. There was obviously something about Cassie he did not know. He raised his left eyebrow, questioning what Benko was thinking.

"When I realized Cassie had telepathic abilities, I did teach her how to manipulate thoughts in case any of my father's Gatherers found her," Benko admitted. "She was a natural. I never saw anything like it. We practiced on merchants, encouraging them to lower the cost of things we wanted to purchase. No one ever appeared to experience any adverse effects, either. Whenever we trained, I was there to pull her out of the subject's mind if I sensed any issues. We only *talked* about what the differences would be if she was trying to influence a hostile person."

Darden frowned in confusion at the news. Cassie regularly claimed she did not know how to use the abilities she inherited. Now Benko was claiming he had trained his daughter to protect herself telepathically. He knew Benko was holding something back.

"Shortly before we met you," Benko continued, "a Gatherer tried to abduct Cassie from our house when she was alone. I was not sure how he found us. When I got home the man was dead on the floor. His head imploded as a result of telepathic powers. Cassie was hiding in her closet, shell-shocked. It appeared she first tried to hold him off physically. She had a black eye and some bruises. Cassie finally was forced to use her telepathic powers against him."

"She never told me," Darden said. "What did she say happened?"

"Cassie never talks about it," Benko answered. "Although I tried to draw the story out of her, she refused to discuss it. My ten-year-old little girl wanted to pretend it was all a bad dream and I let her. I was not in the position where I could have her seek psychological help. The authorities would have asked too many questions. I kept her home until she healed. We had yet another secret to keep. For months she had nightmares and was unusually moody. I was sure she was suffering from some type of post-traumatic stress."

"When did it stop?" Darden asked.

Benko smiled. "When she met you. I do not believe she ever forgot what happened, but she had something else to concentrate on. You."

Crystal telepaths disappeared from time to time, never returning from a mission. No one would have automatically considered the missing man tangled with Benko Jarlyn and lost. They certainly had not been aware of Cassie's existence. Whoever Cassie killed would have been written off as a result of a bad wormhole or entering a hostile world. Before his first trip to Gingko Terra, the only information Darden had about that world was Gatherers suffered headaches when in that dimension.

"You can understand why I have encouraged you not to start a sexual relationship with my daughter," Benko finally said. "If she had the capacity to do that as a child, there is no way to tell what a mated fifth-generation telepath's abilities might be. JoAnna struggles with her abilities and she has the maturity to deal with it. Cassie is still very much a child."

"Yet, JoAnna and Shirl talked Cassie into entering the portal that would take her to the Troyk universe," Darden said. "They must know something we do not."

It hurt Darden that Cassie would make such a decision without discussing it with him. They were partners and such a radical move should have merited a discussion between the two of them. Darden knew he was being hypocritical since he made unilateral decisions all the time that impacted the two of them. He and Benko had meticulously outlined when Darden would bring each of the orphaned girls back to the Troyk universe. Not once had either discussed Cassie's return. It was understood that Cassie would not enter the Troyk universe until Benko had control of the world.

"Shirl and JoAnna both felt that Cassie would never reach her true potential until she went to our world," Benko said. "They had more faith in my daughter than either of us. For that, I am ashamed. Chartail warned her not to go, but that most likely pushed Cassie to leave."

Darden knew there was no love lost between Cassie and Benko's soul mate. Chartail unintentionally managed to prey on Cassie's insecurities. He only further added salt to the wound by rejecting Cassie's physical advances. The more he thought about it, he understood why Cassie joined her two friends.

He had once again failed his soul mate. Now his presence in the Troyk universe would only complicate matters. The last thing anyone of them wanted was to have Jeryl Jarlyn know the true nature of their relationship. The elder Jarlyn would not hesitate to force them to mate to increase Cassie's powers substantially. Darden was now stuck in the penal colony, unable to assist her should she find herself in mortal danger.

Chapter 4

Cassie re-entered her bedroom after taking a much needed shower. To her surprise, a tunic and leggings were laid out on the bed. Leenea Childers had somehow managed to move all of JoAnna's belongings and provide her a change of clothing in the short period of time Cassie took to bathe. The clothing was in a blend of white, gold, and tan colors. She slipped the tunic on over her head and put on the accompanying slacks.

There was a knock on her door and Alex stuck her head in. "Are you decent?"

"Come in," Cassie answered. To be honest, she wanted the company. All she could think about was how much she missed Darden. Alex was a nice distraction.

"My cousin, Solfa, and one of her intelligence officers are here to meet you," Alex said.

Cassie initially started to panic until she remembered someone telling her Solfa was one of the good guys. How they managed to keep the growing network of dissidents from her grandfather was a mystery. The larger the group, the more risk that communication would slip into a communal channel. Every day, the warrior link grew with new members entering the pathway.

"Is the intelligence officer one of us or is this official business?" Cassie asked. She was unsure what happened when someone entered their dimension for the first time. True, she was the Prime Ruler's granddaughter, but procedures had to be followed.

"Intelligence officer Karlon Flonder is one of us," Alex informed her. "He entered the warrior channel soon after Solfa did. My aunt and Solfa's mother will be over later to meet you. We did not want to overwhelm you with everyone at once."

"I appreciate it," Cassie said. "Remembering everyone's names is not one of my strengths. We may have to cheat and share some names through our closed channel. I know it's cheating, but I need all the help I can get."

"Gee, you talk fast," Alex stated. "I don't remember that about you. We'll have Tolfer teach you how to talk orally, as well as pushing the same information through our channel. Telepathic communication is not affected by how quickly we talk, but sometimes by the speed the brain interprets what was communicated."

Cassie knew she spoke rapidly when she was excited. Learning how to repeat her thoughts telepathically would reduce the funny looks she received and eliminate the embarrassment of the listener having to ask her to repeat what she said. It was her understanding Tolfer was a master at what he did and she needed the help.

The two women headed for the common room where everyone congregated. Cassie stopped dead in her tracks when she saw the second C.T. Guard from earlier today. The nondescript man was standing next to a stunning woman with rich chestnut brown hair. It was several shades lighter than Cassie's mahogany locks.

"This is my cousin, Solfa, and Karlon Flonder," Alex made the introductions.

"We met this morning," Karlon said. "They were short a C.T. Guard, so I accompanied Barash. Most of the time our alarms are set off by insects entering the dimension during the intervals other dimensional portals open and close. I felt like a little exercise, so I volunteered instead of allowing them to pull one of the trainees."

"Why were you silent the entire walk to town?" Cassie asked. "It was a little odd, considering I am the Prime Ruler's granddaughter. I know you wanted to keep your involvement with the resistance a secret, but any normal person would have tried to ingratiate themselves with a relative of the man in charge."

Karlon smiled, which made his face anything but ordinary. "But my job is not to be noticed. I blend into the shadows and learn what I can from people who let their guard down. Barash would have become suspicious if I started to act out of character. Besides, he would not have appreciated the competition."

Everything Karlon said made sense. They all had roles to play and Cassie needed to make sure she kept that in mind. One slip and she could topple her father's plans and those who plotted along with him.

"It is nice to meet you, Cassie," Solfa came forward and extended her hand. The woman had a penetrating glance. Considering Cassie was surrounded by friends, she was not concerned by the way the woman glared at her. "Your grandfather has asked me to start screening men for you to meet tomorrow night. A procession of gentlemen will be brought before you and they will kiss your hand. The general population will think it is a means for these subjects to welcome the granddaughter of the Prime Ruler, but it's Jeryl's way of finding your soul mate."

Silence met Solfa's last statement. Everyone in the room knew Darden was her soul mate.

"Well, Jeryl is not wasting any time," a voice from the entryway sounded.

Cassie turned to see Candy Phillips come into the common room. The woman was covered in mud from head to toe. Some things had not changed since they were kids. Candy had always been a tomboy. Uncaring how filthy Candy was, Cassie ran toward her old friend, but Candy put up her hands to stop her.

"I am a sweaty mess," Candy said. "There is nothing I hate more than being sent to Terra Flora to gather crystals. We tangled with a giant larma beast." She shuddered indelicately. "When is that man ever going to be satisfied with what he has?"

Candy was no doubt talking about her grandfather. As she grew up, Cassie's father taught her about the different crystals that could be used to enhance their telepathic gift. Cassie feared most of her abilities except the ones that would safeguard her against danger. She paid little attention to most of her father's lessons. Now it appeared her grandfather mastered pulling power from the stones.

"We can chat after I shower," Candy said. "I am going to grab Tolfer and then clean-up. He can finish cooking dinner after he scrubs my back." With a saucy wink she flounced out of the room.

A pang of jealousy hit Cassie. Her friends had soul mates they could depend on and enjoy intimately. That thought brought her back to what her grandfather planned for tomorrow night. He was going to be disappointed. Nothing was going to occur, regardless of how many men he paraded in front of her. As far as Cassie knew, her grandfather was only aware of two pairings: Shirl's to Starc and JoAnna's to Koel.

"What else does my grandfather have in store for me?" Cassie asked.

"That is it for now, as far as I know," Solfa said. "Jeryl has not shared anything else with me. He has, however, asked for JoAnna to be present in The Palace tomorrow afternoon."

"I am not surprised," JoAnna said. "He continues to train me, but has barely used my mind control gift in any capacity since my return from Gingko Terra. My mind closed its telepathic link to him before I mated with Koel."

"See if you can connect with Cassie," Shirl suggested. "If she has a natural barrier, Jeryl will be unable to control her mind, too."

Cassie was hesitant to have JoAnna do as Shirl suggested. It was not that she feared JoAnna. Actually, it was exactly the opposite. She did not want to damage JoAnna's brain. When she was younger she inadvertently entered some of her classmates' minds and caused their noses to bleed. Once she was aware of what she had done, Cassie had pulled out of their minds.

"I don't think that is a good idea," Cassie cautioned.

JoAnna came to stand beside Cassie. "Let's sit down," JoAnna suggested. "Like you, I am a fifth-generation mind control telepath. If I sense something is wrong, I will release you and no harm will occur to either of us."

"I think we should listen to Cassie and not tempt fate," Alex wearily said.

Cassie looked between JoAnna and Alex. She was not dealing with non-telepathic children. JoAnna was more powerful than Cassie was, since she used her gifts. This was the perfect time for her to try and learn to control her powers. Cassie reminded herself the man she killed all those years ago meant to do her harm, JoAnna was her friend. She could only pray neither of them did harm to the other.

Cassie and JoAnna sat next to each other on one of the sofas. Koel was beside his soul mate, holding JoAnna's hand. Since Koel was able to enter both JoAnna's mind and the brain she connected to, he could monitor their exchange. If he sensed anything was wrong, they would break any bond the two women happened to create.

Cassie took a deep, cleansing breath. She had recently entered one other mind and inherently knew what she needed to do. Afton's nose had bled when she invaded her brain. The last thing she wanted to do was hurt JoAnna. They stared into each other's eyes and Cassie cautiously reached out telepathically to JoAnna. A barrier existed that stalled her ability to penetrate JoAnna's mind.

Cassie felt pressure. Although she had been unable to enter JoAnna's mind, her friend appeared to have successfully entered hers. She tried to relax and welcome the intrusion. If she fought, Cassie knew temporary to permanent damage would result.

"Can you turn off your thoughts, like you do when you turn down the volume of conversations in your brain?" JoAnna asked telepathically. *"I have a natural telepathic wall, but you can erect your own by concentrating on turning off the noise. It will not be permanent, but it will safeguard you if Jeryl tries to enter your mind. He will not know the difference and will cease trying."*

JoAnna was not using a channel to communicate, but was in her mind. The pressure continued to increase as Cassie did as the other mind control telepath suggested. She could feel JoAnna's presence, but was unable to block her intrusion.

Cassie felt liquid running down her lip and she wiped it away with her hand. She continued to concentrate on stopping JoAnna from penetrating her mind. Everything she tried failed.

"You need to stop," Alex cried. "She's bleeding."

It was as if Alex's warning was said in a cave. Her words echoed in Cassie's mind, but did not interrupt what she was trying to do to stop JoAnna.

"We all bled." Shirl's words were even more diluted when she responded to Alex. "If she starts bleeding from anywhere other than her nose, we'll stop. Koel has not pulled JoAnna from Cassie's mind yet."

The pressure in her head lessened. Whatever she was doing was on the right track. Cassie put more energy in pushing the unwanted thoughts from her mind and building an impenetrable wall against future attacks. She made a mental note of where she placed the barrier so she could continually check the strength of the telepathic shield.

"Did I erect a barrier you can't enter?" Cassie asked. She was fairly certain she had, but she needed JoAnna's validation to confirm she had been successful.

"Yes," JoAnna responded, *"But more importantly, we are able to communicate this way without entry to the functioning of your brain. Tomorrow, if Jeryl tries to enter your mind, I can join you and be invisible to him."*

"What's happening?" Alex asked anxiously. Cassie could feel her friend's agitation through their closed telepathic bond, even while she was connected to JoAnna.

"Everything is fine, Alex," JoAnna responded. "We have an ability to connect on the surface of consciousness which Jeryl Jarlyn will not be able to detect. It's almost like another telepathic channel, but unique to mind control telepaths."

"Will Jeryl be able to enter the pathway?" Shirl inquired.

"No," JoAnna answered. "I believe, since we are fifth-generation mind control telepaths, we have abilities unique to only the two of us. At no point did Jeryl ever try to communicate with me in this manner. Believe me, if he had this ability he would certainly use it. The man wants control over everything he can. We need to keep this ability to ourselves."

"I still do not like Cassie being forced to spend time with her grandfather," Alex said. "Candy, do you sense any impending danger?"

Candy had the gift of premonition and her visions became more vivid as an event neared. At this point, Candy would only be able to get an impression of danger without anything concrete for them to help prepare themselves. Worse, Candy could not always determine who was in danger.

"I do not sense anything," Candy said. "However, we must diligently protect both Cassie and JoAnna. There are rebel contingents out there who already consider JoAnna a threat. Now that the communal channels have announced Cassie's arrival, she, too, is in danger."

Two attempts had already been made on JoAnna's life that Candy and JoAnna herself were able to prevent. Cassie knew the risks when she entered the Troyk universe. Even after her father took over the government, she imagined there would always be someone out to get her or her dad. It was not something she had dealt with in Gingko Terra, but knew her life was imperiled the moment she left that realm.

"Like it or not," Shirl said, "Jeryl Jarlyn is never going to be alone with Cassie and she will not walk the streets of Aster Province without one of us by her side."

It was touching her friends were willing to risk their lives for her. Cassie could only pray that nothing happened to them while protecting her. How could she live with herself if any of them were harmed? In the Childers's household she could relax. Tomorrow, when she returned to her grandfather's palace, everyone would be at risk.

Chapter 5

Cassie fidgeted with the bracelet Darden gave her on her eighteenth birthday. It was a beautiful gold tennis bracelet set with a variety of gemstones. The slim bracelet graced her left wrist while a cuff graced her right. When she left Gingko Terra for the Troyk penal colony she began wearing her mother's familial bracelet. Benko had told her very little over the years about the woman who gave birth to her. Perhaps he was afraid she would want to leave for the Troyk universe to find her mother's family.

She sat in her grandfather's receiving room with Shirl, Candy, and JoAnna. Shirl and JoAnna now lived with their soul mates, but returned to the Childers's home for the mid-day meal and to accompany her to The Palace. Candy had originally been assigned to protect Shirl, but they would now ensure she was at Cassie's side for the foreseeable future.

They had been in The Palace for half an hour and her grandfather had not yet made an appearance. Had she known, she would have stayed longer with Alex, Alex's aunt Norrie, and Solfa's mother Pattrice. Solfa's mother was a trip. She kept crying and hugging Cassie as if she were her long-lost daughter. Norrie admitted to having a crush on Benko Jarlyn when she was younger. It was weird thinking of someone being attracted to her father.

Whatever delayed her grandfather was not in any of the information being communicated through the variety of communal pathways that linked the province's population. There had been a little blip in activity when it was announced Cassandra Jarlyn had entered the Troyk universe. As soon as it was clear Benko was not with her, conversations about Cassie had diminished. The return of the children of Benko's followers had become old news.

When her grandfather finally joined them, he seemed flustered. Something had occurred, but Jeryl Jarlyn was clearly not going to discuss it with the four women before him. He seemed surprised to see the entourage Cassie had with her.

"You girls are no longer required," the Prime Ruler said, "you are dismissed."

Cassie needed to make it clear these women would stay as long as they desired, and her grandfather did not have a say in the matter. "I need them with me as I learn about this world and my capabilities," Cassie informed her grandfather. "JoAnna has the same telepathic gift I have and there is so much I can learn from her. Shirl and Candy are like sisters to me, having visited them as often as I did in the orphanage. Although we are blood, you are a stranger to me, Grandfather."

"That was your father's doing," Jeryl growled. "That boy had no right to keep you from me once you were born."

They were going around in circles. Cassie had no desire to repeat the same conversation they had yesterday. Although, it would keep him from asking the inevitable question about where Benko could be found today. She would leave breadcrumbs that would lead the Gatherers anywhere but where her father resided.

"My father is aware you are looking for him," Cassie informed her grandfather. "He always knew you would never give up searching for us. I was taught at an early age how to protect myself from your men. When Shirl returned to the Troyk universe, father knew his life on Gingko Terra was never going to be the same. As soon as JoAnna returned to this world, he left Scottsdale for parts unknown. My dad knew there was a possibility I would follow my friends. He wanted to give me the freedom to make my own choice where I ultimately may desire to live."

Her grandfather stared at her. She could see his mouth twitch as she told him of Benko's latest disappearing act. Cassie tested the fortitude of her telepathic barrier knowing her grandfather would shortly try to connect with her telepathically. That was the power he wielded and she figured he was past due trying to manipulate her that way.

"He is trying to enter your mind," JoAnna warned. *"Can you feel his presence?"*

She felt no pressure or assault on her mind. Her grandfather failed to connect with her brain and discovered the barrier that kept him from JoAnna's mind also prevented him from entering his grand-daughter's thoughts. It was easy to believe the shield was a common characteristic of the rare fifth-generation mind control telepath.

Jeryl Jarlyn stood and walked to the small bar in the corner of the room and poured himself a drink. He must be frustrated by his failed attempt to use his mind control capabilities against his granddaugh-ter. Her grandfather took several gulps of his drink and rejoined them.

"A seamstress will be arriving in an hour to design several gowns for you," Jeryl shared with her. "Several off-the-rack dresses will also arrive from the very best shops in the area for you to try on and wear until the custom couture clothing is ready. Tonight you will be presented as my granddaughter and heir."

Cassie had not expected to be named his heir, and certainly not this evening. She had no desire to rule a universe or use her powers against the Troyk people. Her father had warned her this would happen if either of them had ever returned to the Troyk universe. Jeryl wanted to start a dynasty and live through them once he was gone.

"Surely there are Prime Representatives more qualified to rule when you are ready to step down and enjoy the remainder of your life, Grandfather," Cassie said.

"None have children who inherited the telepathic capabilities the Supreme Being gave us to rule over his people," Jeryl said. "You and Benko are both blessed with the ability to lead the citizens of this great community. It is God's way of taking care of his followers."

Her father told her Jeryl believed it was his God-given duty to rule because of the telepathic gifts. The Prime Ruler did not believe it obscene to utilize those abilities to control the actions of others. Cassie had been taught everything to the contrary. Did she play along or confront him for his beliefs?

"Grandfather, I have no desire or ability to rule as you have," Cassie admitted. "I'm eighteen years old and barely made it through high school."

That part was true, Cassie was a terrible student. She had too many distractions to want to study, mostly Darden. Cassie would be outside gathering herbs as often as she could, so when her soul mate entered her dimension they did not have to waste time collecting the items he had to return to the Troyk universe with.

She knew it would be easy for her to enter the mind of her teachers and convince them to give her better grades. However, she never considered that option. That would be cheating. Cassie received what she earned and was content to live with that.

"That is why we will spend time together," her grandfather replied. "JoAnna will become a valuable asset at your side as her uncle was to me. You even have both your own crystal telepath and built-in security force. Do you not see how the four of you were brought together for a purpose?"

Cassie believed there was a reason they were together, but it was not to rule over the Troyk people. The population needed to be able to make their own decisions about how they wanted to live their lives as she and her friends did. It was senseless to argue with her grandfather. She would take in everything he had to teach to buy her father time to mount his revolution.

"We might as well begin," Cassie conceded. "There is a lot of work to be done."

"There is plenty of time for that," Jeryl responded. "It is imperative you are a success tonight. We never get a second chance to make a good first impression."

Cassie did not respond to the ridiculous statement her grandfather made. If she did something incorrect tonight, Jeryl Jarlyn would merely convince the city's population it never occurred. Any poor impression she made would be changed to a favorable one in anyone's mind. Right or wrong, her grandfather would make sure of it. However, she wanted to represent herself as Benko Jarlyn's daughter in a positive light. Tonight was the first step in preparing the Aster Province for the return of the True Ruler.

"I can't wear this gown," Cassie stated, "I might as well arrive naked."

"Do not be over dramatic, dear," the owner of the poshest clothing boutique responded. "You are not used to how we dress in our world. I can only imagine what passes for evening wear in Gingko Terra."

The shopkeeper shifted her gaze and turned her nose up at the gym shorts and T-shirt Candy wore. Her friend alternated between her Troyk tunics and leggings with the clothing she was comfortable wearing in Phoenix.

"Relax," Candy replied. "I have one of your creations in the other room and I will change before the event this evening."

Shirl and JoAnna were stunning in what they wore and they had yet to change into their formal wear. She imagined her two fashion plate friends would see to her clothing as they had with Alex and Candy. Cassie was closer to the other two when it came to what she wore. Comfort first, fashion not even in the running.

"You represent your grandfather and his government tonight, young woman," the lady responded. She had introduced herself, but Cassie had not been paying attention when the shopkeeper started talking. Cassie was engrossed in looking at the sheer, barely there clothing she was laying out.

"*Do any of you know this woman's name?*" Cassie asked.

"*Madame Gigi,*" JoAnna answered. "*For some reason, this dimension is captivated by French designers from Earth. They have tailored a segment of their high end outfits from the latest French fashions. Several shop owners pay a crystal telepath to open a portal to Paris and stay long enough to grab the latest fashion magazine. They put their own Troyk spin on the outfits, though.*"

"*What is the other segment?*" Cassie asked.

"*Sheer tunics and leggings for second seating at local restaurants,*" Shirl answered. "*If you think these are obscene, just wait until we go out to dinner when Darden returns.*"

Cassie did not know how she felt about Darden seeing nearly naked women when they went out. Not to mention what the outfit exposed of her body. He had never seen her naked. The closest they got to nudity was a bikini she wore when they went swimming in her Scottsdale home's pool.

"The rest of you should start dressing while I finish with the Prime Ruler's granddaughter," Madame Gigi said. "Guests begin arriving in an hour. Your grandfather will greet the guests and you are to make your grand entrance as soon as the last guest arrives."

"JoAnna and I will change," Shirl said. "When we return, Candy can go dress while we do your makeup and hair."

Her friends were true to their word. Since arriving this afternoon she had never been alone. They had not left her grandfather's receiving room. At one point, Candy even accompanied her to the restroom. Until they returned to Zane and Leenea's, at least one of her friends was attached at the hip.

"If she sticks you with a pin, do you want me to kill her?" Candy asked. Cassie knew she was kidding, but the levity in the question helped to boost her spirits. She was more nervous about tonight then she expected.

Madame Gigi finished making the minor alterations to the outfit and left Cassie alone in the room with Candy. She was dreading this evening and was uncomfortable in the clothing she was forced to wear. Her eyes continually wandered down to her exposed breasts.

"Just pretend you are in some strange fairytale dream and have fun," Candy said.

Cassie's nervousness must have been obvious to Candy. She would have preferred to return to the Childers's home and visit with her friends and get to know their soul mates better. All the men were very sweet and doted on their mates, particularly Tarsea now that Alex was pregnant.

"I was expecting intrigue and boring governmental discussions, not parties," Cassie admitted. "We lived a very solitary life on Gingko Terra. None of us wanted to draw attention to ourselves."

"Don't worry," Candy said. "Shirl and JoAnna will make you beautiful, so all you have to do is stand around and let people worship you. Haven't you ever noticed how men start acting stupid around those two? It's actually quite amusing to watch."

"If I knew I was going to have to wear outfits like this, I would have gone on a diet before entering the portal," Cassie admitted.

"You're perfect," Candy said. "Women are supposed to have curves. All that work Chartail probably forced upon you has toned your body. It's probably a good thing Darden is not going to be there tonight. I don't think he would be too happy about how you look in that outfit or the adoration you are going to receive."

JoAnna and Shirl entered the room in their finery and Cassie felt a little better. No one was going to bother to look at her with these two around. They herded her out of the receiving room and into one of the bedroom's bathrooms so they could work on her hair and make-up.

Shirl worked on her face while JoAnna used the Troyk version of a curling iron. Cassie followed every instruction Shirl gave related to closing her eyes, looking up, pursing her lips, and a myriad of other commands. When both women moved away from the mirror, Cassie saw herself for the first time. She was shocked by her appearance.

Her mildly wavy hair was in an array of curls, crowning her face. Cassie's eyelids were highlighted with a black liner and a very dark shade of brown while her lips had a nude shade of lipstick that shimmered. She looked like she could be on the cover of Vogue.

"Wow!" was all Cassie managed to say. She could barely believe the woman she saw in the mirror was her. Once again, she wished Darden was by her side.

"Let's get Candy and conquer this party," Shirl said.

Cassie followed in shoes she struggled to walk in. As long as she never had to move, Cassie might make it through the night. They would wait in the receiving room until they called for her. The party was on the first floor and Cassie was going to take the elevator down. If she wanted to live through the evening, she was not going to traverse the stairs in the high-heeled shoes.

Candy joined them and was white as a ghost.

"What's wrong," Cassie asked anxiously.

"I'm not sure," Candy said. "It's just a feeling. Whatever is causing my anxiety may have nothing to do with you or this evening."

Something was wrong and Cassie knew she was somehow involved. Candy's feelings of impending doom usually proved to be worth consideration. Was she attending a party or her funeral?

Chapter 6

If another man slobbered on her hand, Cassie was going to scream. The first few kisses were flattering, but the adoration over the Prime Ruler's granddaughter shtick grew old fast. Jeryl Jarlyn was going to have a long wait if he expected she was going to react to any of these men.

"Evening, Cassandra," a familiar voice said.

Cassie looked up from her hand and stared into the light brown eyes of Barash, the C.T. Guard she met yesterday on the mountain trail. He looked handsome in his Troyk formal wear. His dark brown hair curled over his tunic's high collar.

"Barash's father was just elected to the Prime Council," her grandfather informed her. "He ran a successful business before running for office. His family has produced several crystal telepathic offspring in the past."

Jeryl Jarlyn provided the pedigree of several of the men after the initial introduction. He probably believed the likelihood of finding her soul mate was slim, so he was calculating which mating would produce a superior great-grandchild. After all, he never found his soul mate.

"It would be my honor to escort you to The Palace after buying you lunch tomorrow afternoon," Barash said.

Before Cassie could reject his proposal, her grandfather accepted on her behalf. It would be rude to do anything but smile and prepare for the next introduction. The line of eager men seemed to only get longer as the evening progressed.

A man with a lazy eye came forward and placed a wet kiss on her hand. She had the urge to wipe her hand against her sheer clothing. How much more of this was she going to have to endure?

"Your beauty suits the granddaughter of such an austere man as the Prime Ruler," the stranger before her said. She noted his eyes rotated between her breasts and her grandfather.

"Oh, God," Shirl communicated through their closed channel. *"I have to get some air."*

"No fair!" Cassie exclaimed. *"If I have to suffer through this, so do you."*

"That's the beauty of there being three of us and only one of you," Shirl replied. *"Candy and JoAnna are better suited to protect you in this environment, anyway. I would only create a spectacle."*

Cassie still did not have a clue of the power contained within her blond friend. She continued to ponder that thought as another man came forward. It was going to be a long evening.

After another thirty minutes of greeting strangers, a familiar face stood before her. Karlon Flonder was a sight for sore eyes. A friend in hostile territory, he had a faint smile on his nondescript face.

"Prime Ruler, your granddaughter has been receiving your subjects for over two hours," Karlon said. "Perhaps a short break is called for where she can stretch her legs. The orchestra is about to play a waltz. There are many beautiful women who would be honored to dance with you."

Her grandfather considered Karlon's recommendation. A grin crossed his wrinkled face and Cassie breathed a sigh of relief.

"That is an excellent idea, young man," Jeryl Jarlyn replied. "It would appear my head of intelligence surrounds herself with bright individuals."

"Solfa is merely an extension of your ability to select the right people for the job," her soon to be dance partner responded.

"A bit of a sycophant, are we?" Cassie said in a volume only Karlon would be able to hear. "I would be honored to dance with you." The last sentence she said loud enough for her grandfather and the line of gentlemen to overhear.

Cassie took Karlon's hand and he led them to the dance floor. It finally dawned on Cassie she had no idea how to waltz. She had taken social dancing in junior high school, but did not learn that particular dance.

"I can't waltz," Cassie whispered.

"Open your mind to me and I will lead you through it," her partner answered in a barely audible voice.

She had no idea he was a mind control telepath. Solfa had not mentioned that fact, neither had any of their friends.

"You are full of surprises, aren't you?" Cassie commented.

Cassie opened her mind to Karlon. He was only the fourth person she allowed in her head. His entry was subtle, barely noticeable.

"It makes things interesting," Karlon said. *"My abilities came upon me later than usual. By that point, I had already determined how the government's manipulation of the population was wrong. I never bothered to share what had occurred."*

"Even to Solfa?" Cassie asked.

"Some secrets are best kept to oneself," Karlon stated. *"As more people enter the warrior pathway, it is only a matter of time before someone slips up. The fewer people who know of my capabilities, the better."*

"But you shared it with me," Cassie pointed out.

"You are different," he admitted. *"As soon as you connected in the warrior link, I knew it."*

Cassie felt sick to her stomach. No one had ever sensed her in that particular channel before. "As you said, some secrets are meant to be kept."

She had been waltzing and had not noticed her graceful movements. Her motor functions were taken over and she danced perfectly in three quarter time in his arms. She wondered how many crystal telepaths danced in European ballrooms over the years.

Karlon whirled her around the dance floor. Cassie felt like she was floating. She wished she could keep this up all night and not be forced back into the receiving line.

"May I cut in?" a beloved voice asked.

Cassie's legs were once again hers as Karlon released her mind. She looked up into her soul mate's face.

"With pleasure," Karlon replied and went to seek another partner.

Darden took her into his arms and they moved together, no longer waltzing. Couples skirted around them but Cassie was oblivious to them. She was in a world of her own.

The planet's axis had righted itself. She was back in Darden's arms. He had not dressed for the occasion, but he outshined every man in the ballroom.

"*How?*" Cassie asked in wonderment.

"*Shirl,*" Darden simply replied. "*She has since returned to the Childers's household to protect Alex and the baby in case things go badly here with my unexpected appearance.*"

The female crystal telepath took it upon herself to bring Darden back from the Troyk penal world without consulting her. Darden was in danger in this dimension and had followed Cassie without considering the consequences. No wonder Candy was antsy.

"Oh, I know the consequences, my love," Darden replied to thoughts she did not intentionally share with him. They were linked, emotions permeated their connection.

"Darden Lours, you are to come with us," a member of The Palace Guard demanded.

It did not take long for his presence to be noted and her grandfather or other official took notice. Her lean, tall soul mate's bleached long blond hair made him stand out. The communal pathways became overloaded with chatter about what was occurring.

Cassie followed the two men who came to arrest Darden, walking beside him. Orders were changed to escort the couple to the fourth floor once it was clear Cassie would accompany Darden. No one bothered to try and stop her. She slipped her shoes off and ascended the four flights of stairs.

They entered her grandfather's greeting room to find him already present. Cassie had not noticed that Candy and JoAnna had followed them until the door was closed. Cassie finally looked directly at Jeryl Jarlyn and saw his face mottled in fury. She was about to experience her grandfather's wrath.

Darden knew the risk when he entered the portal with Shirl. He saw danger reflected in Jeryl Jarlyn's eyes. He was surprised he had not been immediately thrown in the cells located in the basement of The Palace.

He brought Cassie into his embrace. They would face the Prime Ruler and his anger together. The warrior link was active with communication about what could be done to rescue them once sentences were handed down.

"What happened when the two of you touched for the first time?" Jeryl asked.

He was surprised by Jarlyn's insight. The Prime Ruler obviously knew what they were to each other. There was no reason to continue the pretense of what he and Cassie were.

"An electric current ran through me when the soul mate channel opened," Darden replied.

The Prime Ruler understood the significance of the exchange. "When did this occur?"

"When I was ten years old," Cassie responded.

That answer startled her grandfather. For eight years, Darden had lied to everyone. Until recently, that charade included his friends as well.

"Benko and Cassandra had the capability to return home for the last eight years," Jeryl Jarlyn muttered. Darden imagined he spoke the thought aloud, rather than purposely addressing the crowd populating the room.

"We planned to return the girls home when their headaches became an issue," Darden admitted. "Shirl was to be the first since her migraines were becoming problematic."

The Prime Ruler surprised everyone by ordering the presence of Tarsea Childers through the communal pathway. It appeared their secrets were slowly unraveling.

"Have you had sex?" Cassie's grandfather demanded.

His soul mate tightened her grip on his hand, reacting to her grandfather's query. He could feel her discomfort through their link.

"We have not," Darden quickly answered. He did not want Cassie responding to that particular question. The poor thing must be mortified, if not already scared to death about what might happen when the conversation was over.

Jarlyn nodded at Darden's reply. "You fear what you will unleash."

JoAnna stepped forward. "You cannot force them to be together as you did with me and Koel," JoAnna declared. "I used my powers most of my life where Cassie has not. She is not physically ready to absorb additional abilities."

The Prime Ruler's face reddened with anger. "We are talking about my granddaughter, young woman. I am the victim here. For eight years, I have been lied to. Denied the ability to see my grand-daughter, let alone know of her existence. Cassandra is my legacy. What kind of monster do you take me for?"

No one bothered to respond to that particular question. They knew exactly what they were dealing with. An outsider would feel pity for the man before them, but this group knew what Jeryl Jarlyn was capable of.

"Where is my son?" Jeryl demanded.

"My father is safe," Cassie responded. "All he wants is to be left alone to live his life in peace. Because you hounded him, I grew up learning how to protect myself against your Gatherers."

"All I wanted was my son back," Jarlyn said driving a fist into the crystal stand next to where he stood. The geode fell and pieces of the crystal broke off.

No one knelt to clean up the mess. Darden believed the outburst was out of frustration, not anger. Regardless, he gently moved Cassie to stand behind him.

As the drama played out in the room, Darden warned Tarsea of what he would be walking into through the warrior channel. Koel was on his way to be beside JoAnna, while Shirl was prepared to evacuate Alex to the Nightshade universe. No one would consider looking for her in the parallel dimension populated by vampires. The most powerful vampire among them would protect Alex since she carried his soul mate in her womb.

Everyone's focus changed when Tarsea Childers entered the room. He was Darden's best friend from the moment they met. Darden had spent so much time at the Childers's home when they were growing up, Tarsea's parents considered him a third son. He was closer to this man than he was to his twin brother.

"Who is your girlfriend?" Jeryl Jarlyn asked.

"*Tell the truth as we discussed,*" Darden instructed his friend. It was clear the Prime Ruler knew exactly who Alex was.

"She is the daughter of Troyk dissidents, born in the Gingko Terra dimension," Tarsea admitted. "Alex was hiking in Sedona and was accidentally pulled through the inter-dimensional portal Darden opened before it closed. As soon as I saw her, I knew she was my soul mate. She was hurt and all I could think to do was protect her. We brought in her bereaved aunt to lie for us. Solfa and her mother bought the lie, happy a part of their family was returned to them."

"How did you pass our interrogation?" Jeryl asked.

"When we made love for the first time, we gained additional powers," Tarsea admitted. "Mind control telepaths cannot detect when I tell a half-truth. If Alex concentrates, she can read the mind of others. That was how we discovered Chartail was guilty of the attempt on your life."

"That little girl was responsible for Chartail's capture?" the Prime Ruler asked in astonishment.

"Despite our lies, we are loyal to you," Tarsea claimed. "Alex believed Chartail needed to be brought to justice before she hatched another plot."

Tarsea was masterfully weaving a tale of mostly truths. The Prime Ruler appeared entranced with what was being presented to him. It had been a wise decision to turn Chartail in for her crimes. Everything seemed to fall in place with that one act.

"Does Alexia still have that capability?" Jeryl Jarlyn asked. Darden could almost hear the Prime Ruler's mind calculating how he could use such a gift.

"Her pregnancy has temporarily interfered with her ability," Tarsea said. "Her telepathic powers are limited to the connection she shares with our unborn daughter. Alex, however, has been able to link into our familial channel months before she ordinarily would have. Her access to communal channels has also been cut off."

"Fascinating," Jeryl responded. "All we know of soul mates is what we have observed with JoAnna and Koel, as well as Shirl and Starc. Now we have a pregnant soul mate. It is interesting how all the Gingko Terra women found their soul mates in a close set of friends and family."

Candy shuffled in place under Jeryl Jarlyn's scrutiny. Before she sought advice in the warrior channel, Candy also started her own confession.

"Tolfer Childers is my soul mate," Candy admitted. "My telepathic enhancement is the gift of foresight. That is why I need to be assigned to your granddaughter for her protection."

The Prime Ruler's eyes opened wide in alarm. "Is she in danger?"

"Being your granddaughter and heir apparent puts her in danger," Candy said. "I have not picked up anything more specific."

"Then you are so assigned," Jeryl said. "Are there other secrets you are keeping from me?"

"There are only the five of us," Cassie spoke up. "Leave my father alone and I will learn all you have to teach me. Benko's presence will only rile up a history best kept in the past."

They shared all they planned to reveal. The warrior link was still a channel of legend. Zane and Leenea's status as soul mates was still protected. Their dissident network was safe, as well as Solfa's involvement. There were still many secrets to be kept and they would be under more scrutiny than before.

"Cassandra will continue to stay in the Childers's household, sharing a room with Darden." The Prime Ruler held up his hand before JoAnna could protest. "I am not forcing the two of you together, merely letting nature run its course. Darden will turn over his crystals. A C.T. Guard will be assigned to retrieve Shirl's crystals. Both will stay in this dimension until I say otherwise."

Darden could not have asked for a better interim outcome. He did not fool himself for a moment that Jeryl Jarlyn could pull the rug out from under them without a moment's notice and without hesitation. None of them would be truly safe until Benko took his father's place, and Jeryl Jarlyn had just cut them off from his son.

Chapter 7

Cassie did not utter a word on the way back to the Childers's residence. She had closed herself to him as well. Never in their relationship had Darden not known how Cassie was feeling. He was unaware she had developed the ability to block him from her mind. Because he could not feel her emotions, Darden did not know if she felt angry, afraid, or a plethora of other feelings.

As soon as they reached the house, Cassie went directly to her room. Darden headed for the makeshift bar. If he was going to share a bed with her, he needed several drinks to calm his nerves. He stopped dead in his tracks as soon as he entered the common room.

Drake, the powerful vampire from the Nightshade universe, was sitting next to Alex. They were carrying on a conversation as close friends were wont to do. Shirl sat nearby, throwing daggers at Drake with her looks.

Darden had never felt comfortable in the company of this lethal creature. They had an uneasy alliance with Drake and his blood brothers, particularly because Drake believed Alex's child was his soul mate. All visitations would end if Alex said the word. For some incomprehensible reason, she enjoyed the monster's company.

"What is *he* doing here?" Tarsea growled. His best friend could barely tolerate Drake's presence.

"The Nightshade universe is going through power struggles to fill the void left when Yorik was killed," Starc advised. Yorik was the master vampire who victimized Chartail. Had Drake not claimed

Shirl, the female crystal telepath would have met the same fate. "Drake thought it wise we returned to the Troyk universe and he would protect Alex and his soul mate in this dimension."

"Good Lord," JoAnna said in response to seeing the vampire for the second time. JoAnna had only been in the Nightshade universe a short period of time and had just nearly killed her stalker. She never gave herself time to truly come to grips with the terror and lust incited by this frightening creature.

Drake appeared human, although he was a monster. His jet black hair and eyes seemed to mesmerize any female he came in contact with. Once the vampire used his powers, women fell at his feet. Darden was relieved Cassie was in her bedroom.

"Nice to see you gentlemen, again," Drake said. He purposely took Alex's hand and raised it to his lips, placing a gentle kiss on it. "If you cannot deal properly with your Prime Ruler, I will be happy to take care of the problem."

He heard JoAnna catch her breath. Drake did not recognize the other women in the room, but was aware of the impact he had on them. The whole thing sickened Darden.

Tarsea stepped forward to separate his soul mate from the amorous vampire. Darden placed his hand on his friend's shoulder to stop him. There was no sense in enraging Drake. The creature and his friends were their allies for now. He never considered setting the vampires free in the Troyk universe to assist with their political revolution. However, Darden was not prepared to totally rule out the possibility by alienating the being before him. His immediate concern was how dangerous Drake was to the others in the room.

"I presume you fed before arriving in our dimension," Darden said.

"Yes," Drake responded. "I feasted on a beautiful blonde, not unlike our stunning Shirl here."

Starc uttered some words under his breath. His twin brother showed remarkable constraint. Drake had glamoured Shirl when he held her captive. Shirl barely tolerated his presence while Drake did everything he could to aggravate her. It was a game the two played. However, they never crossed a line that would enrage Alex.

"My mate is no longer in danger," Tarsea stated. "The truth about who she is has been revealed. Jeryl Jarlyn is more fascinated by what Alex can do than the lies we told. You can return to the Nightshade universe. I am sure your friends in that dimension are more in need of your assistance with the mayhem occurring there."

"Alas, I was just getting comfortable," Drake responded. "Your daughter is soothed by my presence. The turmoil and lies present in this realm make her uneasy."

Drake leaned back, stretched his long legs, and placed his feet on the table in front of him. His movement brought Alex into his body. The vampire's hand rested upon Alex's womb where his soul mate grew.

"Better here than in your world," Tarsea countered. "My daughter is human and you are not. Humans are sustenance in your world. She will never join you in the horror you call home. Benko has only offered you the opportunity to see Alex and my daughter, not to take either away from this world."

"One day your daughter will be grown and able to make her own decisions," Drake asserted. "Just as the wondrous Alexandra has been able to do. She chose to stay in this dimension with you, rather than return to the world of her birth. One day, Star will be free to make that same decision."

"*Over my dead body,*" Tarsea communicated in the warrior channel. Drake and Alex did not hear his comment. Alex's access to the link was temporarily shut-off because of her pregnancy. Darden was not sure what telepathic capabilities Drake had, but he did not react to Tarsea's statement.

Alex must have sensed Tarsea was about to erupt. She rose from the sofa and went into her soul mate's arms. "Let's not get all bent out of shape over something that will not occur for years. Now that the danger has passed, Drake should return to the Nightshade universe."

"You and Star can return with me," Drake said. "I will ensure your safety. My blood brothers' soul mates have become powerful elementals and will help to protect you."

Before Tarsea could explode, Alex quickly responded to Drake's invitation. "My place is here, Drake. I can finally be who I am and not pretend to be a distant cousin. Shirl knows how to find you if the situation worsens."

Before she could be asked, Shirl was on her feet and opened a portal. "Go," she commanded.

"If you believe I am walking blindly into a portal you opened, you are delusional, my dear," Drake addressed Shirl. "You first and I will follow."

"Crap," Shirl said to herself. The crystal telepath closed the gateway and opened another.

Drake rose and headed toward Koel, JoAnna, and Candy who stood in the rear of the room. None of the three had interacted with Drake. It was clear Candy did not see him as a threat and Drake appreciated Koel's tactical talents.

"We are prepared to aid you in relieving this world of the negative aspects of the mind control government," Drake advised his cousin. "Under your leadership, we made short work of the Portal Guardians in the penal world and rescued Candy. It will be a pleasure to fight with you again."

"I will take that under advisement," Koel said. "A prudent man would leave now and make his case under better circumstances. The child is not born as of yet, there is time."

"So there is," Drake responded.

He walked next to Shirl and entered the portal after her, with Starc following. Darden felt the tension in the room ease immediately with the vampire's exit. Shirl and Starc would return to his apartment, rather than the common room. He imagined they would be greeted by the C.T. Guard Jeryl Jarlyn had sent to collect Shirl's crystals.

With the drama for the evening over, Tarsea headed for the bar and poured a number of drinks for the people in the room. He prepared a glass of water for his pregnant mate. Darden gladly accepted the shot of stoak. The liquor made from the Troyk grain keen burned on the way down his throat.

It was time he headed for the room he would share with Cassie. His mind and body were fatigued by the eventful evening, so Darden was not concerned about the temptation Cassie presented. He was dead tired.

He walked down the hall, knocked on the door, and entered. Cassie wore a long T-shirt and nothing else. The shirt was short and Cassie's legs were long. Darden did not think he had ever seen anything sexier. So much for not being tempted by her tonight. Once he got over the initial shock of how she looked, Darden noticed she was placing pillows on the floor next to a blanket.

"What is that for?" he asked

Cassie looked at him, pushing her wild hair out of her face. "My grandfather said we had to share a room. He said nothing about sharing a bed."

At this point, Darden figured he would rather deal with Drake than the woman before him. He could still not read her emotions and grew more frustrated when Cassie placed another blanket on the floor. There was no way he was sleeping on the floor when he could be holding his mate.

"Why can I no longer feel your emotions?" Darden asked. He wanted to distract her from the task she was performing.

"JoAnna taught me how to bring up a shield in my mind," Cassie answered. "Tonight I opened myself to Karlon. When I let him into my mind, I also realized another means to keep people out of my head. This evening has been very enlightening for a variety of reasons."

Discussion about the hidden talents belonging to a member of their group could wait until tomorrow. Darden had to correct his soul mate's misconception he would willingly sleep on the floor.

"We are sharing a bed, Cassie," Darden said.

"I don't think so," Cassie replied. She stood tall, her hand resting on her hip. Her long fingers grazed her naked upper thigh. "Tomorrow I have my first lessons with my grandfather, so I want to get a good night's sleep. Besides, I think I have a lunch date tomorrow."

Darden stared at her, temporarily dumbstruck. When he finally found his voice, he could only utter one word. "What?"

"Barash asked me out and my grandfather accepted," Cassie admitted. "He comes from a good family and Jeryl wants me to cultivate certain friendships."

He could not believe what he was hearing. In all the years he had known Cassie, Darden did not believe she had gone on a single date. Two days in the Troyk universe and she already had her first date. There was no way she was going to spend an instant alone with Barash Kleyman.

"I assume this date was arranged before your grandfather was aware we were soul mates," Darden said. "Regardless, if Barash shows up tomorrow, we will both join him. From this moment on, you are not going anywhere without me."

Cassie stood staring at him. There was something about her that had changed. It was as if she had grown up overnight. His soul mate stood before him, not a little girl. He could resist her no longer. At this point in time, he did not care what he unleashed. Whatever she would become, he no longer had the self-control to deprive himself of making love to his soul mate.

Cassie could not read the expression on Darden's face. She had never seen him look at her with such determination. When she closed herself off from Darden it also rendered her unable to read him. Suggesting Darden sleep on the floor had probably caused something inside him to snap. She readied herself for some serious verbal sparring.

When he came charging forward, Cassie was not prepared for the solid mass of her enraged male. Darden's momentum tumbled them onto her bed. His lips were on hers before she could demand he get off her. She opened to him, taking in his intoxicating taste. Her temperature soared in reaction to his simple kiss.

Darden's hands were all over her body. He examined her like a blind man coming upon a new object to discover. When he finally reached her panties, Cassie lifted her hips to help him remove the barrier. She lifted her shoulders to remove her Chicago Bears jersey before Darden tore it from her body. It was amazing she had the wherewithal to consider one of the only keepsakes she brought with her from Earth.

She now lay naked on the bed while Darden remained fully dressed. The idiot was still wearing his shoes while he played with her body. Cassie started to lift the tunic from his abdomen, hoping he would take the hint she wanted his naked flesh on hers. Darden rolled off her and got to his feet. Removing his shoes, he tossed them across the room and she heard them hit the wall before thudding to the floor. Cassie's eyes shone as she watched her soul mate rush to remove his clothing.

Cassie soaked in the sight of him. She had seen him in his swim trunks, but had never seen the part of him he had kept hidden from her. Countless times she had seen the bulge in his pants, his erection pressing against the material that confined it. Now it was before her eyes, ready to be buried deeply inside her.

Her soul mate prowled back to the bed and covered her. Darden's movements were graceful and fluid. His hands slid up and down her body as his mouth continued to devour hers. What little noises escaped her were captured by his kiss. Cassie's hands were buried in his long hair. She held on to him for dear life. Part of her was afraid she was dreaming and would wake to find herself once again alone.

"Never alone again, darling," Darden communicated telepathically. Whatever barriers she had erected came tumbling down with his all-consuming kiss. *"We will never be apart again."*

His right hand ran along her waist, down her hip, and then rested on her upper thigh. She knew what would happen next. Cassie had wanted this moment to happen from the time she reached her sixteenth birthday. For over two years she waited for Darden to claim her.

She moved her leg as an invitation to Darden. Before she settled her leg back on the mattress, Darden's hand rested on the juncture between her legs. His index finger gently brushed along her feminine folds until it entered her. A second finger soon followed. He moved within her, preparing her for him.

The temporary discomfort was quickly turning into something quite different as his fingers continued to rhythmically move within her slick passage. His fingers were soon coated with the proof of her passion. Darden removed his fingers and rested his hips against hers, ready to drive home his erect member.

"I love you, Cassie," Darden shared with her.

He drove inside her with a single thrust, his mouth absorbing her cry as he broke through the membrane of her innocence. The slight ache was soon forgotten as she took him into her core. There was a momentary feeling of loss as he left her body, only to be delighted when he reentered. She adjusted as he increased his pace, meeting his body's rhythm.

Darden continued to ride her as Cassie's breathing became labored. Her body was on the brink of something wonderful. God knows, she had read enough books on the subject. They all paled in comparison to what she was feeling. This wasn't just sex, but a true mating of their very souls.

She brought her legs to his hips, allowing him to drive deeper inside her. For an instant, Cassie feared she would not survive the sensations building in her body before she fractured. How long could Darden keep up the frantic pace before he climaxed?

An orgasm came upon her the instant Darden experienced one of his own. Her euphoria was multiplied by their soul mate link. His physical rapture and his joy made her feel whole. A scream came from her, echoed by a guttural groan from her mate. They were truly one.

Cassie knew what would happen next and she welcomed it. As her cry waned, she felt her brain excrete the hormone they had all feared. What telepathic gifts she possessed before would now be eclipsed by her new abilities. As she had barely scratched the surface of her powers, it was unlikely she would be able to decipher her original powers from her enhanced ones.

"Are you all right?" Darden asked.

He moved damp wisps of hair from her face. Darden looked at her with such love, it took her breath away. She never believed she could love this man more than she had, but she was wrong. They were entering a new phase of their relationship. Now, they were truly partners.

"I'm wonderful," Cassie answered. It was a partial truth.

She wanted to concentrate on what it felt like to be in Darden's arms, not dwell on the telepathic changes occurring. They had made love to share a passion that was long denied, not to make her more powerful.

"Everything will be all right, I promise," Darden said. He reacted to the confusion and turmoil that engulfed her. She could not hide her innermost thoughts from him.

"It's not fair," Cassie cried. "We should be basking in the aftermath of what we are together, not wondering what we both will experience because we made love."

"Any changes will be gradual, based on the past experience of our friends," Darden assured her. "You will adjust to the powers, just as your lifelong friends have. JoAnna did not turn into a monster, and neither will you. Benko did you no favors in not fully training you and scaring us out of not having sex. Legends of soul mates are positive tales, not horror stories."

"But what about what haunts Shirl?" Cassie asked. "I've known her my whole life, something about her powers terrifies her."

"Shirl is no monster," Darden responded. "She knows what she is capable of and controls her power because she is a good person and so are you. Regardless, you are not alone. You have me, along with the rest of our family, to help you navigate your new future. Try to sleep. As you noted earlier, you have a full day tomorrow."

Darden rolled over and brought her into his arms as he adjusted their positions. Her head rested in the crook of his neck. She took in his scent and closed her eyes. Cassie would try to rest. It was doubtful she would be able to sleep. She was worried about what had they just released.

Chapter 8

Darden woke to find Cassie sleeping soundly in his arms. She had struggled to find peace after the hormone was excreted, plagued by what would occur. He had developed new abilities of his own over the years. Although he was a crystal telepath, early on he discovered other gifts. Gifts he shared with no one.

Cassie had been so young when they met. The first time they touched, not only did a telepathic channel open, but he also developed a means to soothe her when required. Adolescence was hard for anyone, but it was harder for Cassie. Her refugee status, her father making her fear her powers, and a soul mate she was ill-equipped to deal with at such a tender age, all made her burden greater.

Darden struggled over the years to adjust to the role he would play in his soul mate's life. How do you transition from older brother or friend to lover? As her body developed it was hard not to have a physical relationship with her. They shared their first kiss when she was sixteen.

Benko could not deny her anything. It seemed easier to meet her every request rather than dwell on their predicament. When Darden entered the picture, he followed Benko's example. Anything Cassie wanted was hers, except for the sexual relationship she had been demanding once she turned sixteen. They inadvertently created a spoiled brat.

Benko monopolized their time when Darden was in Gingko Terra and he did not want her father to know he had any additional powers or that they affected Cassie. At first, he was relieved by Benko's presence. As time passed, he began to resent the intrusion. Fortunately, he could differentiate his frustration with Benko related to his interference with Cassie and his admiration of, and loyalty to, the True Ruler of the Troyk universe.

Darden held her through the night, sending her feelings of love, security, and peace. Everything had changed. Cassie still needed protection, but not from herself.

He heard muffled voices down the hall. The household was stirring. Candy was probably in the kitchen drinking coffee while Tolfer cooked. Zane and Leenea would join those two after breakfast was finished. Leenea knew she was an atrocious cook and did not want to stop her son from finishing the meal out a sense of loyalty to his mother.

His right hand caressed the side of Cassie's neck. Waves of mahogany hair were spread across the pillow. Her toned body still rested beside his, generating a comfortable heat that made him want to lounge longer in bed next to his mate. Had he followed his heart, Darden could have enjoyed mornings like this in the penal colony, rather than waking cold and alone.

"Morning," Cassie muttered, sleep still partially embracing her. "What time is it?"

"Early," Darden replied. "Go back to sleep. I will wake you when breakfast is ready."

The aroma of bacon started to permeate the room. His stomach complained. When was the last time he ate? He had barely eaten a bite once he returned to the penal world to discover Cassie gone.

"I have to pee," Cassie complained. He found her unguarded words adorable. She felt comfortable enough in his presence not to put on any pretense.

Darden smiled to himself as Cassie rolled over and slowly rose. He enjoyed the view of her naked backside as she staggered to the bathroom. Her long hair cascaded down her back and swayed as she moved. If he was lucky, there was no clothing in the bathroom and Cassie would return in all her glory.

Unfortunately, ten minutes later a fully dressed Cassie emerged. Her face was newly scrubbed and the hair surrounding her face was slightly damp. She bent down to kiss him good morning. Cassie tasted of mint, having just brushed her teeth.

"I'm famished," Cassie admitted. "Get dressed and join me in the kitchen before Alex gets up. I understand she can pile away the food."

Cassie was right about Alex's ability to eat. How the little auburn haired woman could eat everything and not gain an ounce was a miracle. He imagined Tarsea kept Alex active in bed burning every calorie she consumed. Darden planned to do the same with Cassie.

"Barash Kleyman is bragging about his lunch date with Cassie," Starc communicated in their private channel. Although they were not identical twins, they shared a link just accessible to the two of them. *"What is going on?"*

"Jeryl Jarlyn set it up," Darden communicated. *"He did not know Cassie and I were soul mates when he did."*

Silence answered his comment. Rarely speechless, it was not like Starc not to have the last word. His taciturn brother rarely spoke to others, but that did not apply to conversations with his twin. Darden had been sent for training as soon as his abilities were discovered. Starc had all the normal childhood experiences and shared his activities and what they were like with Darden. That continued well into their adulthood.

"What is wrong, Starc?" Darden inquired. Something was bothering his brother about the arranged date and he needed to know what his concerns were.

"Jeryl Jarlyn is always looking to garner more power," his brother shared. *"We are not an influential family like the Kleymans. The Prime Ruler will not gain anything with a permanent mating between you and his granddaughter. Once Cassie comes into her powers, you are expendable unless your physical presence enhances her abilities."*

Darden had not considered what his brother suggested. Would Jeryl Jarlyn separate a pair of soul mates for his own gain? The answer to that question caused Darden to jump out of bed.

"Koel. JoAnna. I need you to come to the Childers's home as soon as possible," Darden communicated through the warrior channel. Everyone would have heard the request and he imagined more than Koel and JoAnna would arrive. Hopefully, Tolfer made enough food to feed an army.

He quickly dressed and headed for the kitchen. As expected, Candy was enjoying her morning beverage and Tolfer was plating the meal he just finished. The talented cook quickly started to prepare additional food for the unexpected guests he had just sent for. Cassie and Candy quickly filled their plates and started to eat.

Tarsea entered the kitchen and poured himself coffee. He imagined his friend's mate was still sleeping in their bed. With Alex's pregnancy, she would not have received the communication he sent through the warrior link. As expected, Tarsea immediately rose and was ready to hear what Darden planned to share.

"Start laying out the problem before the others arrive," Tarsea requested. His best friend was the unofficial leader of their group.

"The Prime Ruler has arranged a date between Cassie and Barash Kleyman," Darden said. "Starc is afraid Jeryl Jarlyn will want to set up an advantageous marriage between his granddaughter and another powerful family. I may be expendable once he learns Cassie and I have been sexually active."

Darden had not planned to share with everyone that Cassie and he had made love. However, it was critical everyone knew all the facts. Although he spoke aloud to everyone in the kitchen, Darden also communicated through the warrior link.

"My grandfather cannot force me to marry anyone against my will," Cassie said. "If things become too difficult, we can always return to the penal world. Shirl does not need a crystal to open a naturally occurring portal. Besides, I can play the blushing virgin and declare I won't have sex until Darden puts a ring on my finger. Why would I want to be with anyone other than my soul mate?"

The conversation was temporarily stalled when Alex entered the kitchen. She passed the coffee and sighed. Since her pregnancy, one of Alex's many complaints was her inability to drink caffeine. It made her especially moody in the morning.

Tarsea rose and poured his mate a glass of juice. Alex accepted it without a word and sat next to Cassie, mumbling some kind of greeting. Neither appeared to be morning people, but Cassie was able to drink coffee and let the wondrous beverage clear off her brain's morning fog.

"What do we know about Barash Kleyman?" Tarsea asked.

"*He supports the government and never deviates from procedure,*" Starc responded through the warrior link. "*Otherwise, he is a decent guy. Barash worked on his father's campaign. The new Prime is a mind control telepath; the son is not.*"

"Barash follows the straight and narrow," Candy commented out loud. She translated what was communicated in the warrior link to her two friends who did not have access to it. "Otherwise, he's cool. Cassie's new beau is not a mind control telepath and does not appear to be a fanatic. He has never entered the warrior channel, that much I know."

Darden thought it odd Cassie was unable to link into the warrior pathway. Being so close to both him and Benko over the past few weeks, Darden had assumed she would be able to connect. He never considered Cassie was not loyal to her father, the True Ruler of the Troyk universe. All of a sudden he looked at Cassie differently. Was there more to her growing relationship with her grandfather?

Cassie cast her eyes down to the coffee mug. Darden was giving her looks full of doubt and suspicion, and she could feel the same emotions through their private telepathic link. He had never looked at her quite like this before. She knew exactly what had sparked the distrust from her soul mate—the stupid warrior link.

When the warrior channel first opened, she was too blown away by what had occurred between her and Darden to acknowledge the pathway. Besides, the soul mate channel was the stronger of the two pathways opened to her. So, she didn't need the secondary access.

Benko did not enter the warrior link until she was a teenager. Darden had wrongly assumed he and her father were the only two who had access to the channel because she never communicated through it. As soon as Tarsea and the others joined the link, all of a sudden they believed the legendary warrior channel had revealed itself. Cassie never bothered to correct the misconception. Now it had come back to bite her in the ass.

How Cassie wished she could enlighten Darden that he was very wrong. One thing she knew about soul mates—they were immune from the power the other wielded. At no point had she ever tried to use her mind control talents to get anything from her father or

Darden. She was unsure how she was going to rectify this problem without giving too much away.

"Barash never said or did anything for me to be concerned about," Cassie said. She was going to get involved in the conversation and hopefully refocus Darden's thoughts. "We should not assume everyone who cannot access the warrior channel is an enemy. Legend only has the closest advisors to the True Ruler having the ability to enter, not every supporter. If the coup we plan is to be successful, it is the common Troyk citizens we communicate with through the communal channels that will help us win the day."

Cassie was working herself into an agitated state. She seldom joined political discussions. She often wanted to tell her father and his advisors the focus should be on the people they needed support from, not the politicians they planned to overthrow. She knew they all regarded her as a spoiled brat and feared they would simply discount anything she said, so she remained silent.

Alex placed her hand on Cassie's forearm. "Maybe we should focus on Barash's arrival and how we will explain the small army accompanying them on their date. Besides, our biggest challenge is Cassie's meeting with Jeryl Jarlyn. Let's not lose focus on what's most important."

If they had been alone, Cassie would have hugged Alex. She did not know if her friend picked up her discomfort or just wanted to put in her two cents. Alex's baby was a telepathic empath. Chartail had temporarily developed mind control abilities while pregnant; it was not a stretch to figure Alex's unborn daughter was sharing her powers. Regardless, Cassie was happy for Alex's support.

By this time, Tolfer had finished his second batch of breakfast food and Darden piled his plate with protein. Cassie figured she had a reprieve where the warrior channel was concerned. When Koel arrived, they would concentrate on the tactical aspects required for the day. Darden's cousin was a talented tactician. He had planned Candy and Tolfer's rescue from the Troyk penal colony. The rescue included coordinating the entry of people from four different parallel dimensions, including the Nightshade universe.

Once Darden's attention was on his food, Cassie was able to continue eating her own breakfast. Although she was nervous about spending time with her grandfather, her stress had no affect on her appetite until Darden threw her questioning looks. When was he going to trust her? She needed to keep her composure and not lapse into her spoiled brat persona.

Cassie was relieved when JoAnna and Koel arrived. She and JoAnna went to her room and worked on her telepathic shield while the rest of the group moved to the common room to devise strategies to handle Barash. By some miracle, Cassie was able to put up her shield against JoAnna's assault, as well as listen to the discussion taking place in another part of the house through the warrior channel.

"JoAnna, how did you deal with everyone not trusting you when you first arrived in the Troyk universe?" Cassie asked. Her new friend experienced some of the same issues Cassie was struggling with now. Perhaps she could learn from JoAnna how to combat the doubt.

"I just had to have faith in myself," JoAnna answered, shrugging her shoulders. "Everyone was fighting a power I manipulated most of my life without realizing it. Koel knew what we were to each other, yet he did his best to stay away from me. Finally, he had no choice but to trust I would be able to control my additional telepathic abilities. The same is true with you and Darden. He has known you since you were a little girl. I don't understand his behavior."

"That makes two of us," Cassie said. "It really hurts. My father and Darden believe I am going to turn into some kind of monster, yet you girls barely know me and have more confidence in my ability to control myself."

"Maybe because we have all been through the same thing," JoAnna said. "Of the five of us, only we share the same ability. I imagine even mind control telepathic abilities may vary from person to person. It's best to take things one day at a time. Alex, Shirl, Candy, and I are here for you. You are not alone. The men are focusing on Benko and his revolution. We, on the other hand, are focused on you and your safety."

Cassie reached over and hugged JoAnna. Her words and advice were exactly what Cassie needed at this point. Thank goodness she was not the first to enter the Troyk universe. She had a whole new respect for Alex, their trailblazer. Now, she just needed to get through her first date and then the training session with her grandfather.

Barash arrived exactly on time, shortly after Shirl and Starc. Cassie was not present to greet him since she was retouching her makeup. When she joined her date in the common room, poor Barash was surrounded by hostile men all dressed in black. She was not sure when the men changed tunics, but they certainly looked menacing.

"Oh, I see you have met our entourage," Cassie said. "My grandfather considers my safety his number one priority."

Barash would look foolish to argue the point. Jeryl Jarlyn had not set up the security force - that was all her friends and soul mate's doing. If she was being honest, Cassie was relieved she had people around her who cared. There were still factions who wanted to bring down the mind control government without regard for the means or consequences. She now represented that government.

"We should head out," Barash said.

Candy made a pre-emptive move and grabbed Barash's arm. The Warrior Woman started conversing with him about a hand-to-hand training session the C.T. Guards participated in the day before. It gave Darden the opportunity to walk alongside Cassie.

For two people who had made love the night before, they were both tongue tied. Cassie had hurried out of their room this morning anxious about the day's events and they had been surrounded by people all morning. She was not sure how Alex and Tarsea had found any privacy in the house, not to mention Candy and Tolfer.

"We need to present a united front to your grandfather," Darden shared with her through their private channel. *"He needs to understand we are a package deal. I have more of a right to you than he does."*

Cassie counted to ten in her mind. She did not want to show any negative response to Darden's comment. Why he felt he was lord and master over her was beyond Cassie's comprehension. They were soul mates; she was not a piece of chattel.

"My grandfather has not been part of my life," Cassie said. She did not feel the need to keep this part of the conversation private.

"He naturally wants to get to know me. And frankly, I would like to spend time with him as well."

Her date turned from time to time, checking to make sure she was still behind him. Candy continued to monopolize his attention. JoAnna and Shirl were close behind with their men, ready to take Candy's place if necessary. She was not altogether sure whether this was all for her benefit or Darden's.

It did not take long to get to the restaurant where they would dine. The restaurant was located in the gathering place park near the Childers's residence. The park was on the way to The Palace, so it seemed the logical place to share a meal. Barash may have intended for them to enjoy an intimate lunch, but her protectors made them a modest sized group.

They were led to a table set for eight. Lunch was well underway and they attracted a lot of attention. Shirl, Candy, and JoAnna were well-known in the area. They were women of legend living among Troyk citizens. It would only be a matter of time before Cassie would grab that same notoriety. Already, the communal pathways were active with gossip related to who she could be.

Barash quickly snagged the chair next to her, while Darden claimed the chair on her other side. JoAnna sat next to Barash, giving Candy a well needed break. Either of the two mind control telepathic women could convince Barash he was not interested in her. Cassie had never used her power in such a way, but did not rule it out for future use if things became sticky with Barash or any other man her grandfather set her up with. In this particular case, her grandfather would undo anything they attempted.

It was her understanding that a mind control telepath could make the decision for a person who was waffling over a choice. Anyone who was totally committed to an action or person could not be swayed. The victim of a mind control telepath would be unaware the decision was not their own. If new information or some kind of stimulus was introduced, the person would go through their decision-making process again. This time, however, they would make their own decision, assuming a mind control telepath did not interfere.

Although he never admitted it, Cassie was confident her father used his gift from time to time in making business deals. He no doubt justified its usage as a means to make a comfortable life for Cassie in the world they were trapped in. Benko was unusually successful and was able to afford homes in both Scottsdale and Sedona, Arizona.

Cassie looked at the menu and was unsure of what to order. There were several selections that were unfamiliar to her. Darden had been around her enough on Earth to know what she liked and disliked.

"What should I order, Darden?" Cassie asked through their special link.

She knew orders were taken telepathically. As soon as Cassie knew what she would order, she would send it through the communal pathways. There were waitresses in the past Cassie felt had to be telepathic. They would take an order at a large table at an Earth restaurant, never writing anything down.

"Order the chicken and keen dish," Darden responded. *"It is one of Alex's favorites. The spices used are all found on Earth and the keen will pick up those flavors."*

"I will be happy to order for you, Cassie," Barash said aloud. "You have not been here long enough to have clear access to our many telepathic pathways."

"Thank you, Barash," she said. "I'll have the chicken and keen dish."

Cassie did not have the heart to correct Barash's misconception. Besides, the more people underestimated her abilities, the better off she would be. As far as Barash knew, she had never used her telepathic powers until she arrived in the Troyk universe. He assumed Benko never taught her and was ignorant of the time she spent in the penal colony.

She was about to sip from the glass of water when Candy communicated a warning through the warrior channel. *"We've got trouble coming. Darden, you need to get Cassie out of here. Koel, JoAnna, and I will deal with the agitator. Shirl and Starc, you should accompany Cassie and provide back-up."*

Chapter 9

D arden grabbed ahold of Cassie's arm and almost lifted her from the chair. Candy launched herself to her feet and approached the man stalking toward them. The communal pathways were already abuzz concerning the angry man pushing his way through the restaurant. He bumped into various waiters, causing them to drop their trays of food.

Cassie was dragged outside the perimeter of the dining area, but her eyes still fought to witness the altercation. Barash automatically went to Candy's side, rather than reacting to Darden evacuating his date from the scene. She tugged on Darden's arm when they were out of danger huddled within the crowd that gathered around the exterior of the restaurant.

The intruder had some kind of weapon. Cassie could not tell what kind from her vantage point. Candy had the ability to know when the perpetrator would use the firearm or knife and JoAnna could get into his head. It was fascinating to watch the interplay, wondering which power would prevail, the physical or the mental.

She felt a slight pressure in her head. Her mind was not accustomed to all the telepathic communication occurring around her. It was clear, she needed to spend more time with Tolfer to learn how to better manage the various communal channels jockeying for her attention.

"You do not want to cause anyone any harm," JoAnna communicated to the unidentified man. For some reason, Cassie was able to pick

up the telepathic communication. She concentrated on the dialog, rather than why she was picking up the conversation. JoAnna was not using a communal pathway, she had entered the man's mind. *"Violence is never an answer. All you do is bring shame to your family and destroy any sympathy the citizens might have for your cause."*

Somehow, Cassie could feel the man struggling with JoAnna's words. The pressure in her head continued to build. She could not make out individual thoughts, but Cassie could actually feel his confusion. He was fighting what the other mind control telepath was trying to do. The man's emotions were flooding her mind.

Suddenly, she knew his brother was the man Jeryl Jarlyn had executed outside The Palace for trying to kill JoAnna. His anger and sorrow consumed him. He knew he had to do something, but fought with himself over what to do. The man's brother's death had made him reconsider his thoughts about the government and the position he held. She focused on preventing the man's emotions from overwhelming her.

Cassie struggled to release herself from Darden's grasp and moved forward in the crowd before her soul mate could stop her. Cassie knew she could help talk the man off the figurative ledge. Cassie was unsure whether this was a power she always had or a latent ability that emerged after the hormone spread through her brain last night. Cassie knew she could make a difference in whether anyone would die today.

"A martyr can only inspire a cause so far," Cassie communicated to the distressed man. *"It takes the living to make true change. I know you loved your brother and did not condone his actions. Do not make the same mistake he made."*

Cassie had piggybacked off the connection JoAnna had made with the man. She could still feel the other telepath's presence. The man turned and glared at Cassie. His face was a mixture of surprise and confusion. Her heartbeat quickened and she swallowed hard. What had she done?

Her eyes traveled to Candy, who did not seem alarmed. That made her relax a little bit.

"I'm Cassandra Jarlyn," Cassie said aloud. It was weird calling herself by that name. Her last name had been Clark for as long as she could remember. She needed witnesses from this point forward. "My father is Benko Jarlyn. I understand why you fight and know better than most the sacrifices freedom fighters have suffered. Harming JoAnna will not bring about the change your brother wanted."

The communal pathways exploded with conversations once she identified herself and spoke of her father in the present tense. Fear now consumed her. Cassie did not know if it was her fear or the man's. The Palace Guard and a contingent of C.T. Guards had arrived. They held back due to the proximity of the Prime Ruler's granddaughter to the weapon the freedom fighter held.

"Please give yourself up willingly," Cassie said. "Has there not been enough bloodshed? I will see you are sent to the Troyk penal colony where other freedom fighters were sent. No one is going to die because of what happened today."

Cassie was basically sending her father another capable man to support his cause. She did not sense insanity in the man, but over-whelming grief. He acted on impulse, not a premeditated desire to kill. When he saw JoAnna enter the restaurant, something inside him snapped. The man was actually a Palace Guard and had been heading to work.

"Give me your weapon," Cassie said as she moved forward, extending her hand.

Candy came up beside the man and gently placed her hand over the metallic crystal weapon. She moved with grace, no sudden moves that would alarm him. Whatever had alerted Candy was no longer present. Several guards passed her and arrested the man.

"Starc and I will accompany him to The Palace," Shirl said. "We'll make sure your promise is kept. If there are any problems, I'll let you know."

Barash came toward her and stopped. "I should go with them and testify to what I saw and heard. What you just did was very brave and stupid. Your grandfather will also be briefed about what happened."

Cassie was not sure if that was a promise or a threat…perhaps both. Her grandfather was the least of her problems. Darden came up beside her, he was furious.

Darden had never felt such dread as when Cassie put herself in harm's way. She had no business interfering with the capture of the man who had threatened JoAnna. Now that the danger was over, his feeling of helplessness was replaced by anger. He was furious Cassie had endangered her life. She had been reckless with no concern for her own safety.

He took several breaths before approaching his soul mate. For once in his life, he wanted to do her harm. He wanted to make sure she never was so careless with her life again. Darden fisted his hands as he approached Cassie.

She was paler than he had ever seen her. He was not sure if it was because she had faced a madman with a weapon or Cassie feared justifying her actions to him. It took every ounce of self-control he possessed not to yell at her in front of the crowd that continued to grow.

People came forward to meet the daughter of the famous freedom fighter and the granddaughter of the Prime Ruler. He was not sure which facet of Cassie's familial relationships excited the crowd more. Cassie was gracious and greeted the public. JoAnna threw him a concerned look.

"The Prime Ruler is expecting his granddaughter at The Palace," Darden informed the crowd.

His anger had lessened a small amount now that new risks to her safety grabbed his attention. The crowd was becoming more aggressive in their desire to talk with the young woman they felt held their future in her hands, one way or another. It irritated him that both Shirl and Candy had left Cassie's safety to him, JoAnna, and Koel.

"I will speak with my grandfather to set up opportunities for me to meet the general public," Cassie said in a calming voice. "Since I did not grow up in this realm, he has been focusing on my education of the Troyk government and how it runs."

Cassie started moving toward the restaurant's exit, greeting people as she moved through the crowd. Darden was surprised that such a large horde was unusually calm and protective of her instead of pushing and shoving each other to shake her hand or touch her. For the first time, Darden wondered if Cassie had an ability to soothe a group, similar to his ability to calm her. He had been in many mobs in the past and they did not react as this group did.

They walked toward The Palace with each person walking beside her to say a few words, then to be replaced with someone else. Out of the corner of his eye, he saw Candy on the outskirts of the crowd. Her eyes were glued on Cassie, but did not seem alarmed by the people approaching her friend. Darden maneuvered through the mass of humanity and walked beside Candy.

"Do you understand what is happening?" Darden asked.

"It's odd, I admit," Candy said. "I do not pick up any hostility within the crowd. If anything, it's the exact opposite. I get a certain feeling when danger is present, but now it's almost as if I'm entering some kind of Zen state."

"Don't get too comfortable," Darden warned. "I do not like what is happening. Crowds do not behave in this fashion. I am afraid they will turn on her at the slightest provocation. Everyone just witnessed an altercation and an arrest. Something always results from those events until a mind control telepath intervenes."

Candy did not immediately reply to his comment. She seemed to be considering his words. The young woman had spent most of her life in Gingko Terra, ignorant of the Troyk universe, telepathic beings, or her own abilities.

A small smile blossomed on her face. "Cassie is a mind control telepath," Candy finally said. "Have you considered she is responsible for the crowd's behavior?"

He had, but he was not sure if it was intentional on Cassie's part or if she had the power to sustain it. When The Palace came into view, he breathed a sigh of relief. They would soon enter the building and head to a part of the structure the general public could not enter.

Candy and JoAnna both stationed themselves on either side of Cassie as they entered The Palace. The crowd did not seem alarmed or take offense to the young women. They backed off as the three of them passed through a guard station. Various versions of goodbyes were yelled to Cassie as she started to climb the stairs.

Darden never believed spending time with Jeryl Jarlyn would cause him any relief. Today it did. He quickly changed his mind when they entered the greeting room to find the Prime Ruler in the midst of a nosebleed. The old man was clutching a crystal in one hand and tissues in the other.

Alarmed, Cassie ran toward her grandfather, while JoAnna grabbed additional tissues. The blood continued to pour from Jeryl Jarlyn's nose. If it were any other man, Darden would have been concerned about his gray coloring.

"Grandfather," Cassie cried as she took ahold of his arm and led him to a sofa. "How long has this been going on? Has someone contacted a doctor?"

Darden looked around, but there was no one else in the room. Her grandfather had not called for help when this latest attack started. Koel and JoAnna had previously divulged information the Prime Ruler suffered frequent nosebleeds from abusing powerful crystals. JoAnna worked to pry the crystal from his fist while Cassie tried to staunch his nosebleed.

"Benko will be coming to take my place," Jeryl Jarlyn ranted. "My boy intends to take control by force and you are the one he sent to start the process."

The man was fighting Cassie's aid, referring to her as the enemy. There was no evidence the Prime Ruler had attempted to attack JoAnna or Cassie telepathically. Darden looked at Koel for some type of direction. His cousin had been dealing with Jeryl Jarlyn's deterioration since his mating with JoAnna. The general public had no idea the state their ruler was in.

"Grandfather," Cassie once again called out to the old man having some kind of attack.

She was helpless to know what to do. Her father had used crystals from time to time to increase his telepathic gift once he entered the Troyk penal colony. But he never had any adverse side effects, like her grandfather was now experiencing. Tears of concern and frustration fell down her cheeks.

"Why isn't anyone coming?" JoAnna asked. "Koel, see if you can find someone who can call a doctor. At his age, the Prime Ruler must have a physician he sees on a regular basis."

It would have been so easy to reach out telepathically for help. However, Cassie did not want to communicate her grandfather's condition through the communal pathways. Her father would ultimately decide when he was ready to overthrow Jeryl Jarlyn and rule.

"You are all out to get me," Jeryl Jarlyn yelled. He was becoming more agitated with each exchange.

"Grandfather, it's me, Cassie," she cried. "We have finally found each other; please don't leave me now."

His nose stopped bleeding, but he was still out of his mind. Cassie blocked out all the terrible things he was saying, believing it was his illness that caused the outbursts. She was relieved when Koel finally returned with a small contingent of guards and men not in uniform.

"Arrest these people," her grandfather ordered. "They tried to kill me!"

Fortunately, the new arrivals did not react to Jeryl Jarlyn's words. They probably had witnessed the deterioration of their ruler and knew he experienced moments when he was out of his mind. Cassie rose and approached the small party.

"My grandfather had a severe nosebleed," Cassie said. "He needs to be cleaned up and a doctor sent for."

"The Prime Ruler has dismissed his doctors," one of the men commented. He appeared as helpless as Cassie felt. "He should be his old self after he rests."

She could feel her anger slowly simmering. "I do not care what his orders were in the past. My grandfather needs a doctor. If he has been getting regular nosebleeds, he may need a blood transfusion. Look at him!" Cassie screamed.

"I will see to it," a man in the back said. He exited the room and Cassie felt her first sense of relief since finding her grandfather in his current state.

A thousand thoughts cluttered her brain. *"What should we do next?"* Cassie asked Darden through their closed channel. She needed his help. Although he was probably still mad at her, he needed to get over it and aid her now.

"Send for Solfa Theffar," Darden ordered the befuddled guard awaiting instructions. "We do not want to alarm the general public by requesting her presence through any of the communal links."

The guard gazed at Cassie, who nodded in agreement. In everything but name, she was the Prime Ruler until her grandfather recovered from his latest bout of madness. She wondered how much longer Jeryl Jarlyn would be able to hide his illness from the citizens of Aster Province.

Her friends rallied beside her, but Cassie never felt more alone in her life. If only her father were here. Perhaps now was the time to bring Benko Jarlyn back to the Troyk universe.

After thirty minutes, which felt like an eternity, Solfa entered the greeting room. She had visited with the doctor before she joined them. Solfa continually reported her whereabouts through the warrior channel and Cassie yet again pretended she could not receive the telepathic communication. Cassie vacillated as to when she would admit to everyone she could access that pathway.

"The doctor has given your grandfather a clean bill of health," Solfa advised the group. "Jarlyn is working in his study. He used his mind control capabilities to convince the physician he was in remarkable health for a man his age. Your grandfather met with the guards and they are now also ignorant of what happened this afternoon."

"How long has this been going on?" Cassie asked.

"I have no way of knowing," Solfa shrugged. "If I witnessed one of his events, I have no memory of it. Only JoAnna and Koel will recall the nosebleeds and his madness. This can happen indefinitely until your grandfather finally passes."

"It is a good thing we did not act prematurely and bring Benko over," Koel said. "We need to continue our planning as if today did not happen. Nothing has changed as far as the general population is aware. Cassie needs to ingrain herself into her grandfather's life and the government. Jeryl Jarlyn will eventually abdicate part of his control. Only then will Benko return."

Cassie could see JoAnna struggled with her soul mate's declaration. "We have the power to overtake the old man," JoAnna said. "Between my power and Cassie's growing abilities, Jeryl Jarlyn can be brought down."

"It is too risky," Koel said. "I will not risk you or Cassie. The guards are still loyal to Jeryl."

The guard who earlier went to bring a doctor to see her grandfather reentered the room. "Your grandfather wishes to see Cassandra alone in his office. He will not allow anyone but his granddaughter to enter."

Cassie immediately responded to the guard and followed him out of the room. "Stay here, I will return shortly," Cassie ordered the people she left behind. *"I mean everyone, Darden,"* Cassie followed up through the soul mate channel to prevent Darden from having second thoughts.

The walls of the hall she walked down felt like they were closing in on her. She knew it was her imagination caused by her anxiety to meet with her grandfather. Would he be back in his right mind? Cassie stood before the closed door to her grandfather's study. The last thing she wanted to do was enter, but she had no choice. What was she going to find on the other side of the door?

Chapter 10

The room was dimly lit and Cassie's eyes had to adjust. She could barely make out the figure sitting behind the desk. Was her grandfather sane once more? Jeryl Jarlyn was wily enough to wipe the memory of his doctor and guards, meaning he had control of his abilities. Her grandfather could think enough to manipulate people around him to suit his will, but did that make him sane?

"Sit down, Cassandra," her grandfather said in a commanding voice. The frailty she witnessed earlier was gone. Jeryl Jarlyn seemed to have control of his mind and subjects once again. It was as if the earlier attack had not occurred.

Cassie complied with her grandfather's request without a word. She was not sure what to say to him. Would inquiring about his health set off her grandfather? There was too much for her and her friends to lose to antagonize the Prime Ruler.

"I understand you put yourself in danger this afternoon trying to disarm someone who tried to kill JoAnna," her grandfather stated. "What telepathic powers did you use to protect yourself?"

Her grandfather was more concerned with her abilities, than the fact she had endangered her life. A strange reaction, especially considering how furious Darden was at her. Cassie had expected Jeryl Jarlyn's reaction to be similar to her soul mate's.

She took several seconds to consider her answer. He knew Cassie could not have intervened without using her abilities. However, she did not want to reveal too much. It was true, she did not know if she had the ability before she made love to Darden. Cassie figured like any talent, her telepathic abilities needed to be practiced in order to hone and develop them.

"I entered a link JoAnna created between herself and the man," Cassie admitted. Her grandfather already knew JoAnna was a powerful mind control telepath.

Her grandfather rose and walked to a cabinet she had not noticed, as it was so dark in the room. He pulled open a drawer and took out an object. After closing the drawer her grandfather headed for the light switch and made it a little brighter in the room. He did it so gradually, Cassie's eyes adjusted to the additional light without having to squint.

Jeryl Jarlyn took the seat next to her and handed her a number of crystals. She recognized several of them, but a few of them were unknown to her. Her father and JoAnna had mentioned there were crystals that enhanced a telepath's ability, but she had not been interested enough to listen. It appeared she was now going to be educated.

"Do you recognize this stone?" Jeryl asked after he picked up a piece of herderite. She knew her father purchased the golden crystal every time he came across one.

"It's herderite," Cassie responded.

"Did your father teach you how to use it to increase your telepathic power?"

Her dad did everything he could to encourage her not to use her abilities. They were only to be used for self-protection. She had only used her telepathic powers before entering the Troyk penal colony twice in a non-training exercise: Once on a Gatherer when she was ten and again on poor Afton. At no point did he ever encourage her to enhance her abilities.

"No," she answered simply. She figured she did not owe her grandfather an explanation.

"Well, this little gold crystal will amplify your power," her grandfather said. "You take the essence of the crystal into your mind."

Cassie had no idea what he was talking about. Her grandfather held a rock. Did rocks have essences? She didn't know how to even begin.

"Your soul mate Darden and your friend, Shirl, can use their telepathic ability and their crystals to navigate inter-dimensional portals," her grandfather said. "Have you never wondered how they did it?"

To be honest, Cassie never gave it much thought. She always figured it was like adding in your head, it just happened once you learned math. At no point had she considered the mechanics behind how they were able to pull power from a rock.

Her grandfather took the rest of the crystals from her and placed them on the desk. He handed her the herderite. "Place this in your palm and concentrate on the crystal. You want to get in a meditative state and then absorb the waves of power emanating from the herderite."

She was not sure about the mumbo-jumbo her grandfather was spouting. Cassie would talk to JoAnna when they had time alone. There had to be a trick to pulling power from crystals since both JoAnna and her dad did it.

"What do the rest of the crystals do?" Cassie asked.

"One lesson at a time," her grandfather responded. "Your friends were sent to their respective homes under guard. When I said I wanted time alone with you, I meant it. It is charming you have such loyal friends, but their first loyalty is to me."

There was a knock on the door and Barash Kleyman entered after he was granted access. He bowed to her grandfather and stood at attention, ready to receive orders. Her grandfather rose from the chair and took his place behind his desk once again.

"Have a seat, young man," her grandfather said to Barash. Her date from this afternoon sat in the chair The Prime Ruler had just vacated. "I understand you had some excitement at your lunch and some unwanted company. Did you sense anything out of the ordinary during the confrontation between JoAnna and my granddaughter with the man carrying the crystal weapon?"

"Nothing, sir," Barash answered without any elaboration.

"It is my understanding you wished to escort my granddaughter home," her grandfather continued.

"Yes, sir," Barash answered. "I picked her up and feel it is my duty to return her home. After the confrontation, I never should have left her side. My deepest apologies for that oversight, my Prime."

"She was well guarded and you took control of the man who would have done her injury," her grandfather said. "There is nothing to apologize for. You may return my granddaughter to her temporary home. I am tired and will not be officiating at any events this evening. Cassandra may return to her friends."

Barash stood and waited for Cassie to join him. She was relieved she would not have to spend any more time with her grandfather today. It was a good thing he felt he needed sleep. Cassie glanced at the crystals that lay on the desk, wondering what powers each possessed. Her grandfather had cut their lesson short.

Cassie skirted the desk and gave her grandfather an awkward hug and kissed his cheek. "Get some rest, Grandfather," Cassie said. Although there was no longer evidence of his nosebleed, the circles under his eyes had deepened since she entered his study.

They left her grandfather's office and headed down the hallway leading to The Palace's common area exit. Just prior to reaching the end of the corridor, Barash stopped and backed her into a small alcove. Before she could object, Barash handed Cassie a beautiful carved wooden box. It looked hand painted.

"I would like you to have this," he said.

Cassie was shocked at Barash being so forward. She opened the box and found a lovely rose colored crystal on a gold chain. The stone resembled one of the crystals she saw on her grandfather's desk, one she could not identify. Barash took it from the box and placed it over her head. The chain was long enough that the necklace did not have to be clasped behind her neck to be worn.

"Thank you," Cassie said, "it's lovely."

Not wanting to cause a scene in The Palace, Cassie did not attempt to remove the necklace. She would take it off before Darden could see it. There was no sense in making her soul mate any more jealous than he already was.

"I know a short cut that will get you home faster," Barash said.

Cassie was not averse to taking a different route home. She needed to learn the city and returning the way they came would not offer the opportunity to see more of Aster Province. They passed several shops she had not seen before and Barash did not object to her peering in the windows to check out the displays. There were a variety of women's clothing stores that offered Troyk fashion that did not appear to be as risqué as the ones Madame Gigi forced upon her. She would have to return with Shirl and JoAnna.

When they started heading to her left, Cassie believed they were going in the wrong direction. "Shouldn't we be heading toward the gathering place?" she asked. She could see the trees several blocks to the right.

"I want you to meet a friend of mine," Barash said as he shoved her down an alley.

Cassie knew she was in danger and Candy's senses must be having a field day. *"Candy, Barash Kleyman is abducting me. I'm several blocks on the other side of the gathering place. There was a green awning over a woman's clothing store just down from where he is dragging me."*

"Darden," Cassie simultaneously called out to her soul mate through their channel. *"I'm in danger. Head in the direction of the gathering place and over three blocks to the east."*

Reaching out to her friends made more sense than screaming for help and alerting Barash's accomplices, if he had any. The street they had been walking down was deserted. She struggled in Barash's grasp, buying Candy and Darden time to get to her. There were no immediate replies to her pleas for help, which was troubling.

At the end of the alley, a door opened as they approached. She did not recognize the men who made way for her and Barash to enter the apartment. Cassie was dragged forward, although at this point she had stopped struggling. There was something about her new surroundings that did not indicate she was in any danger.

They entered a smartly decorated room. It looked like something that would be laid out in an expensive department store for the very rich. Things were not adding up. A well-dressed woman sat on a cream colored sofa. Something about the woman was familiar. It was as if she was staring in the mirror, reflecting what she would look like in forty years.

Cassie could not believe her eyes. This woman had to be her grandmother, or at least, a close relative. Benko rarely talked about the woman who had given him up at birth to Jeryl Jarlyn.

"I never gave up your father," the woman said. "He was taken from me by that monster."

It alarmed Cassie that her grandmother could read her thoughts and Darden had not responded to her pleas. She needed information and the best way to get it was to cooperate. Cassie sat in a chair next to her grandmother.

"That crystal you wear interferes with your telepathic communication capabilities," her grandmother stated. Cassie pulled it off and handed it to the woman. "Its proximity will still prevent you from calling for help. I mean you no harm. Kidnapping you seemed the most efficient way to meet you. My name is Elyn, by the way."

"Father never mentioned your name," Cassie replied. It was more of a comment to herself than to Elyn.

Her grandmother gave a half-laugh. "I imagined he would not. Benko was the model son. He surprised everyone, including me, when he tried to overthrow his father. Does my son still live?"

Cassie studied her grandmother. She was as leery to provide her news of Benko's whereabouts, lest any of the people in the room report back to her grandfather. It was becoming a well-known fact Benko still lived, so Cassie did not give anything away by letting Elyn know her son was alive.

"My father was fine the last time I saw him," Cassie said in a noncommittal tone. "How do you have the ability to read my mind?"

"Several years after I gave birth to Benko, I met my soul mate," Elyn responded. "After we made love, I had the ability to read people's minds."

It was the same telepathic enhancement that Alex and Tarsea possessed once they mated. Elyn was admitting to being a soul mate and was aware of what could happen when they came together for the first time. Cassie did not have a reason to doubt her grandmother's word.

"What is your association with my grandmother?" Cassie asked Barash.

She could not figure out why he was the one who brought her to this little family reunion. From everything she had gathered, Barash was loyal to Jeryl Jarlyn. However, as far as the general population knew, so was Solfa Theffar.

"You can say we have the same interests," Barash responded. Cassie raised an eyebrow, requesting clarification of that statement.

"I did not like what my father became when he started running for office and what has happened to him since he won the seat. He tolerated the government, but enjoyed the wealth it brought. As he became friendlier with the powerful Prime Representatives, his values changed. Mine have not."

"How did the two of you find each other?" Cassie asked.

Elyn smiled. "People of like beliefs have a tendency to gravitate to one another, even when it is not healthy to do so. I used my ability to read minds to identify others with similar inclinations. We ignored our telepathic abilities and started to meet in crowded locations, speaking in hushed tones. Over the years, we made many unsuccessful attempts to unseat my former lover. Barash is a newer member of our group. When Jeryl Jarlyn threw the two of you together, it seemed like destiny that we would meet. After the display this afternoon, I knew the time had come."

Her grandmother stood and grabbed the rose colored crystal that prevented Cassie from communicating with Darden and her friends. Elyn lifted a heavy metal candleholder and proceeded to crush the stone. Cassie immediately reached out to Darden and Candy, who were frantically transmitting to her through their respective channels.

"Would you like something to eat while we wait for your friends to arrive?" Elyn asked as she pulled a tray of food from the cold storage unit.

Their lunch had been interrupted, so she had not eaten since breakfast. Cassie grabbed some cheese to take the bite off her hunger. She did not want to eat too much, since she was still nervous about her current situation. The food allowed her to better focus and control her emotions. Her behavior would not alert her grandmother she was communicating with Darden and her friends.

Darden, Candy, and Tarsea were led into the living room in less time than she expected. Cassie immediately went into Darden's arms. He kissed her while she telepathically communicated who the woman who kidnapped her was.

"How did you get here so fast?" Cassie asked Darden through the soul mate channel.

"Candy became uneasy, so we evaded the guards surrounding the house," Darden shared telepathically. He did not want to give

anything away to a room full of strangers. *"Shirl and JoAnna were able to distract the men, while the three of us went looking for you. There were various sightings of you along this street. Sometimes communal pathways can be very informative."*

"What is it you want?" Tarsea asked her grandmother. She could hear the anger and impatience in his voice.

"That is easy," Elyn answered. "I want your assistance in overthrowing Jeryl Jarlyn and bringing my son home."

"That is easy?" Tarsea responded. "What makes you believe we will not turn you over to the Palace Guard? You speak of treason."

Cassie was surprised the strangers in the room did not react violently to Tarsea's threat. Her grandmother just responded to Tarsea's words with another knowing smile. Her calmness was unsettling. She could not read her grandmother's emotions from her expressions or body language. Although she had struggled against it, Cassie finally used her abilities to enter her grandmother's mind.

She ran against a strong barrier that prevented her access into Elyn's mind. Her grandmother continued to stare at her, fully aware of what Cassie was trying to attempt.

"What will you do if I let you in?" Her grandmother connected with her mind as JoAnna had in the past. Was her grandmother a mind control telepath and failed to mention that tidbit of information?

"I need to know if I can trust you with my life, the life of my father, and my friends," Cassie responded. *"You are a stranger to me. This could be an elaborate trap my grandfather concocted to test my loyalty to him."*

"Fair enough," Elyn said.

The barrier to her grandmother's mind disappeared and Cassie entered her thoughts. She could detect no trickery or deception, only a desire to be reunited with her son. Cassie could not locate any distinct thoughts, just emotions of a distraught mother who had been separated from her child for too long. Somehow she knew her grandmother was dying and desperate.

"You found what you were looking for?" Elyn asked.

"She can be trusted," Cassie informed the others.

Tarsea exchanged a look with Darden. It was obvious he was not convinced. This group only accepted entry into the warrior channel as a sign of trustworthiness. Something they did not believe Cassie had been able to do.

"We will consider what you have shared," Darden said. "If we wish to meet again with you, we will contact Barash. Under no circumstances do you take Cassie by force again."

Darden did not share the nature of their relationship with her grandmother. The seeds of distrust that had been brewing in Darden had begun to grow. It was not a question of whether her soul mate trusted Elyn, but whether he trusted her. Cassie was not looking forward to the explanations she would have to make once everyone knew the truth.

Chapter 11

Candy chattered as they walked back to the Childers's home. Cassie only took in every third word, not bothering to make any sense of what her friend was rambling on about. Her mind was overwhelmed at how angry her soul mate was. She turned off the link between them, but was pre-occupied by what was going through his mind.

Darden was seething mad. She had felt him trying to rein in his nearly out of control fury before she broke their connection. It wouldn't surprise her if he took her by the arm and dragged her back like some kind of caveman. His barely controlled rage made her stay close to Candy.

When they reached their destination, Cassie had planned to join the others in the common room. There was so much to discuss, especially now that part of the group had met her grandmother. She was still a little shell-shocked by the encounter.

Darden, however, had other ideas. As soon as she stepped through the threshold of the house, Darden wrapped his arm around her waist and led her to the room they shared. She figured it would not be a good idea to fight him, especially with most of her friends present. The last thing she wanted was to start a civil war in the Childers's household.

As soon as they entered their quarters, Darden shut and locked the door. His normal warm blue eyes were an icy gray. Cassie took a step back, unsure if her soul mate meant her harm. She had never seen his irises that color before.

Darden removed his shirt, exposing his sinewy upper body. There was not an ounce of fat, just pure muscle. He pulled down and stepped out of his leggings. His fully erect member surged forward. Cassie swallowed hard as her eyes took in the magnificent being before her. Regardless of his anger, he was hers.

"Remove your clothing and get into bed," Darden ordered.

Obviously, he was not in the mood for seduction. He did not move forward but waited for her to comply with his demand. Cassie could feel his patience was wearing thin.

Rather than removing her clothing slowly or seductively, Cassie undressed as if her clothing was on fire. She scurried under the covers, only to have him whip the sheets from the bed. She lay there naked, exposed.

"Do not move," Darden said. His voice was cold, without emotion. This was not the man she had dreamt being with for the last eight years.

This Darden was a little dangerous and unpredictable. She had never seen this side of his personality. Cassie could not help being turned on by his attempt to dominate her.

He walked to the end of the bed and grabbed her left ankle. Darden reached to grab something from the chair behind him. Cassie took in a breath when she saw what he had retrieved. A black silk rope was tied around her ankle and then secured to the bedpost. Where the hell had the rope come from?

"I had plenty of time to contemplate how to punish you for today's recklessness," Darden answered her unasked question.

The rope had so shocked her, she temporarily released the shield blocking Darden's anger. Cassie brought the shield to full strength and checked out her bound leg. She tugged on it lightly, hoping Darden would not notice. He seemed distracted by binding her other ankle. The rope had a coating on it that did not chafe her skin, but was secure enough she could not release herself with a more powerful tug.

This macho crap both alarmed and excited Cassie. If she were truly in danger, Candy would be charging through the locked door. She might as well lay back and enjoy her 'punishment'. It was as if one of her fantasies, or one of the hot kinky scenes in her favorite romance novel, was coming to life. Excitement, not fear, made her weak with want.

Cassie's right ankle was now tied to the other post. Her sex was now fully exposed. Rather than tightening with fear, her body throbbed with anticipation. She watched Darden as he examined his handiwork and then drew his sight to her spread legs. Her breath quickened as she watched his eyes lose their icy shade. They now burned for her, as her body burned for him.

As if sensing her desire, Darden leaned over her body. He captured both her wrists and raised them over her head while laying his torso next to her, one leg in between hers. Her wrists in his right hand, he slowly explored her with his left. Her skin warmed to his touch. Need rocked through her as his fingers tantalized her flesh.

When he got to her left breast, his thumb and index finger took hold of its nipple. Pinching and releasing the nub a bit harder each time, he relished in both nipples hardening in response to his ministrations. Cassie closed her eyes and took in all the sensations rushing through her body. She cried out when his lips replaced his fingers. He sucked harder, bringing more of her into his mouth.

Cassie was barely aware of the hand that stroked down her body. Darden's mouth on her breast had most of her attention. The harder he sucked, the more Cassie enjoyed it. She made no attempt to free her hands or fight the restraints that bound her legs. Various moans escaped which she did not attempt to stifle.

She was totally aware of his hand when his fingers caressed the juncture between her legs. His tongue lathed her nipple and two of his fingers entered through her feminine folds. When a third finger joined the others, Cassie nearly bucked Darden off the bed.

His fingers fucked her hard. Cassie always hated that word. It was crass and poorly described the act of making love, but she couldn't think of a more appropriate word to better describe what he was doing. She could feel an incredible orgasm building in her core. His fingers were like the kindling used before the logs in a fireplace started to glow. Her breathing quickened as she gasped for air.

Just short of her climax Darden stopped. If her hands had been free she would have smacked him. She finally realized that was her punishment—orgasm denial. Darden had led her to the promised land, just to leave her stranded in the barren plains outside paradise.

Darden shifted his weight, released her arms, and moved down her body. She brought her freed hands down to rest naturally at her side. The problem was, she wasn't quite sure what to do with them. Cassie was too focused on her frustration to consider any of the weapons now at her disposal.

All thoughts fled when his tongue entered her. Darden secured his positioning and then lifted her hips to give him better access. The ropes had enough slack to allow him a little more freedom of motion where her legs were concerned.

She'd never experienced giving or receiving oral sex before and was both embarrassed and entranced by what he was doing. His tongue lapped up the result of her passion, not unlike a cat consuming cream. Her hands grabbed ahold of the mattress as he continued to devour her. Cassie was once again having difficulty maintaining the mental barrier. She was close to giving up every thought and control of her body to the wonderful things Darden was doing to her.

As soon as his tongue brushed her clit, Cassie's shield came tumbling down. Everything she was feeling and experiencing now seeped into their telepathic channel. Darden hesitated as he took in the emotions she was helpless to keep hidden from him. Cassie felt his response through the same channel.

Darden's anger cooled when his mind could once again connect with hers. He realized he loved her too much to use sex as a weapon. He wanted to give her pleasure, not frustration. Withholding her orgasm was the closest he could get to show her the agony he experienced twice today.

She felt movement on the bed as Darden reached down and released her legs. With their freedom, Cassie captured the lower section of his body. He brought her into his arms as her legs rose and tightened around his waist.

"Take me," she said before she bit his ear. "I want you inside me."

Darden pushed back the hair plastered to her forehead and examined her face. She was not sure if her expression revealed the love she bore him. Cassie was certainly pushing those feelings through their channel. He simply kissed her. Where his fingers had been relentless, his lips were tentative. She knew he was questioning whether he had been too rough earlier. Cassie deepened the kiss and tightened her hold on him, communicating without words she was not a china doll. Cassie silently reassured him she would have told him had he truly hurt her.

As cautious as his kiss had been, there was no mistaking his intent when he entered her with a single powerful thrust. Cassie cried out in surprise and then placed her lips against those of her soul mate.

Darden rode her hard, releasing the last of his pent up anger. Cassie kept pace with him. Her mind's barrier was down, allowing him access to her physically and telepathically. She could have uttered words of love, which could have been meaningless, but one cannot manufacture emotions passed between soul mates.

The rapture she was denied earlier came upon her at the same time Darden fractured. True soul mates climaxed together. The sharing of the experience made love's pinnacle that much more intense. They both cried out, unconcerned about the people gathered in the common room. Thank goodness they were in the bedroom farthest from the house's epicenter.

She was truly joined with Darden. It was a perfect moment in time. There were more secrets she kept well hidden, even from Darden. Once he learned the truth, would they ever be like this again?

He could watch Cassie's face when she climaxed again and again. It was a sight he would never tire of. During her orgasm, Darden knew she was beyond happy and safe.

Twice today, he worried for her safety. First in the restaurant and again this evening when no one could reach her telepathically. Darden finally realized the horror Tarsea experienced when Alex fell off the telepathic radar.

In Alex's case, it was because she was pregnant. In Cassie's, it was the manipulation of a crystal. Koel's sister, Tarah, had gone through a similar experience when she was held captive by Jeryl Jarlyn to ensure Koel and JoAnna consummated their relationship.

He behaved poorly when they were reunited. Darden thought by dominating her physically, Cassie might behave differently in the future. Although he had watched the relationship between Tarsea and Alex, he never caught on how Alex had always been able to get the upper hand when Tarsea tried to control her. Now he knew the truth. Soul mates were partners — one didn't dominate the other. There seemed to be symmetry in each of the relationships.

Tolfer was someone who needed to nurture and Candy was convinced she needed no one. When Candy broke down, it was Tolfer who lifted her up. At first, they seemed like unlikely partners, but in the end they were perfect for each other. His own twin had given up on women when Shirl entered his life. Starc had lived in Darden's shadow and needed a mate who equaled the strength that lay dormant within him. The two were inseparable and Shirl's telepathic powers were magnified with Starc by her side. Koel helped to balance the terribly powerful abilities JoAnna possessed by entering her mind. Now he needed to find out why he and Cassie were soul mates. What did he have to offer the girl he held and, in fact, helped to raise?

"Cassie, when you left my side this afternoon and interceded with that man, my heart stopped," Darden said. "All I could think about was how I could live if I ever lost you."

She let out a long, loud sigh. "That was really your first thought?" Cassie asked. "Not if I could be injured or that my life might be tragically cut short? Although we've seen each other off and on for the past eight years, I really have not been a part of your life."

Instead of expressing the terror he felt when she was in mortal danger, Darden had said the first thing that entered his head. Surely, she could feel the emotions that spilled into their shared link during and after the event. She had become the axis to his world.

"How can you say that?" Darden asked. "Cassie, I have been celibate for eight years waiting for you to grow up."

Cassie lifted her head and gave him a look indicating she thought he had lost his mind. "How are you going to keep living without me? You were celibate for eight years. It's all about you. Do you have an inkling about what I have been through the last eight years, including the time when we were in the penal colony and you would barely touch me in fear of what you would unleash? I don't care what my grandfather thinks or does. Get out!"

He lay there flabbergasted. Was she really kicking him out of their bed? When he did not comply with her order, Cassie wriggled out of his embrace and got up from the bed. She stormed into the bathroom, slamming the door behind her. How had things deteriorated so badly, so quickly? He used to be so smooth with women and now the most important person in his life locked herself in the bathroom to get away from him.

Darden got up and approached the bathroom door. He turned the doorknob to find she had, indeed, locked the door. His little girl was having a temper tantrum. Well, he had the maturity to wait her out. This was not the first time her emotions got the best of her.

When Cassie finally opened the door, she was fully dressed. Her hair was a tousled mess and her lips were swollen, signs she had just been well loved. He did not believe he had ever seen a sexier woman.

"I am not having a temper tantrum, you Neanderthal," Cassie said as she pushed passed him.

"With everything I am feeling, that is what you picked up through our channel?" Darden asked incredulously.

Things had spun out of control. He was not sure what really set Cassie off, but he was not leaving and neither was she. Darden placed his hands on her upper arms to stop from leaving their bedroom. He needed to talk to her and calm her down.

"Don't touch me," Cassie cried out. "I think you have proven you are physically stronger than me enough for one night!"

"Are you going to run back to Daddy in the penal colony?" Darden taunted her. He was frustrated he could not control Cassie.

If she was going to act like a child, he was going to treat her like one. He tried to figure out what Cassie's next move would be. Her life had centered around Benko Jarlyn for too long.

"No, I am going to run to Granddaddy," Cassie spit out. "My grandmother wants him dead and my father wants him overthrown. It's time I see for myself what type of condition he is in and if he is worth saving. The best way I can do that is to live with him. I don't need to be babysat by you or my friends. It may have escaped your notice, but I am a powerful mind control telepath in my own right. I know my father told you about the man I killed prior to meeting you. It was unintentional, but it gave us an idea of how powerful I would become and that was before I made love to you. Excuse me, before we had sex. I don't know if what we did the last two nights could be classified as making love."

She stormed out of the room, yet again, slamming the door to dramatize her exit. He heard another door slam. Cassie had not bothered to say goodbye to Alex or Candy who were somewhere in the house. The guards stationed outside the structure would make sure she got to The Palace safely. If Darden followed, he would only aggravate her more. He continued to stand there stupefied by what occurred.

There was a knock on the door and Alex entered. "What happened?"

After things were squared away with Cassie, they had to move into his apartment. There were too many people residing in this household. Starc and Shirl, who temporarily used his apartment, would have to find another place to live.

"We had a fight," Darden responded. "Mind your own business, Alex."

"Maybe you should put on some clothes, Romeo," Alex said. "You better figure out what you did to piss her off and what you are going to do to fix it."

Darden reached for the sheets that covered the floor at the end of the bed. He wrapped them around his waist. If Tarsea was behind Alex, the last thing Darden wanted to deal with was Alex's incensed mate.

"What did I do?" Darden asked. "Maybe it was what Cassie did and this is all her fault."

"No," Alex answered calmly. "It's always the guy's fault. Figure out how you are going to make this right."

Alex turned and left him to discover on his own what really drove Cassie away. Replaying their argument in his memory, he smacked himself in the head. Cassie was right—he was a selfish son of a bitch. He concentrated on himself and how their relationship affected him. He did not spend enough time focusing on everything Cassie had been through or how she might feel. It was not Cassie's fault they met when she was a child. It was not Cassie's fault that he ignored her attempts at flirtation and acted like her brother instead of her suitor. He complained about being celibate, but she had desired a physical relationship a couple of years ago. He made the choice for both of them – and out of fear no less - to keep their relationship platonic.

Tonight his soul mate did not whine like a spoiled brat. No, she was a furious woman and he had responded to her like the arrogant, overbearing male she accused him of being. Alex was right. He needed to figure out how to fix this and fix it fast. The prospect of Cassie under Jeryl Jarlyn's guardianship scared him to death.

Chapter 12

What was wrong with her? So Darden looked at their relationship concerning how it affected him. She had done the same thing. For years, Benko and Darden had directed her life and she fought them tooth and nail the only way she could - emotionally.

She finally had what she wanted, a sexual relationship with Darden. So why had she reacted so dramatically? She realized that acting like a spoiled brat was like pulling a favorite blanket around her, it was a defense mechanism. Was what he said so wrong? If something happened to Darden, wouldn't her first thoughts be if she would be able to survive without him?

"I have changed my mind," Cassie informed the two guards who marched no more than three feet behind her.

The two men exchanged glances. "The Prime Ruler was advised you were moving in with him," the taller of two informed her. "Your grandfather will be disappointed with your change of plans. Various announcements were communicated through the communal pathways. An official proclamation is scheduled tomorrow during the Prime Council session announcing you are his heir."

Her grandfather had wasted no time indoctrinating her into his life once she advised him through their familial link of her hasty decision. Any way she looked at it, she was stuck. Her rash behavior sealed her fate for the time being. She'll have to look for an opportunity to free herself of the obligation she now had to her grandfather.

When she left the Childers's home, Cassie had closed off all her telepathic channels, which was how she missed the announcement of what was planned for tomorrow. Conversations assaulted her mind as the shield went down. Cassie staggered as the onslaught made her dizzy.

The two Palace Guards quickly came on either side of Cassie and steadied her. She was quickly becoming a mess. All she wanted was Darden, and her stupidity made that impossible for the time being.

She reached out to him telepathically. *"I'm so sorry, Darden,"* she shared through their channel. *"I don't know what came over me."*

Cassie waited for Darden's reply. As far as she knew, he did not have the capability to turn off telepathic transmissions. The longer she waited, the more she became concerned over his silence. Had she done permanent damage to their relationship? Couples fought all the time and still managed to stay together.

"I apologize, as well," Darden finally communicated. She felt his apprehension through their channel, even at this distance. Cassie believed he felt like he was walking on eggshells where she was concerned. *"Come back home, baby."*

How she wished she could. Cassie had backed herself into a corner and knew she could only go forward. She would have to find another way to be with Darden. She needed to concentrate on building a relationship with Jeryl Jarlyn. Once things were squared away with her grandfather, she could return to her soul mate.

"The Prime Council is accepting me as his heir tomorrow. My grandfather is expecting me tonight," Cassie admitted. *"It would draw unwanted attention in the communal channels if I try to back out now. There is already too much focus on me as it stands. It would be dangerous if the populace thought me impulsive. And the last thing I want is to draw anyone's attention to my friends, Tarsea's network, or expose Solfa."*

"It appears you have thought this through," Darden said. *"I cannot argue with a single point you raised. Your grandfather knows what we are to each other. He will want to know how I enhance your powers."*

"I still plan to keep the extent of our physical relationship from my grandfather," Cassie said. She couldn't put the words sex and grandfather in the same sentence. It would be hard enough to admit to her father when they were reunited.

"That is for the best, I suppose," Darden responded. *"Sleep well. I will see you in the morning."*

Cassie turned off access to all channels but the soul mate, the warrior, and the link she shared with her friends. The volume of conversations was drastically reduced. Her mind could now rest.

The Palace came into view and Cassie was surprised by the anxiety growing inside her. She was alone. This was the first time she entered her grandfather's lair without one of her friends or Darden by her side.

A woman dressed in what Cassie believed was a maid's uniform was present to greet her. Rather than taking the stairs, the woman led her to a hidden elevator. They rode to the fourth floor in silence. Her maid had not bothered to introduce herself.

Cassie walked down the hall that led to Jeryl Jarlyn's private living area. They passed her grandfather's greeting room, his private office, and finally stopped in front of the last room on the right side of the hallway. The woman opened the door and Cassie followed.

The room was filled with vases of violet and dark purple roses. She wondered if the city had a single rose blossom on any of the bushes. A delicate aroma scented the room. With so many flowers, Cassie was surprised the room was not overpowered by a cloying sweet smell.

"My name is Flora," the maid said. Cassie was not sure if she was serious about her name. Flora did not respond to the questioning look Cassie cast in her direction. The maid obviously did not grasp the irony of her name to the environment.

"Thank you, Flora," Cassie finally said.

"The clothing designed for you is in the closet, as is new sleepwear," Flora shared with her. "There are various toiletries in the restroom. If you would like a different scent, please ask. I serve at your pleasure."

Cassie had taken care of herself and her father as long as she could remember. It was odd to have someone dedicated to seeing to her every need. Leenea and Alex tried to fawn over her earlier, but Cassie did not want them to bother. If something was done for the group's benefit she partook, but she did not want anyone troubling themselves solely on her behalf.

"Thank you," Cassie replied. "I am tired and plan to go to bed."

"I will wake you at eight," Flora said. "It will give you an hour to prepare for breakfast with your grandfather and the ceremony will take place at eleven. Everyone is very excited."

It was odd having the adoration of perfect strangers. She grew up hearing all sorts of terrible things about her grandfather and his government. Since her arrival, all the people she encountered appeared happy. Naturally, they were ignorant of what was being done to corrupt their brains and their inability to make their own decisions.

The room was decorated with cream and mauve colors. Despite the turmoil shredding her nerves, her surroundings started to relax her. She was physically and emotionally exhausted. Maybe a good night's sleep would help her control her emotions and help her think straight.

Cassie removed her clothing and slipped on a nightshirt she found in one of the drawers. The satin felt decadent against her skin. Normally, she showered at night, but she did not want to wash Darden's touch from her naked body.

She crawled into bed. Cassie touched the vacant pillow next to her head. How she wanted Darden to be beside her. A chill ran down her spine. What if she could never be with Darden again?

A very loud squawk came from outside her window. Cassie opened one eye and glared at the bird that woke her from a sound sleep. She had dreamt of Darden. They were back in the penal colony and sharing a hut. Her dream had just gotten steamy when the damned bird announced its presence.

The bed next to her was stone cold. Her erotic romp with Darden had only been a dream. She was unsure what time it was, but the sun had barely risen. Liking to sleep in, Cassie had not seen many dawns. She rose from her bed and looked out the window.

Very little stirred on the nearly deserted street in front of The Palace. The pavement was wet from a light rain. A more violent storm would have disturbed her sleep before the bird had. She opened the window and took the fresh morning air into her lungs.

Cassie went to the closet and stared at the volume of different outfits hanging from a variety of hangers. It appeared no parallel dimension had come up with a better way to store clothing. She didn't have a clue what to wear. Flora would arrive at eight and recommend the correct outfit.

As she had not showered the night before, Cassie decided she'd bathe. She removed her nightshirt and stood in the corner of the shower and avoided the water until it was the perfect temperature. She adjusted the showerhead to stream water in a massaging flow. The water pounded on her tight shoulder muscles. It felt wonderful, just what she needed.

Cassie poured shampoo into her palm. The lavender scent filled the stall. It was her favorite fragrance and she was pleased the hair conditioner was similarly scented. A lilac enhanced body wash was in the third bottle.

When she finished bathing, Cassie wrapped herself in a bath sheet. It was the largest towel she had seen not meant for the beach. The cushy towel was warm and embraced her body. She could easily get used to starting her day in this fashion.

Cassie grabbed another towel and secured her dripping wet hair. She would deal with working out any tangles later. Right now, she wanted to crawl back into bed. There was something decadent about sliding her towel-clad body between the silk sheets.

She tried to open one communal channel at a time and listened for Darden to share something. She didn't want to wake him. If he had as bad a night as she had, he would still be asleep. The damned bird woke her hours before she planned to rise. Cassie got more static than conversations through the pathways.

In the background, she could hear people stirring around The Palace. Employees were starting to arrive for work. It would only be a matter of time before she would hear Flora's footsteps coming down the hall.

Somewhere along the way, Cassie had fallen back to sleep. She was shaken awake by Flora's gentle nudges. In the time she slept, Cassie had not dreamt. It was odd not having Darden being her first thought upon waking.

There was a cup of tea now on her nightstand. Flora must have brought it with her. The beverage had cooled enough to allow her to immediately start sipping the tea.

Flora headed for the closet and pulled out one of the outfits. "This will be more than appropriate for breakfast with your grandfather and attending the Prime Council's celebration this morning. Dress and I will be back shortly to help with your hair."

The last time she went out, Shirl and JoAnna took care of her hair and makeup. Although Flora was sweet, Cassie missed her friends dreadfully. Moving into The Palace cost her immediate access to Darden and her friends.

Cassie slipped on the gold tunic and the earth toned leggings. The material caressed her body. For this morning's celebration, she added a rust colored jacket to her ensemble. Cassie looked at her reflection in the mirror and was relieved her breasts were properly covered. The outfit was flattering, making her appear leaner than she was.

Flora returned as promised and made quick work styling her hair. She created a French braid. It was a hairstyle she always envied, but never could figure out how to master the look.

"You will find your grandfather in his greeting room," Flora informed her. "He is waiting for you. Jeryl Jarlyn is a great man, just not a patient one. I would run off if I were you."

It was a poor choice of words, but Cassie got the gist of what Flora meant. Her grandfather's greeting room was an odd place to have breakfast. Perhaps, he was just meeting her there and then they would head to wherever the dining room was.

When she entered the greeting room, Cassie noticed plates piled high with food. It was obvious they were to eat here. Based on the volume of food, her grandfather must be expecting an army.

"Good morning, Grandfather," Cassie said. She leaned over and gently kissed his cheek. "Do you always have breakfast here?"

"Morning, dear," her grandfather replied. "I usually have my meals at province functions or in my study. With you living here, I will have to come up with another solution so we may dine together."

Cassie grabbed a plate and pulled items she recognized. For other dishes, she let her nose guide whether she would try the new food. Generally, if she liked how something smelled, she also enjoyed its taste.

"Who else will be joining us?" Cassie asked. The amount of food she took barely made a dent in what was available.

Her grandfather took a sip of his coffee and savored the flavor of his beverage. Cassie preferred tea or soda in the morning. If only coffee was available, she would have it with lots of milk and tons of sugar in it. Coffee was too bitter to drink black.

"There are only the two of us, Cassandra," her grandfather replied. "I did not know what you liked, so I ordered everything Benko enjoyed when he was your age. That boy sure did love to eat. He never gained an ounce. Is he still slim?"

Cassie considered her answer, as she always did when her father was the topic of the discussion. "He still enjoys eating and works out at the gym to burn off excess calories. I wish I had inherited his metabolism."

She watched her grandfather's face as she answered his question. There was such love reflected there. Regardless of everything Benko had done, his father still loved him. She wished her telepathic gift worked across dimensions. Cassie would have wanted to share this with her father.

Their special moment was interrupted by a boisterous group forcefully entering the room. When Cassie looked in the direction of the new arrivals, she was surprised to see Candy, JoAnna, and Darden. Shirl and Starc were the last to enter.

"What is the meaning of this?" her grandfather bellowed. "You were not invited."

"We are family," Candy said lightly before she bit into a crispy piece of bacon. "Wow, you have quite a spread here."

Although Cassie imagined Tolfer had cooked a spectacular breakfast for Candy, her friend piled her plate high with food. Shirl and JoAnna merely picked at various goodies. Darden and Starc stood at attention, less at ease in the Prime Ruler's presence. It was rare she got to see the twins side by side like this. Cassie imagined Koel was nearby surveying his surroundings.

"There is plenty of food, Grandfather," Cassie added. "Besides, Candy is right. They are an extension of my Gingko Terra family." It was strange calling Earth by its Troyk name.

Her grandfather got back to his breakfast realizing he had lost this battle. Jeryl knew her friends were mated couples and would be unable to use his telepathic powers to make them leave. Cassie attacked the mound of food before her.

After she miraculously cleared her plate, Cassie began to wonder why the presence of her friends had surprised her. She had closed the communal pathways, but not the other links. Why hadn't she received any communication from anyone in the room this morning? Cassie used her telepathic abilities so infrequently, she had not considered anything was wrong when she did not hear any chatter in any of their channels.

"Why didn't you tell me you were coming?" Cassie asked Darden through their pathway.

There was no reply. When she looked at Darden, he appeared not to have received her communication. Cassie reached into the pathway she shared with her friends and received the same result. Nothing. Finally, Cassie tried to communicate with her grandfather through their familial link. Something was dreadfully wrong.

"Why can't I communicate through any of the telepathic channels, Grandfather?" Cassie immediately laid blame where she believed it belonged.

"I wanted you to concentrate on what was going to occur today and not be distracted by the communal pathways starting to bombard your mind," her grandfather replied.

Her grandfather would not have a clue how many channels she had access to, many of which he could not enter. Regardless of what she was capable of doing, Jeryl Jarlyn had no right to try and manipulate her powers.

"What have you done?" Cassie cried.

Her eyes scanned the room looking for the rose-colored crystal Barash had given her that interfered with her telepathic powers. There were a multitude of different crystals surrounding her, but she did not see the one she sought.

"I had flentium ground up and put in the hot chocolate you drank last night and the tea this morning," her grandfather admitted.

She had never heard of flentium, but that was irrelevant. Her father had never mentioned the crystal, so Cassie figured it did not exist on Earth. Nor did she have any idea of the long-lasting effects she would suffer consuming the mineral.

Cassie was speechless. However, her soul mate was not. "You had no right drugging Cassie," Darden growled. The telepathic connection between them was null and void for the time being. She could not feel Darden's anger, but it was obvious when she looked at his face. It was bright red with rage.

"She is my granddaughter," Jeryl Jarlyn screamed at Darden. "I have every right to see to her health and happiness."

"And I am her soul mate," Darden countered. "The Supreme Being has joined us, body and soul. I am taking her out of here right now."

Cassie was afraid her grandfather was going to have Darden arrested. She did not want to do anything to further antagonize Jeryl Jarlyn. In desperation, Cassie looked at JoAnna for assistance.

"Let's all calm down," JoAnna said. "How long will Cassie be affected by the crystals? Jeryl, Cassie is an adult. You should have asked if she needed something to help her manage the communal channels. When we work together, you always gave me options about how far I would go with the crystals you showed me. Cassie should be given the same consideration."

"Everything I do is for the health of my granddaughter and the good of the Troyk people," her grandfather answered defensively. "The ground crystals will exit her body within four to eight hours. That is why I had her given more this morning. This afternoon she will have all her abilities back with no adverse side effects."

Her grandfather abused crystals. His opinion of what was harmless and what was dangerous was worthless. Fortunately, she did not currently feel any different, other than not being able to access the pathways.

"Grandfather," Cassie said sadly, "how can I trust anything I eat or drink in The Palace again? I need to learn to use and control my powers, not eliminate them for short periods of time. I think it best I return to the Childers's home. After the ceremony I will move back in with them. We will explain my presence here last night was to prepare for today's celebration."

She had been looking for an opportunity to return to the Childers's household and was happy to take advantage of the unexpected out. Jeryl Jarlyn was guilty of a major lapse in judgment. For her own safety, regardless of her prior motives, she needed to get away from him.

Her grandfather rose and exited the room. He mumbled various statements on his way out, but Cassie did not understand a single word he said. She would find a way to mend their relationship without placing herself at his mercy.

"Try as many channels as you can," JoAnna said. "Based on past experience, the soul mate channel will mend itself first."

Cassie pushed a thought to Darden through their link. His color had returned to normal, but she could not feel him. Based on his non-reaction, her communication was still blocked.

Candy handed her the glass of water she had been drinking. "I can still pick up all the telepathic channels. Finish drinking this and try to wash out the remainder of the pulverized crystals. I can't believe he did that to you."

"As far as I am concerned," Darden said, "everything has changed."

Although he did not elaborate, Cassie knew he was referring to her father's return to the Troyk universe. She could not trust her grandfather to not try to impede her talents again, possibly more dramatically the next time. Perhaps it was time she returned to the Troyk penal colony. She missed her father, Beatrice, and even Chartail.

A Palace Guard entered the room and stood before Cassie. "The ceremony has been pushed back until noon. You are all to wait here until you are sent for. Guards will be situated outside to assure you comply with the Prime Ruler's orders."

Cassie looked at her friends wondering what her grandfather had up his sleeve?

Chapter 13

The Prime Council chamber was teeming with people. Every square foot of available space was filled with Troyk citizens who came to see Cassie named Jeryl Jarlyn's official heir. Was there a term beyond "standing room only" she wondered? She continued to drink tested water, hoping to flush the crystals from her body.

Her friends had accompanied her downstairs and were seated behind all the Prime members and their families. Cassie's telepathic abilities had not returned, so she had no means to communicate with Darden or the others. Once again, she was on her own.

After her friends were shown to their seats, Cassie was instructed to go into a room near the front of the chamber and change clothing. A beautiful white and cream lace dress awaited her. If she did not know any better, she would have sworn she was putting on a wedding gown. Fortunately, there was no veil that would have caused her to panic.

The dress was tight and fit her like a second skin. Although it hugged her figure, the gown was flattering. She unbraided her hair and it now flowed loosely over her shoulders and down her back.

Cassie re-entered the hall and the whole chamber rose to their feet. A sea of people was before her, but Cassie could not make out a single face. She was led to a small dais where Jeryl Jarlyn stood. There was a small platform in front with a large pillow on top. She was instructed to kneel in front of her grandfather. Was Jeryl Jarlyn going to produce a sword and dub her his heir like in a scene out of *Camelot*? It felt like she was in another place and time.

Cassie became alarmed when Barash came to kneel beside her. This felt like a wedding, not a symbolic transfer of power to a younger generation. She was about to stand when Barash grasped her hand and held her down.

"Relax," Barash whispered. "I represent the acceptance of another powerful Troyk family accepting the future Prime Ruler."

Cassie did not believe a single word. He had proved untrustworthy from the very beginning. Two people kneeling before an official implied a totally different ceremony, one she certainly had not agreed to. It would be very different if Darden knelt next to her. Jeryl Jarlyn knew she had a soul mate.

There was a commotion in the back of the hall. It was easy to believe Darden was involved, but Cassie could not see what was happening. She could not communicate with anyone and Barash did not seem inclined to release her.

"My friends and subjects," her grandfather shouted. "Thank you for joining me on this important day. As many of you know, Benko's daughter has graced my life with her presence. It is my intention to train Cassandra to be my successor. The peace and harmony we enjoy will be secured in my granddaughter's capable hands for generations to come."

The chamber erupted in applause. "Jarlyn, Jarlyn," echoed throughout the room. Cassie was not altogether sure who they were chanting for, her grandfather or his legacy.

"Cassandra Jarlyn and Barash Kleyman represent the future of our fine universe," her grandfather continued. "Together they are going to bring the Troyk dimension to new heights."

Applause once again broke out at her grandfather's announcement. Cassie had no idea what her grandfather meant when he referred to her and Barash being together. She had not spoken any vows, nor had Barash. The two of them could have been a symbolic couple, as Barash had indicated earlier. Being ignorant of Troyk traditions, Cassie did not know what to believe.

Barash stood, pulling her up in the process. He raised the hand that held hers and the crowd started chanting, "Jarlyn, Jarlyn," again. Cassie was helpless to do anything other than raise her other hand and wave.

Fortunately, no rings were exchanged or other symbolic items that would designate a joining had occurred. It was frustrating she still could not communicate with Darden. Anger built within her that felt more like her soul mate's, than her own. That made her believe the crystal particles were losing their effectiveness.

"I, Jeryl Jarlyn, pronounce my granddaughter, Cassandra Jarlyn, the next Prime Ruler of the Troyk universe."

Her grandfather came up beside her and put an amethyst ring on her right hand's middle finger. Cassie's first thought upon seeing the ring was Shirl could use it to evacuate her and Darden from this dimension. It was only then that she realized how she emphatically wanted to leave her grandfather's universe.

Before Cassie could shift gears and pay attention to Barash again, she found herself in his arms with his lips plastered to hers. Her initial response was surprise, followed by revulsion. Even if she did not have a soul mate, she had not given Barash permission to kiss her.

The more Cassie fought his embrace, the more Barash tightened his hold on her. Anger the likes she never felt before continued to build within her. She knew it was not her anger, but Darden's. Their soul mate channel was mending and Darden was mad enough to kill.

She hoped the bastard would stick his tongue in her mouth so she could bite it off. Although she continued to struggle, no one around her seemed to notice or care that Cassie did not welcome Barash's attention or touch. The crowd had been worked up into a frenzy and Barash was feeding off the power the group generated. There was no question that her grandfather was not the only man in this universe to fear.

It was unlikely Darden and her friends were going to be able to work their way through the crowd and liberate her from Barash. Cassie took her fingernails and started to claw at Barash's face. She felt herself lifted off the floor and Barash started to carry her out of the chamber. He carried her as if she weighed no more than a feather. The crowd started chanting something she did not understand. Where was he taking her and what was his purpose? She doubted he was taking her to her grandmother's house.

Darden and his friends fought the crowd. They struggled to reach Cassie, but people were trying to exit through the doors behind them. His single focus was to rescue Cassie from her grandfather and Barash Kleyman. Neither of the men had Cassie's interests as their number one priority.

He felt the soul mate channel grow in strength, but it did not have the capacity to carry conversations. At this point, only feelings were transmittable. From Cassie he felt anger, frustration, and fear. As the volume in the chamber increased, so did Cassie's anxiety level. Darden needed to reach his soul mate before either Jeryl Jarlyn or Barash Kleyman rushed her out of the Prime Council's chamber.

The communal pathways were filled with nothing but adoration for the young woman who would replace her grandfather one day. Most of Darden's focus was on the communication coming through the warrior channel. Koel was able to situate himself closer to Cassie during the ceremony. He had not been caught with the rest of them in Jeryl Jarlyn's greeting room. His cousin's tactical thinking helped him stay one step ahead of their group.

"*Barash Kleyman is attempting to carry Cassie out of the hall,*" Koel communicated through the warrior link. "*She is putting up a hell of a fight. That girl is as slippery as a bar of soap in the shower. The Palace Guard are surrounding both the couple and Jeryl Jarlyn. Their first priority will be to see to the safety of the Prime Ruler and then Cassie. I will try to get to her before they are able to evacuate Jeryl Jarlyn.*"

Darden could only hope his cousin would be able to accomplish the task. He was not making much progress in moving forward. If anything, they were being pushed back.

"*I've had enough of this,*" Candy said. "*Follow me, I've got an idea.*"

The next time he picked up a conversation from Candy, it was through one of the communal pathways. She utilized multiple channels to communicate her message. "*We need to properly welcome our future leader. She belongs to the people of the Aster Province. Let us go and meet her now. When are we going to have a better opportunity to shake her hand?*"

As if by magic, the current of the crowd changed and they were now moving forward toward Cassie. More communication entered the communal pathways to stay Cassie's exit along with demands for her to address the crowd. Candy's plan was working perfectly.

"We should hear from all the girls who grew up in Gingko Terra," Shirl added to the noise within the pathways. *"We have heard so many stories about them being the embodiment of women from our folk tales. There may be a mated crystal telepath and the Warrior Woman among the girls. They have been hidden from us for too long."*

If Candy had been stoking a flame, Shirl had just thrown alcohol on it. The crowd got louder and pushier. Conversations called for the exits to be blocked so no one could escape with their future ruler. Darden could only hope they got to Cassie before the crowd got out of hand.

"Our girl is being held against her will," someone communicated through one of the communal links. Darden was surveying every telepathic conversation within the chamber.

"Liberate the girl," Darden ordered through the channels, *"but make sure not to harm her. She is our future. We want to hear her address the crowd with the other girls from Gingko Terra."*

Various shouts of encouragement echoed through the chamber. An impromptu army had been built with one single purpose — rescue Cassie. Darden felt love for Jeryl's granddaughter flow through the communal channels. She represented a new start in their eyes. The daughter of Benko Jarlyn, raised by the man himself had come home to rule them with her father's ideals.

Darden finally got within sight of Cassie. The crowd was pulling her from Barash's clutches. He did not need to excite the crowd anymore. From what he could see, they were doing their best to incapacitate Barash and rescue Cassie without injury. The bastard holding his soul mate finally succumbed to the crowd and placed Cassie on her feet. Cassie ran toward Darden, the crowd making way for her as she escaped her captor.

A tremendous sense of relief came over him when Cassie launched herself into his arms. She covered his face with kisses as the crowd watched, wondering what was going on. They had witnessed some type of union take place between her and Barash Kleyman, yet here she was showing outward affection for another. The crowd chanted for Cassie to address them.

"It is time you meet your people, baby," Darden said. "Tell them what is in your heart. You have their support."

He walked Cassie to the podium where Prime Representatives addressed the chamber. Today they were going to hear a very different type of speech and speaker. Darden was not sure what she was going to share, but he would support her in whatever she decided. She looked so young standing before the crowd. A scared eighteen-year-old girl stood before a mob of excited people. They waited for her to share whatever she was going to say.

"I'm Cassie Jarlyn, daughter of Benko Jarlyn, and granddaughter of Jeryl Jarlyn," Cassie said. She looked at him and extended her hand, inviting him to join her. Darden had no choice but to stand beside the girl he fell in love with somewhere along the way.

"My father told me stories of soul mates when I was a little girl on Gingko Terra. I used to think the stories were wonderful fairytales, like the ones told in the world where I grew up. They are not merely tales of legend. I met mine when I was ten years old - a crystal telepath traveling to my world collecting herbs. The minute we touched it felt like static electricity zapped me and a telepathic channel opened allowing us to communicate privately. Soul mates exist, and mine is Darden Lours."

The crystal drug was wearing off. Portions of what she was saying were coming through the communal pathways. People in attendance were actively filling in the gaps caused by the crystals still in her system. Regardless of what Jeryl Jarlyn's next move was, the people knew he was her soul mate and he was not so easily gotten rid of. She also laid the foundation for other soul mates to come forward, no longer afraid to hide their true relationships.

Shirl came to stand by Cassie. His brother's soul mate was about to share the true nature of their relationship as well. With Jeryl Jarlyn already aware of what they were to each other, Shirl must not have seen the harm in telling the truth. She pretty much admitted who she was when she entered the communal pathway earlier.

"I am Shirl Thork," Shirl shouted. "My mother was Benko Jarlyn's crystal telepath. The one who helped him escape after their failed attempt to unseat Jeryl Jarlyn. I am a crystal telepath and, unlike my mother, I have a soul mate. Starc Lours is mine, and I am a mated female crystal telepath. Another legend proves true and we stand beside Cassie to bring the Troyk universe a new beginning."

It was finally Candy's time to admit to the crowd who she was. Candy had become a favorite in the Aster Province after she was rescued from the Troyk penal colony, but few knew the real story behind what happened there.

"My name is Candy Phillips," Candy said. "Benko Jarlyn led my parents and other dissidents against Jeryl Jarlyn and fled this dimension. Their lives were cut short in the Gingko Terra universe and I grew up in an orphanage with Shirl. I, too, met my soul mate Tolfer Childers in this dimension. They say I am the Warrior Woman of legend. It is time for soul mates to stop hiding in the shadows and come forward to celebrate what they have together. No one should hide when they meet the one created specifically for them."

JoAnna remained quiet. She probably felt her mind control abilities would scare people, especially when they learned she was mated. Besides, JoAnna had already received more attention than her friend desired. Two attempts on her life was more than anyone could handle.

The communal channels were active with soul mates across the province admitting who they were, their soul mate, and they would no longer hide what they were to each other. Cassie was praised for coming out and telling others who shared a special bond to no longer fear being hunted down for the special abilities coupling with their soul mates brought them. They were immune to mind control.

Cassie did not start a revolution against her grandfather, but she activated a hidden force of advanced telepaths who, when the time came for Benko Jarlyn to return, would stand beside Cassie. Darden did not know when he ever was more proud of the woman his soul mate had become.

The Palace Guard entered the chamber and started to break up the crowd. Cassie and her friends were corralled and once again called before the Prime Ruler. This time Darden would not be separated from his soul mate, regardless of Jeryl Jarlyn's wishes.

Chapter 14

Cassie's stomach fell with each step she took toward her grandfather's greeting room. The beautiful dress she wore was tight and cut off her circulation, making her lightheaded. If she had a choice, she'd crawl into bed and disappear for at least a day. If Darden wanted to join her, even better.

She had managed to manipulate the link between her and Darden temporarily, and used the power of the soul mate link to enter the communal pathways. Although her connection was weak, she had managed to get some broken sentences out. Cassie was able to hear others share through the pathways what she could not.

When they arrived in the room where they were to await her grandfather, Cassie collapsed onto one of the couches. The cushions molded to her bottom and she was glad for the back support. Now, she just needed to build her defenses and prepare to confront her grandfather. She was not sure what he would do next.

In the short time since they left the greeting room, the chamber was filled with the rose-colored crystal that would prevent telepathic communication. Her grandfather had intentionally cut off the telepathic channel between soul mates and all the other pathways they used.

Darden sat beside her. They did not have the intimacy of the soul mate channel to share private thoughts. Emotions flowed through their link and he passed her feelings of reassurance that everything would be all right. It was not until he took her hand that she had any inkling it could be true. Hope was all they had now.

She was overcome with a wave of nausea when her grandfather entered the room. From the expression on his face, she had a reason to be wary. Cassie held her breath, awaiting a tidal wave of condemnation to come her way.

"It will take weeks for my government to undo the damage you did this afternoon," her grandfather said. "What you all are and the abilities you possess are strictly for the use of the ruling party."

"Why?" Cassie managed to squeak out. "We have God-given gifts that can help everyone. There could be more special people out there who have gone through the evolutionary change. They should celebrate what they are, not hide their abilities."

"You are young and naive, Cassandra," Jeryl Jarlyn said. He looked around the room and added, "You all are. Abilities such as yours need to be nurtured and properly directed. None of you have a clue what you are capable of."

Cassie could not comprehend her grandfather's bias. She struggled to see the world through his eyes. Jeryl Jarlyn wanted to stifle the population unless he could gain power from an individual's gifts.

"Jeryl," JoAnna said, "mind control can only go so far. With the revelations communicated this afternoon, more and more people are going to doubt what is right before them. Whatever thoughts implanted in their minds will be reevaluated and another decision will be made. Their decision."

"Power needs to be centralized and controlled," her grandfather argued. "Decentralized control with no clear common direction leads to chaos. That is the mess we inherited and it took years to correct the disharmony and dissension among the population."

"But that was why my father betrayed you," Cassie cried. "How are new ideas going to be eventually adopted unless there is a discussion, regardless of how dysfunctional the rhetoric is in the beginning?"

"Cassandra," her grandfather tried to contain his anger, "pretend it is your time to rule with JoAnna and the rest of your friends by your side. If you wanted to build a children's hospital which scenario would you choose? Building the hospital and opening it within a year or arguing with the different viewpoints and still not get it approved after ten years of debate."

If she were being strictly practical, she would want the hospital functioning within the year. Did she have to give up her principles to get things accomplished? Would she swallow her pride and use her power for the good of the Troyk children? Cassie could see herself becoming her grandfather and it scared her. How could one person dictate what was right for a whole population?

"I'd want the hospital built as quickly as possible," Cassie admitted, "but there has to be a way to work with everyone and bring people together for the common good without manipulation."

"Yes, my dear," Jeryl Jarlyn said, "and you can give up a senior center to get one group on board. Then, to get the majority to agree, you would have to compromise delaying the construction of a pollution-free light rail system to allow people to move across Aster Province faster. People can always continue walking everywhere they need to go in order to get the hospital built."

Cassie's heart sank. She could not argue against the examples her grandfather brought up. They could be fictional extremes or what Jeryl Jarlyn actually encountered daily as he decided when to use his telepathic abilities.

If she had access to her telepathic links, perhaps she could have worked with Darden and her friends to create constructive counterpoints. Her ignorance of the Troyk political system and culture would be demonstrated if she continued her argument. Cassie had so much to learn.

It was best to change the subject and redirect her grandfather's attention.

"What was the business with the white dress and kneeling next to Barash Kleyman?" Cassie asked. "You know perfectly well that Darden is my soul mate."

Jeryl Jarlyn let out a long, pained sigh. "Cassandra, you are my flesh and blood, but I have my limits. There are things I am willing to live with, such as you throwing the ignorant viewpoints my son held in my face. However, I will not tolerate treason. For eight years, Darden Lours knew the whereabouts of the most wanted man in this universe and kept silent. You are the only reason the man you call your soul mate is still breathing."

Tears welled up in Cassie's eyes. Feelings of terror rocked her body, as chills ran up and down her spine. She had inadvertently stepped into quicksand and had no clue how to pull herself and Darden out of the fix she had unintentionally put them in.

"As for Barash Kleyman," her grandfather continued, "and as far as the Prime Council is concerned, the two of you are engaged."

"Over my dead body," Darden blurted out.

Cassie gasped aloud at her soul mate's unguarded words. Candy shifted slightly in Darden's direction, preparing to come to his aid if necessary.

"I can certainly see to that, young man," Jeryl Jarlyn responded venomously. "From this moment on, Cassandra will continue to reside at The Palace. JoAnna, and only JoAnna, may visit her. Your other friends may request an audience with you, but only I can authorize such visitations. You will obey me like a good little girl, or, your soul mate will meet the fate he so richly deserves."

Anger, unlike anything she ever experienced, consumed her. Cassie lashed out with the only weapon she had…telepathy. Focusing on her grandfather's brain, she began using the deadly technique that killed a man when she was younger.

JoAnna grabbed her hand. *"Don't,"* her friend said as she entered her mind. *"You are not powerful enough yet. The only thing you will accomplish is assuring Darden's death."*

JoAnna had somehow managed to negate the power of the crystals surrounding them. It was a testament to how powerful she was. JoAnna had entered the mind melded passage created earlier through some other means than telepathy.

Cassie released the hold she had on Jeryl Jarlyn's mind. It was such a weak attack, she doubted he even felt her presence. There had to be a way of freeing herself from her grandfather's control without causing Darden's execution.

Darden was helpless as he watched the color drain from Cassie's beautiful face. His courageous soul mate tried to stand up to her grandfather and failed. It angered Darden that he was the weapon Jeryl Jarlyn wielded against his granddaughter.

Even more frustrating was his inability to communicate through their channel. There was no guarantee Cassie would not inadvertently consume more of the crystals that blocked her access to every telepathic link. The last thing he wanted was Cassie going on a hunger strike or refusing to drink anything.

He knew Jeryl Jarlyn would give them no time to say their temporary goodbyes. There was so much he wanted to say to Cassie. He never verbally expressed the love he bore her, except the last time they made love. Darden should have continually told her what she meant to him.

Once their channel opened again, he would flood it with sentiments of love. She would never again be unsure of his feelings. He would now dedicate every waking hour to getting Benko Jarlyn back to the Troyk universe. Jeryl Jarlyn was too powerful to fight alone.

He was surrounded by powerful women and could not use them. JoAnna was a mind control telepath of unknown strength. However, she would be the first to admit she was a novice where Jeryl Jarlyn's power was concerned.

The Warrior Woman continued to hone her skills. However, they were defensive in nature. Candy was never an aggressor. He was not sure she had it in her to launch an offensive attack.

Shirl was the most powerful of all the women. All she had to do was open a portal and blast Jeryl Jarlyn to nothingness. He knew he would never ask that of her because, even though Jeryl was dangerously insane, Shirl would feel immense guilt for the rest of her life.

Although he could not send words through the link he shared with Cassie, he pushed the love that scorched his heart to his soul mate. He left the room knowing Cassie had received his feelings. Her face was covered with a light blush that tinted her lovely cheeks.

"*I am heading to Crystal Telepathic Headquarters,*" Darden shared with the others through the warrior channel as soon as he left The Palace. "*Barash Kleyman and I have a few things to get straight.*"

He did not share his destination through the communal channels. The last thing Darden wished was for Barash to know he was coming. Darden wanted the man Jeryl Jarlyn had chosen for Cassie to be unprepared for his visit.

Darden did not know if he was facing an ally or an adversary. Barash's association with Cassie's grandmother did not sway his opinion in either direction. It was unclear what Elyn's true motivations were.

Solfa had been aware of Tarsea's little band of dissidents, but looked the other way. She had never picked up any clues about Elyn and her followers.

It was important for Darden to explain to Barash how things stood between him and Cassie. Barash was never to manhandle Cassie again. Their true relationship had been communicated through the communal pathways, so Barash knew he and Cassie were soul mates.

If Darden had the slightest hint Barash would refuse to cooperate with him, Darden would find some way of separating him from Cassie and warn Tarsea not to use Barash or Cassie's grandmother in any of their operations. His life revolved around those two goals now that he could no longer travel between dimensions.

Crystal Telepathic Headquarters was the hub where both the Gatherers who navigated the inter-dimensional portals and the C.T. Guards who protected them during their missions congregated. The C.T. Guards were greater in number because of the rarity of crystal telepaths and the multitude of additional duties the guards performed.

Because of his past relationship with Cassie, Darden often traveled alone to Gingko Terra. He had been able to go unaccompanied because Troyk citizens experienced terrible headaches in that world. By the time it was known Benko Jarlyn had escaped to that realm, Darden and Cassie were safe in the Troyk penal colony world with her father. Things became complicated when Cassie entered the Troyk universe.

It did not take long for Darden to locate Barash. By the time he did, his twin brother and Shirl joined him to offer their support. Shirl was itching for a fight since Jeryl Jarlyn had not included her with the people who could visit Cassie without his permission. With her crystal telepathic abilities, it had not surprised Darden that Jeryl Jarlyn had cut off Shirl's access to his granddaughter.

As he approached Barash Kleyman, his companions ceased their conversation. All attention focused on him. The communal pathways were flooded with speculation about what would happen next. Darden squared his shoulders, unused to being the center of attention.

"I assume you have come to confront me," Barash Kleyman said in a neutral tone. Barash did not seem the least bit intimidated. The man had a blank expression on his face, so Darden could not read anything that would help him gain the upper hand in the conversation.

"It would be best if we spoke in private," Darden responded. He did not like the number of people who surrounded them.

Barash eyed his twin and Shirl behind him. "If they are coming, I will bring my own witnesses."

"Whatever makes you happy," Darden answered. He wanted to bait some type of reaction from Barash. "I just plan to explain where things stand. If you need help remembering what has been said, by all means, bring as many people your faulty memory may require."

"Do not lose your cool, Darden," his twin warned through their channel. *"Kleyman's power and influence seems to have increased over the last few days. We do not want people choosing sides until Benko is ready to return."*

"It is just a little harmless gamesmanship," Darden assured his brother.

Starc grunted instead of continuing their conversation. Officially, Darden figured his brother still got the last word. He was too focused on Barash to care.

They headed to the second floor where various meeting and training rooms could be found. This time of day, they should have their pick of locations. Training was typically in the mornings.

Barash and two of the men he had been conversing with entered the small training room Darden selected. There was enough space for Darden to pace if he desired, but it was compact enough that Barash could not hide his expressions or body language.

"You were unaware of the relationship between myself and Cassandra Jarlyn earlier this afternoon," Darden said. "Now that you understand how things are, you will cease any physical contact with my soul mate or try to develop any kind of relationship with her."

"Have you had sex with Cassandra?" Barash asked.

"Whether we have or have not had relations is no concern of yours," Darden growled. "Hands off my mate or it will be the last thing you do."

His adversary did not seem affected by their conversation one way or another. If anything, he appeared bored. At a minimum, a C.T.

Guard should show deference to a crystal telepath. Darden rarely expected that type of sycophantic behavior from one of the guards, but from Barash, he demanded it.

"The Prime Ruler expects a union between myself and his granddaughter," Barash said. "He told me the nature of your relationship this morning. Whether she has gone through the evolutionary change is irrelevant to me. A fifth-generation mind control telepath has more than enough power to control the government and its population."

Darden was not prepared for what he heard. What kind of man would want a woman who was a soul mate to another? He was at a loss regarding how to proceed.

"Cassie will never accept you," Shirl interceded.

"We will see," Barash responded.

Barash and his two friends left the conference room. Darden did not bother to lift his head to acknowledge they were gone. Somehow he had managed to make the situation worse.

After several minutes of silence, Darden addressed Starc and Shirl. "The warrior channel is too crowded. Inform Tarsea to keep Barash and Elyn ignorant of his activities. I need to spend the night at my apartment and figure out my next steps."

"We will expect you for breakfast at the Childers's home," Starc said. "I will let Tolfer know you are coming and to make your favorites. Things will work out, brother. Get some rest and we will examine our options tomorrow. I will make sure Koel is there."

Darden remained in the training room for another hour, staring at a blank wall. His mind whirled, but he was unable to come up with anything constructive. Maybe a good night's sleep would help.

His apartment was ten blocks from The Palace. It felt great breathing in fresh, cool air. He took a shortcut through an isolated alley. The last thing he wanted to see were happy couples walking hand-in-hand down the walkway.

A sharp pain in his neck startled Darden. He went to bat away whatever had bitten him and was shocked to feel a small needle protruding from his neck. Before he could send out a telepathic cry for help, he fell unconscious onto the hard, unforgiving ground.

Chapter 15

Cassie had slept like the dead. No impolite bird woke her early this morning. After everything that occurred the previous day, she probably needed a good night's sleep. Flora had most likely been instructed to let her sleep in.

Cassie had not eaten dinner nor had she partaken of any of the beverages offered, afraid everything contained crushed crystals. Last night before bed, she used the faucet in her bathroom to quench her thirst.

Although she was starving, Cassie was not eager to get out of bed. She did not think she could face Jeryl Jarlyn without breaking down in angry tears. From this point forward, she was not going to refer to or think of him as her grandfather. He was the tyrant her father had always warned her about. She wished learning that lesson had not been so costly.

The static in her head proved her access to the telepathic pathways was being restored. Yesterday's proximity to all the flentium no longer altered her abilities. She immediately reached out to Darden, but was unable to make contact with him. Cassie next focused on the warrior channel, which was active with conversations about a manhunt underway. They were searching for someone who had disappeared and she instinctively knew they were looking for Darden.

Cassie flew out of bed and quickly dressed. She was uncertain what kind of resistance she might face while attempting to leave The

Palace. Cassie vowed she would mow down anyone who got in her way, including Jeryl Jarlyn.

"I'm on my way to meet up with everyone at the Childers's residence," Cassie communicated through the warrior link.

Candy immediately responded through the same channel. *"I am downstairs in the Grand Hall,"* Candy informed her. *"JoAnna is on the way to your rooms and planned to break the news to you about Darden."*

Opening her door, Cassie observed two guards were stationed on either side of the entrance. She had heard murmured discussions when she rose this morning. These two men were not going to stop her from leaving.

"The Prime Ruler has not sent for you, miss," the blond guard said. "You are to stay in your rooms until you are summoned."

Cassie did not have the time or the patience to deal with these two men. "Let me pass or you will be sorry," she warned them. There was an edge to her voice, indicating she was serious.

When the dark haired guard approached her, Cassie dug into the recesses of her mind where she stored the deadly power she possessed. She had not been confident or determined enough to reach this far into the darkness of her powers when she attempted to attack Jeryl Jarlyn yesterday. A man died the last time she called upon the power, but today, she would hold nothing back.

Both men grabbed their heads in pain, helpless to stop her from leaving. A third guard made way for her, not wanting to meet the same fate. Cassie released her hold on the two men and left the private quarters of her prison. If the guards were smart, they would not follow. Better a headache for several hours than dying from a brain hemorrhage.

JoAnna was waiting for her and had already dealt with the guards stationed at the threshold to the public area. Unless you got too close, the guards were positioned to look like they were reading. A civilian would believe the guards were lazy, not unconscious.

"Did you have to kill anyone?" JoAnna asked through the channel she shared with the other girls.

"Not yet," Cassie responded. *"If anyone else tries to stop me, I can't guarantee I won't. Everyone is concerned about what I will become. Well, we may very well find out if Darden is not found quickly."*

They made their way unchallenged to the Grand Hall. Candy was surrounded by people asking her a variety of questions. Her return from the penal colony had made her a celebrity long before revealing she was a legendary soul mate.

A momentary hush fell over the crowd when Cassie and JoAnna joined the group. People quickly realized the Prime Ruler's granddaughter was among them. Cassie did not like how the crowd changed from elated to reverent. She was one of them and had no intention of being placed on a pedestal.

"How is everyone this fine morning?" Cassie asked the crowd cheerfully. "We are going to a friend's house for breakfast, would you like to walk with us? I can tell you all about Gingko Terra, the world I call Earth."

Her grandfather could easily discover her intended destination, so she may as well inform the whole Aster Province and have a large civilian army accompany her. Jeryl Jarlyn would create a scene if he tried to stop her or bring her back against her will. The more minds he had to manipulate to do damage control, the better off Cassie would be.

En masse, they walked through the streets of Aster Province and Cassie told the people about Sedona, Arizona, the Grand Canyon, Casa Grande, and anything else she could think of. When they asked about her father, Cassie readily answered them. She spoke lovingly about a man who had become a folk hero to them.

Cassie could feel the energy she drew from the crowd and the harmony she spread to those around her. As they continued through the walkways, more people joined them.

"*Do you feel what is happening to the crowd?*" Cassie asked JoAnna through the link she shared with her friends.

"*I don't think you are using your mind control telepathic gift,*" JoAnna conjectured. "*You are pulling psychic energy and pushing something that is causing the brain to excrete a chemical making the people closest to you happy and content. I also think they are spreading it to the rest of the crowd. I wish I paid more attention in science class.*"

"*They are producing endorphins, which are neutron transmitters,*" Alex communicated through the link. "*Unlike the two of you, I paid attention. Tolfer is cooking up a storm and we are awaiting your arrival. Cassie, you must be starving.*"

With so much else going on, Cassie had forgotten all about being hungry. She was doing something to affect the people around her and Darden still had not communicated through their pathway.

A million thoughts about what happened to her soul mate fluttered in her brain. They were all bad and involved Jeryl Jarlyn. The people around her helped Cassie concentrate on something other than worrying herself sick about her soul mate. As it was, tears welled in her eyes, ready to fall down her cheeks.

"We always go to Alex for answers," Candy said. Somehow Candy knew her friend needed to be distracted. The more the girls rattled on, the less she obsessed over Darden's disappearance.

While they walked, Cassie talked aloud to the people around her, commenting about what she saw through the communal pathways, and conversed with her friends through their closed channel. She monitored what was communicated through the warrior pathway. No one had remarked on her earlier entry into that particular link. There was still no sign of Darden.

Cassie could no longer hold back the tears she so bravely fought. She could feel the concern of those around her as she started to cry. Love seeped through the communal pathways directed toward her. As far as Cassie understood, what was happening was impossible.

"Oh, my God!" JoAnna exclaimed. She must have sensed what Cassie picked up.

"What?" Candy inquired.

"I don't know how it's possible," JoAnna said, "but emotions are coming through the communal channels, all focused on Cassie."

"That must be why my receptors are getting that Zen-like feeling again," Candy commented.

The small group closest to Cassie took turns kissing Cassie's cheeks and comforting her with hugs. After each embrace, the stunned citizen made way for the next to comfort Cassie. As one turned, Cassie could have sworn she heard him refer to her as 'The True Ruler'.

Everything around her became surreal. Although their progress to their destination was slow, she gained physical and mental strength from her well-wishers. Cassie wondered if this was real or some strange mass hallucination. The citizens around her seemed as dazed and confused as she was.

Leenea opened the door for them when they arrived at her home. For a moment, Cassie was afraid the throng would try to follow her into the home. The group disbanded, sending telepathic good wishes through the communal pathways.

As soon as she entered the house, the aroma of delectable goodies made her mouth water and her stomach grumbled loudly. She followed her nose into the kitchen where Tolfer put down his spoon and embraced Candy.

Candy had always been so self-reliant. It was nice knowing someone took such good care of her friend. Cassie could not remember a time she had seen Candy so happy. Even though Benko had stopped taking her to see her friends at the orphanage, Cassie had ways to keep track of their lives.

JoAnna grabbed a plate full of food with one hand and Cassie's hand with another. She dragged her into the common room where Alex was setting the table.

"Where is Shirl?" Cassie asked. For some reason, she thought the female crystal telepath would be here to greet her.

"She's out hunting for Darden with the men," Alex answered. "A contingent of crystal telepaths and C.T. Guards who are loyal to Darden and Starc have joined the search. A warrant was never taken out against Darden, so assisting us is not considered treason."

Since Cassie had temporarily lost access to the telepathic channels, she had no idea when Darden disappeared. Initially, she was not interested in what had happened, but focused on getting Darden back. Now she wanted all the information she could gather. Even with her minimal knowledge of the Troyk universe, she could offer a recommendation or two.

"When was the last time anyone could place him somewhere?" Cassie asked.

"Last night at the Crystal Telepathic Headquarters," Candy answered. "Darden, Starc, and Shirl went to confront Barash Kleyman about what had occurred during the ceremony."

Cassie was taken aback by the news. She had immediately placed the blame on her grandfather. She never once considered Barash. It made perfect sense that Barash wanted Darden to disappear. Even so, Cassie was convinced Jeryl Jarlyn was ultimately behind everything bad that happened in the Troyk universe.

"Was my grandmother questioned? Cassie asked.

"Elyn has conveniently disappeared," Candy replied. "The apartment where Barash took you to meet her was one of the first places they looked. The place has been cleaned out."

That piece of news did not surprise Cassie. For some reason, Cassie believed finding her grandmother would get them closer to finding Darden. She did not question Elyn was her grandmother, the resemblance she bore to the woman was unmistakable. However, Elyn's motives were another story. If she conspired with Barash, she would at least know the places the C.T. Guard liked to hang out.

"Have Solfa put out a warrant for Elyn's arrest, or whatever you call it in this universe," Cassie ordered. "That woman knows more than she divulged originally."

"What charge?" Alex asked.

"Treason," Cassie answered. "She did ask Tarsea to help overthrow the government. Tarsea reported it to Solfa, and Jeryl Jarlyn's Head of Intelligence tried to handle things covertly. Now, without an arrest, Solfa is making the treasonous act public. Plus, for the time being, Tarsea's fictitious allegiance to the Prime Ruler is reinforced."

"What if she is innocent?" Alex inquired. "She may also have been duped by Barash."

"Somehow, I doubt it," Cassie responded. "The communal pathways make no mention of Elyn. If Barash had betrayed her, the channels would be teeming with conversations. Can you imagine the chatter if an arrest warrant was executed for Benko Jarlyn's mother?"

"We can always apologize to your grandmother later," Candy commented. "Desperate times and all…"

Cassie pushed her plate away. Although her empty stomach growled, she had no appetite. All of the people around her were looking at her with a variety of expressions on their faces. She wished she could tell her friends she was all right, but that would be a lie.

All Cassie could think about was Darden. Was he hurt? Was he in the bottomless pit Jeryl Jarlyn put crystal telepaths he wanted to get rid of?

Darden woke to the worst migraine he had ever experienced. Had he somehow ended up in the Gingko Terra universe? He tried to roll over, but for some reason could not.

When the fog lifted from his brain, he realized he was chained to the wall. His wrists and ankles were bound by metal braces and attached by short chains allowing prisoners of varying heights to be secured.

The muscles in the back of his neck cried out in pain as he shifted his head to examine his surroundings. The cell was dark so he could not determine how large it was. There was a distinct smell of decay and human waste.

He heard metal scraping against the stone floor as the door to his prison opened. A flash of light illuminated his world as a torch held by someone entered. When his eyes adjusted, Darden recognized Barash Kleyman.

"I should have figured you were behind this," Darden growled. "You are not going to get away with kidnapping me."

Barash laughed as if something he said was funny. "Try to summon help from your soul mate."

Darden reached out to Cassie, but was unsuccessful making a connection. There was no static in his mind. The communal pathways were gone. Whatever they had fed Cassie was now impairing his ability to communicate telepathically.

"Where am I?" Darden asked.

If Darden stood any chance of getting out of this alive, he needed information. The more confident Barash was his fate was sealed, the more facts he would let slip.

"You are where crystal telepaths are brought to die," Barash answered. "Very few know about the prison located underneath The Palace. Even fewer know there is another level below the temporary holding cells."

He was in the middle of the Aster Province, but he might as well be on the moon. They had only found out about the subterranean prison when Starc and Chartail were arrested some time ago. His brother would find a way to search below The Palace, but would not have a clue he was so close. It was doubtful the entry to the lower level would be obvious.

"How did you manage to engineer this?" Darden inquired.

"Oh, you believe I am behind this?" Barash said in surprise. "Jeryl Jarlyn arranged for your abduction, not me. He wants you out of his granddaughter's life. I suppose she will mourn for you, but eventually she will warm my bed. Cassandra is young; she will recover quickly."

Darden fought against his restraints. He wanted to pry himself loose and tighten his hands around Barash's neck. The thought of the bastard touching Cassie was more than he could bear. Barash would be the first suspect Starc and the others would go after to find him.

His jailer placed his torch in a holder and picked up a pail of water. He taunted Darden by scooping up ladles of the precious liquid and throwing it at his feet. Darden's throat was parched.

"Would you like a drink of water?" Barash asked. "It is laced with crushed flentium. What is more important, not dying of thirst or hoping the telepathic channels will open again in your mind before you die? Either way, you are going to perish down here."

"You can go fuck yourself," Darden sneered.

"Why would I do that when I can slide my cock into the Prime Ruler's gorgeous granddaughter?" Barash gibed. "I wonder if you will still be breathing when I drive into her and she gasps for air, crying out with pleasure. Here is my one gift to you. I will treat her right. She will come to love me while we rule side by side."

He actually believed Barash was sincere, but it was irrelevant. Somehow, someway, he was going to find a way out of this prison. Darden had the most powerful beings in the Troyk universe searching for him. After eight years of denying himself, he had finally joined with Cassie. Fate was not so cruel that his story would end down here. Cassie, Starc, and the rest of his friends would not leave a stone unturned until they found him.

Barash left without saying another word. Darden was relieved he was not tortured with more imaginings of Barash and Cassie's supposed future. Even if he died down here, Cassie would never find what she could have shared with him. He cursed his temper for getting himself in this position and not only endangering his future, but Cassie's as well.

Darden was helpless without a crystal. There were thousands of them directly above him. Jeryl Jarlyn hoarded them for his own use. He had traveled enough with Shirl to know crystals called to her.

Darden closed his eyes and reached out for the power directly over his head. He could feel the power vibrate, but he had no clue how to harness the energy at this distance. If he was going to survive, he would have to find a way.

Chapter 16

Putting a warrant out for her grandmother's arrest did the trick. Within two hours of announcing Elyn's treasonous behavior, her grandmother was brought to the Crystal Telepathic Headquarters.

People were generally interrogated in The Palace, but Cassie did not want to chance running into Jeryl Jarlyn. It also made sense to keep her father's parents separated. There was no telling what would happen if the two were reunited.

When Cassie entered the conference room, Elyn was visibly upset. Being arrested in the Troyk universe was no small matter. At one time, anyone convicted of a crime either served a life sentence in the Troyk penal colony or were sent to the Nightshade universe to die. The vast majority of Troyk citizens were unaware a blood lusting, vicious vampire handed down the death sentence. Jeryl Jarlyn traded their blood for crystals. Both practices had ceased and no new solution had been agreed upon.

"Where can we find Darden Lours?" Tarsea asked. He had taken command of the search for Darden. Solfa had brought him into her organization, so his questioning the prisoner was not out of line and would not draw unnecessary scrutiny. They had enough visibility as it was.

"How would I know?" Cassie's grandmother replied, seemingly innocent of any wrongdoing. "I was not involved in his abduction."

"Then how do you know he is missing?" Tarsea asked immediately after hearing Elyn's answer.

Tarsea had trapped her grandmother. Cassie moved forward in her chair. She could barely disguise her excitement. It would only be a matter of time before they liberated Darden.

"An unusual channel opened the evening we met," her grandmother claimed. "There has been chatter all day in that pathway, but the communal channels have made no mention of Darden's disappearance."

"Shit," Tarsea mumbled under his breath.

Elyn's entry into the warrior channel made her an ally and beyond suspicion. Now, they not only had to find and rescue Darden, they had to exonerate her grandmother. Cassie was crushed, but tried not to show it.

"How did you meet Barash Kleyman?" Cassie asked. "Where does he live? Are there places he likes to hang out? Is there a specific place he would go to hide?"

Cassie's anxiety caused her to rapid-fire question after question at her grandmother. Elyn didn't seem overwhelmed by the barrage and merely waited for her to finish before attempting to answer.

"Since Barash has aligned himself with Jeryl Jarlyn," Elyn said, "I imagine he will not leave The Palace unless he must."

"Barash was last seen entering The Palace early this morning," Koel informed the group. "No one witnessed him leave and we have had people searching every spot open to the public without success. He may have left The Palace and we missed him."

The discussion stopped when Shirl and Starc entered the room. Her soul mate's twin looked exhausted and defeated. What little optimism Cassie had in finding Darden quickly was destroyed when she looked at Starc's face.

"What are you picking up, Candy?" Cassie asked. She was grasping at straws, but odds were if Candy had a premonition, she would have told the group.

"I've got nothing," Candy admitted. "As my powers have grown, I've discovered I can reach out and get impressions about people. Normally it's nothing I can use, but I at least feel something. With Darden, it's almost as if he's disappeared from the pathways I use."

"Do you think he is off world?" Cassie asked.

"Doubtful, since he is a crystal telepath," Tarsea responded. "No one would risk Darden getting ahold of a crystal and escaping. I would imagine he is either unconscious or his access to the pathways have been severed. Cassie mentioned she consumed a crystal inhibitor and Tarah was also unable to enter any links when The Prime Ruler held her."

Not a single person in the room mentioned the possibility Darden was dead. Wouldn't Cassie know if that was the case? She imagined she'd feel a crippling sense of loss if Darden had been killed.

"We should keep looking," Koel suggested. "In the meantime, Cassie should be sent back to the Troyk penal world."

"No!" Cassie cried. "I can help. My mind control capabilities continue to improve. I have abilities we can use."

"Cassie," Koel cajoled, "we will find my cousin; I promise. If I have to, I will ask the vampires from the Nightshade universe for help. We cannot afford Jeryl Jarlyn getting his hands on you and using Darden as a pawn to get you to do his bidding. We cannot verify the Prime Ruler has him, but it is too risky having you in this dimension."

All eyes were now glued on Cassie. How could she argue with Koel when she knew he was right? The last thing she wanted was Jeryl Jarlyn harming Darden, forcing her to bend to his will. She was surprised he was not already blackmailing her through their familial channel.

"We draw a crowd everywhere we go," Cassie said. The trip they made to the Crystal Telepathic Headquarters was as crazy as a Mardi Gras parade in New Orleans. She was surprised they didn't start throwing beads as they made their way through the streets. "How are we going to get to the mountain portal without a crowd following us?"

"Look at your finger, Cassie," Shirl said. "Dorothy had her ruby slippers, and you have an amethyst. That crystal is emitting so much power, I could transport an army with it."

"You just may have to, Shirl," Tarsea said.

Shirl touched her ring's stone and a gateway opened. The crystal telepath entered first, in order to manipulate the harmonics that would open a portal to the Troyk penal colony. Everyone entered behind Shirl. Cassie wondered if she would ever return to the Troyk universe or be held in her soul mate's arms again.

THE TROYK PENAL COLONY WORLD

They exited the portal just as the community gathered for their evening meal. Shirl opened another portal and brought the rest of their friends to the colony. No one was safe in the Troyk universe anymore.

Cassie spotted her father and immediately ran into his extended arms. She had a short-lived sense of home and safety. He was her anchor to the past, but Darden was her future.

She felt her father suck in a breath. Without turning, Cassie knew he was reacting to seeing his mother, perhaps for the first time in his life. It was high time Benko met the woman who gave birth to him.

"Daddy," Cassie said, "Jeryl Jarlyn ripped you from your mother's arms as soon as you were born. She never wanted to give you up."

Benko Jarlyn released Cassie and she watched him tentatively walk toward his mother. She had never seen her father do anything with hesitation. Cassie never realized what his mother's abandonment had done to her father's psyche.

Elyn closed the distance between them and took her son into her trembling arms. Tears of joy fell from her grandmother's eyes. Cassie wiped away the moisture from her own cheeks.

What had started as a typical evening meal turned into a celebration. The children squealed when Tolfer walked through the portal. Candy's soul mate was a particular favorite among the colony's young. When he and Candy had been stranded in the penal world, Tolfer had gone out of his way to bond with, and be there for, the children. He had a talent working with the young ones to help them manage their multiple telepathic channels and reduce the pain they experienced until mastering the techniques.

Chartail and Elyn hit it off immediately once her grandmother recovered from the difference in their ages. The older woman must have felt it was some kind of favorable reflection on her that her son had such a young soul mate. There did not seem to be a single soul

Chartail could not charm. Even Alex, who loathed Chartail in the beginning, was in an intimate discussion with her stepmother about their pregnancies. She needed to put her jealousy aside and make Darden's rescue her primary concern.

As the evening wound down, Tolfer took the children to the lake to build a bonfire and tell them stories about Troyk's legendary women. The celebratory part of the evening was done and the adults had more pressing matters to discuss.

Cassie had been barely able to carry on a conversation during dinner. She moved the food around on her plate to make it appear she was eating. An occasional nod also masked her distraction. Her attention was not focused until Darden was mentioned.

"Are there sections of The Palace the general population does not know about where they could be holding Darden?" Tarsea asked Benko. Her father was in the best position to answer that question since he once resided there.

"There are cells directly below the Grand Hall," Benko answered.

"I am painfully aware of those," Starc said.

Although Starc had not been tortured while he was a prisoner in The Palace, Cassie figured Starc and Chartail had been anxious about their fates as The Prime Ruler talked to Shirl during their captivity. Fortunately, Jeryl Jarlyn released Starc, and Chartail was sent to the Troyk penal colony dimension for her crime.

"As a child, my father terrorized me to break me of any habit he found distasteful and mentioned a place no one ever returned from," Benko added. "Unfortunately, he never showed me the location, so I am not sure such a place exists."

"I wish I could help," Kelog said. "Although I heard rumors of such a place, I was never asked to escort a prisoner there."

"There has to be a place criminal or dissident crystal telepaths were sent," Koel said. "They disappeared without protest or commotion as they were not transported through the streets. The prison has to be under The Palace or Crystal Telepathic Headquarters. My guess would be The Palace. There are more deliveries at that location. The guards used to transport prisoners would have taken advantage of all the activity bringing items in and out of The Palace."

"I can read each guard's mind until I find the one with the information," Alex offered.

"You are staying here where it is safe until Benko has control of Aster Province," Tarsea stated. "If you will not consider your own life, remember you are carrying our daughter."

It first appeared Alex was going to challenge Tarsea. Cassie knew the exact moment her friend acquiesced, Alex's shoulders slumped in defeat. All Tarsea had to do was mention their child and his soul mate folded. She did not expect her to do anything else. Cassie figured Tarsea was going to be as overprotective a father, as he was a controlling mate. Alex will have to teach Star how to wind Tarsea around her little finger like Alex had.

"Cassie can keep Alex company," Benko said.

Unlike her friend, that was one dictate Cassie was not going to tolerate. "I am going with you to find Darden," Cassie declared. "The soul mate channel is the first telepathic link to mend. I may be the only one capable of communicating with him. Besides, he is *my* soul mate. No one has the right to tell me I am not going to be part of his rescue. That includes you, Dad."

"Baby girl, you do not understand; this will be an all or nothing attack," her father said. "Either I unseat my father or we will be joining Darden or dead. This will not be a stealth attack. Everyone will be exposed."

There was an uneasy silence between Cassie and her father. She knew he wanted her to be safe, but there was no way she would wait on the side lines hoping the mission was successful. The future of the Troyk universe rested in this small group's hands.

"As much as I hate to say it," Koel said, "Drake has offered his support. It would be foolish if we do not take him up on his offer. Our attack will be at night, so casualties should be low. I hope there will be a good number of guards who will switch allegiances once they realize who they are fighting. The vampires will only make our force stronger."

"Once news of the invasion enters the communal pathways, the citizens of Aster Province will hit the streets," Candy said. "I don't know how I feel about letting a bunch of blood thirsty vampires loose on innocent bystanders. They were able to only attack our enemies when they helped liberate Tolfer and me from this world. Drake and his blood brothers may not be able to tell our supporters from our foes."

"And we will?" laughed JoAnna. "We have three powerful mind control telepaths. That has to count for something."

"Make that four," Chartail announced. Although she did not naturally have the ability, her pregnancy temporarily gave her the telepathic gift.

All eyes shifted to Benko Jarlyn. Chartail carried his unborn son. His soul mate had almost successfully executed a plan to assassinate Jeryl Jarlyn. The baby notwithstanding, how could Cassie go and Chartail not be allowed. Her father was not in an enviable position.

"Cassie," her father sighed, "as much as I would like to command you to stay behind, Darden is your soul mate. I must respect and live with the decision you make. Chartail, I have made no oral commitment to you or our child. For that unforgivable oversight, I have no control over you."

"We are both going," Chartail said before her soul mate could change his mind. "I have sat in all the planning sessions. Nobody knows the plan better than I do, with the exception of Koel."

Her father slightly nodded, acknowledging Chartail's decision. Although Cassie was ambivalent regarding Chartail, she admired her courage. Her child would grow up in the Troyk universe if they were successful. Not one more child would be born in the primitive world where the former dissidents lived in exile.

"Are we sure about Drake?" Shirl asked.

"I know what his demand will be for aiding us, and I am willing to pay it for Darden's life," Tarsea stated. "He will be able to control himself and his blood brothers while they are in the Troyk universe. Drake has too much to lose if he angers Alex or me. As long as he is convinced our daughter is his soul mate, the creature is controllable."

"All right then," Shirl said. "He is expecting a visit from me in the next day or so. Drake and his brothers will be at Lorenz's settlement awaiting my return. I will be right back."

Shirl opened a portal and entered it with Starc. Cassie imagined the vampires would have to feed before returning with Shirl. Koel, in the meantime, worked with Tarsea and Benko to revise their plans to include a contingent of the freedom fighters to find and rescue Darden. They also had to determine how best to use the vampires and provide as little risk to the Troyk population as possible.

Cassie soaked in as much of the plan as she could. Unlike Chartail, she had not attended many of her father's planning sessions. Rather than stepping up and learning to lead, Cassie was often off brooding about her relationship with Darden. She could have kicked herself for her immaturity. Now, she needed to be the warrior her friends had become. They were fearless, and she needed to be the same. Her soul mate's life depended on it.

Half the members of the penal colony would join the fight. Darden had been searching worlds to find exiled dissidents to help rage war. The other half would evacuate the settlement with the children. If any of the exiled freedom fighters were identified in the Troyk universe, they would know where Benko had initiated his plans. There was the possibility of reprisals were they unsuccessful in overthrowing Jeryl Jarlyn.

Shirl and Darden had been smuggling crystals and the weapons they powered to the penal colony for the day they would take back the Troyk universe. Cassie watched as the items were distributed. A number of the people did not want to take any armaments. No one wanted to use the weapons, but they would more than likely run into resistance before they reached Jeryl Jarlyn. The Prime Ruler surrounded himself with zealots, willing to die to protect their leader. Her grandfather would not go down without a fight. Cassie accepted the weapon her father handed her.

"Point and shoot, baby girl," he said. "It is as simple as that. Living with the consequences is something very different. If it is between your life or your adversary's, do not hesitate. Shoot to kill."

Cassie hefted the weapon. It was surprisingly light. Most of the weight was at the rear of the metal device where the crystal was embedded. Each crystal weapon fired three shots. She put additional crystals in her pockets as they were handed out. Koel gave her and Chartail a quick lesson on how to unload and reload the weapon. They were not going to waste any crystal ammunition to practice shooting. Everyone, except Cassie, had weapons training.

A portal opened and five large men and a woman exited behind Shirl and Starc. Cassie missed seeing Drake earlier, but immediately knew which man he was. Shirl and Alex's descriptions had not done justice to the devastatingly handsome creature before her. The pale complexion of his skin brought out his incredible eyes. They had been described to her as black, but they were actually a dark purple.

Drake immediately headed to Alex. He knelt and kissed her abdomen as Alex rolled her eyes. Cassie found it utterly touching and nothing she would have expected from a vampire. Her mental picture of Drake changed dramatically with this first impression. A weight was lifted off her shoulders. They were not taking a blood-crazed lunatic into the Troyk universe.

A second vampire followed Drake to Alex's side. He could not have been more than a boy when he was converted into a creature of the night. Cassie almost laughed at the over dramatization going on in her mind. It was not every day one met vampires. Like most women, Cassie was drawn to the romanticized vampire films. The boy had beautiful wavy brown hair and she imagined had DaVinci seen him, Leonardo would have wanted to paint him. Cassie heard Drake introduce him as Jace.

The other three males did not appear to be vampires, if their tan faces were any indication. Cassie would have liked the strength three more vampires would have brought. However, these men looked like they would do great in a battle. They were huge!

One of the largest Nightshade men approached Cassie with Koel by his side. "This is Frazour," Koel said. "He will not leave your side once we return to the Troyk universe."

Cassie looked at the menacing figure before her and his lethal looking sword. No one with half a brain would challenge this gorilla. He had dark features like Drake, but appeared far more dangerous.

"I fought beside your soul mate," Frazour said. "He is an honorable man. We will not rest until he is found. My blood brother, Drake, has demanded more time with his mate for his services. I fight because of my respect for Darden."

She looked between Drake and Frazour. Cassie was aware Drake had four blood brothers, but was unaware human relations existed.

"Now I'm lost," Cassie admitted. "I thought Drake's blood brothers were all vampires."

Frazour's smile lit his face and made him appear less threatening. "Once we make love to our soul mates we transform into what nature had originally planned for The Creator to be. We are all becoming elementals. My soul mate, Emma, is a water elemental. She gifted me the sun. Our women are transforming faster than we are. Sammuel and his mate are land elementals. Lorenz and Afton can wield fire."

Cassie looked past the blond Adonis to the woman who stood beside him. The black haired statuesque woman could not be Afton. Yorik's half-ling daughter had been a malnourished, slight girl. Shirl and Candy said Afton had transformed, but she was not expecting such a dramatic change.

"Afton?" Cassie asked.

The raven-haired Amazon turned in her direction. Her eyes widened upon recognizing Cassie. She said something to Shirl and made her way to Cassie.

"I was hoping to see you," Afton said. "Miranda always mentions you after visiting Beatrice. It had always been my intention to join Miranda on one of her visits, but things have been crazy."

"Yes, I heard about Yorik's death," Cassie said.

Afton had orchestrated her vicious father's death upon learning he planned to force himself on Miranda to produce another half-ling child. It would not be appropriate to express her condolences. After all, ultimately it was Benko's mind control telepathic abilities that killed Afton's vampire father.

There was momentary unease between the two women. Cassie and Benko had been the ones responsible for Afton leaving Earth and entering the horrific Nightshade universe. They had been willing to sacrifice Afton for Shirl's life.

"I need to..." Cassie started to apologize before she was cut off.

"There is no need," Afton said immediately. It was clear from Cassie's tone and lowered eyes what her intention had been. "I would have eventually starved to death on Earth and never would have mated with Lorenz. He would have faced eternity alone if you had not used your telepathic gift to trick me into returning to my father's world."

The blond vampire who entered their world with Afton came to her side. This must be her soul mate, Lorenz. Afton raised her head and there was such a look of love on her face, it took Cassie's breath away. Did she look at Darden that way? It only caused her to long for Darden that much more.

"And for that," Lorenz said as he entered the conversation, "we fight to reunite you with your soul mate."

Although Cassie had felt guilty about her role in Afton's abduction, she had not realized how it had weighed her down. Tears of relief and gratitude fell from her eyes. Afton took her into her powerful arms.

"Don't worry," Afton said. "We'll find Darden. Frazour won't leave your side until you are once again with your soul mate. Frazour has been a warrior his whole existence. For a period of time, he was so obsessed with killing, his blood brothers considered him more of a feral animal than a man. His mate, Emma, changed everything."

Cassie was not sure if she should be relieved or petrified. The bottom-line? If Frazour was helping to free Darden, she wanted him to be a vicious animal.

Koel wanted to go over the plan several more times. He laid out where each person would enter the Troyk universe and the role they played. This late in the planning period, there were still a number of questions from the participants.

As far as Cassie was concerned, they were taking too long. Minutes could be the difference between finding Darden alive or dead.

Chapter 17

Darden could barely open his right eye. Not that it mattered. It was so dark in his cell, there was nothing to see. Barash had beaten the crap out of him. The orders had supposedly come from the Prime Ruler to make Darden's incarceration as miserable as possible.

Jeryl Jarlyn had always wanted to have the ability to control the portal frequencies. He never left the Troyk universe because he trusted no one else to control the wormhole's harmonics. Even though he was a valued crystal telepath, Jeryl Jarlyn considered Darden expendable. The Prime Ruler wanted him out of Cassie's life.

Darden wondered how long they would keep him alive. Barash seemed to get a perverse thrill slamming fists into his face and ribs. During one beating, it felt like Barash was hitting him with some kind of blunt object. He had not been conscious enough to determine if there was a weapon or if it was all his imagination. If not rescued soon, Darden knew he may be beyond any help a med-tech could offer. Troyk medicine could cure just about anything except when the patient bled out or there was major damage to an internal organ.

Some crystal telepaths treated C.T. Guards as if they were beneath them. Darden never did because Starc had chosen that profession to be near his twin. As far as he was concerned, there was no better man than his brother. He was thrilled when Starc discovered Shirl was his soul mate. Together Starc could navigate the portals with the woman he loved beside him. Although Darden had always treated

Barash with respect, his adversary took out his frustration over the disdain of other crystal telepaths out on his hide.

Chained as he was, Darden was forced to stand. Extreme fatigue set in and he hoped he would dream of Cassie. She was all he thought about, every waking hour. Now he could only think of how to keep the pain at a manageable level. Darden prayed for sleep. It would release his body from the pain and let him be with Cassie.

He was about to pass out again when a frequency started to play in his mind. It was similar to the sounds produced when he navigated the inter-dimensional portal. There were similarities, but there were also distinct differences.

Darden had been so focused on what mating would do to Cassie, he had not given his own evolutionary change much thought. The female's transformations seemed to be more extreme. He never once considered that he might develop any mind control abilities.

The frequency grew louder in his head as he concentrated his telepathic powers on it, using the same technique he used when his crystal was low in energy. Although he did not possess the crystal physically, the same process should work. There were so many crystals in The Palace. Darden wondered if the mated enhancements he was gifted allowed him to access them, even when not holding one.

Although his focus was on manipulating the power growing in his mind, Darden did not miss the sound of the metal door scraping against the floor. Barash had returned.

"Good, you are awake," Barash commented. "I will not have to wait to pass on our Prime Ruler's regards. My future bride has disappeared. Do you have any idea where our little Cassie has run off to?"

Thank the Supreme Being! Tarsea had ordered Shirl to get Cassie out of the Troyk universe, a simple request he made as a backup plan if anything happened to him. It would be easy enough for them to find a crystal Shirl could use. The stone did not have to be charged for her to pull power from it. A mated female crystal telepath could use a simple piece of jewelry and be successful. Jeryl Jarlyn was still unaware of the enormous power Shirl possessed.

"You will never find her," Darden growled. "Cassie is safe from both you and her grandfather."

"Gatherers have been sent to Gingko Terra and other worlds we have found dissidents over the years," Barash informed him. "We will find Cassie, and I will rule by her side when the old goat dies. The more he abuses pulling power from the crystals he possesses, the sooner I will rule. He is half-mad already."

"Cassie will rule," Darden said. "You are no one and have no special telepathic gift."

Barash slammed his right fist into his side. Darden swallowed the groan from the all-encompassing pain. Fury gleamed in Barash's eyes. Darden unintentionally fueled Barash's insecurities concerning his inadequate telepathic gift.

Darden had seen firsthand how much Chartail was bothered by such treatment. It caused her to plan Jeryl Jarlyn's death. His focus now should be on his latent powers to see if he could get free himself.

"Oh, but I have an incentive for Cassie to be a good little girl," Barash replied.

It did not take any stretch of the imagination to figure out the bastard meant him. The last thing he wanted was his life to be held over Cassie's head to force her compliance. He would will himself to die before that happened. However, he was far from surrendering at this point.

Darden channeled the pain and pulled on the crystals' power. He imagined himself within the core of the wormhole. When Barash came at him again, Darden focused his power on his adversary's brain. Contained within the mind was the mechanism that directed motor function. All he had to do was turn off Barash's ability to move, particularly his right arm.

He ignored the arm's forward momentum and concentrated on stopping the fist. Even though it stopped within an inch of his bruised cheek, Darden did not relinquish his assault on Barash's mind. Darden could feel blood running from his nose, but continued pushing his telepathic power outward.

Barash's eyes widened, surprised by his inability to move. "What are you doing? You are not a mind control telepath you do not have the power to control me."

He did not bother to argue the point, but pulled in the power of the crystals that had sung to him earlier. Liquid ran down the side of his neck. Darden knew his ears were bleeding, his new telepathic powers too much for his untrained brain. He vowed to continue until Barash was dead at his feet or his own brain hemorrhaged from the strain.

Blood started to seep from Barash's head. His hands were cradling his injured skull. Darden could see brain matter starting to seep through the cracks he had created. Again, he refused to stop until one of them was dead.

Cassie entered the Troyk universe through a special portal Shirl opened. They were the fourth of ten groups that entered this universe with two missions: freeing Darden and unseating the current mind control government. Her group consisted of Frazour, Candy, and six of the settlement's best fighters. Frazour hand selected them based how each performed during the battle to defeat the Portal Guardians.

Her father's only demand when creating the teams was that Candy would accompany Cassie. Having Candy by her side relieved some of her anxiety concerning the mission, but there was plenty to spare. Her blood rushed through her head at such a rapid pace, she could barely hear.

Her nose was assaulted by the smell of decay and mildew. The stone structure must have a wood base. She was no expert, but she imagined she smelled dry rot, among other things.

"It really stinks down here," Candy commented as she covered her nose with her hand.

They entered the dimension exactly where the subterranean cells were located. To their surprise, the level was empty. The stench would have been overpowering had the human equation been added in.

"Where are they holding all the criminals they are no longer sending to the penal colony?" Cassie wondered out loud. It was doubtful anyone had an answer. At this point, the information was irrelevant.

"There should be a door that leads into the lower cells, if any exist," Candy commented. "We should search the exterior walls for a hidden door or a trigger to open one. That would be the most likely place for an entrance to another level. If we fail, we'll try searching interior surface structures."

Cassie and Candy moved along the wall closest to where they stood. They could easily move past the area where cells hugged the wall. She was not confident they would find what they were looking for. If such a door existed, it would be a known fact another cellblock lay below. With nine people searching, it took no time to determine there was no visible doorway.

"Let us look for an entrance somewhere in the interior," Frazour said. "Look for any break in the pattern on the floor, footsteps that exist and then disappear, or anything that just looks odd or off kilter."

Once again, Cassie trailed along behind Candy, as they scanned their designated section. Searching the interior was more challenging than the exterior. The few rugs on the floor were pulled back, but nothing indicated there was any entrance to any subterranean area. Cassie grew more frustrated and aggravated as the search continued with nothing to show for their efforts. Could they have been wrong about The Palace? Maybe she should have joined the team searching Crystal Telepathic Headquarters.

Behind the noise in her head was an underlying frequency. Cassie could barely hear it. It was not a natural tone crystals made, but it sounded as if someone was manipulating the tonality. Not unlike a crystal telepath changing the pitch within a portal. Darden was somewhere close. Cassie knew it!

"He's near," Cassie announced to the group. "There has to be another level and a way down."

"There could be an entrance that is not within The Palace, but located somewhere outside," Frazour said. "It is not uncommon for keeps in the Nightshade universe to have subterranean passages that extend past the structure itself."

Cassie was going to be sick. Where would they even begin if the entrance was located outside The Palace? The possibilities were too numerous and their numbers too small.

"I agree, there may be another entrance from the outside to the area below us," Candy said, "but it makes sense to have an entry within The Palace. Having two entrances would allow an easy exit for the Prime Ruler during an attack. Not to mention the practicality in feeding the prisoners. The Grand Hall is too crowded most of the time. It has to be down here. We just need to sweep the areas we already checked. Somehow we missed it."

The idea of searching seventy percent of the large chamber depressed Cassie, but she could not offer a better alternative. They would just have to retrace their steps and look for things they did not notice the first time around. Thank goodness they did not have to cover the whole massive room.

Cassie took a few steps and stopped in her tracks. If she were going to hide something in a room, the best place to store it would be the most unlikely place anyone would look.

Taking in her surroundings with a new perspective, Cassie smiled for the first time in over a day. "Where is the last place anyone would look? In fact, where haven't *we* looked?" she asked.

Candy regarded her quizzically. Her friend did not like riddles. Frazour, on the other hand, looked like he had found the pot of gold at the end of a rainbow.

"You are a worthy soul mate for Darden," Frazour claimed. "We check the cells."

With the acceptance of her idea as worthy, Cassie got a second wind and a thread of hope they would find Darden. Candy followed Cassie to where they originally started their search. Rather than passing the first cell, they entered it. They checked the exterior wall and the cell's floor. The hope that had just blossomed started to wilt. She saw nothing out of the ordinary.

"I have something strange here," one of the men from the penal colony called out. Cassie believed his name was Stellar.

Cassie immediately headed in his direction, daring to hope they had finally found what they sought. Stellar stood in the middle of the cell located in the center of the cavernous room. He had a smug look of triumph on his face. If Stellar found what she hoped, Cassie was going to grant the man anything he desired. She'd find a way to get him whatever he wanted.

"See all the footprints and then clean rock?" Stellar said. "Somewhere close by is something that will open a passage downward which will start right there." Her savior pointed to the area he indicated that looked like foot traffic.

Cassie could clearly see why he felt he found the entrance. Now they just had to find the trigger that would open the hidden passageway leading down to the next chamber. Her eyes surveyed the area, looking for anything odd or out of place.

"We better hurry," Candy warned. "I think we are going to have company fairly soon."

"Chard and Tavlor, guard the entry to this level," Frazour ordered. "If our friends above are as successful as I hope, we could have some of the Palace Guard wanting to secure the prisoners. Shoot to kill. Protect your old home like you did the penal colony against the Portal Guardians."

The adrenaline in her body was pumping at a frantic rate. Cassie could feel the clock ticking down and was worried their rescue attempt may fail. She was about to give up, when a small depression in the stone not far from the footprints caught her eye.

Cassie ran to the spot and got on her hands and knees to examine the oddity. Frazour was right beside her before she had a chance to advise the others of her discovery. She blew into the depression to get a better view of what they were dealing with. A cloud of dust came back at her in response and Cassie quickly turned her face to avoid breathing in the stuff.

"Smart girl," Cassie heard Frazour comment above her. "The depression appears to be the size of one of the bars. Check for a loose one."

She sprung to her feet to help the small group find the piece of metal that would fit into the small hole. For an instant, she thought of all the movies and television shows she watched where prisoners held on to the bars in their cell and tried to shake them loose in frustration. Cassie had a different type of vexation, but was equally motivated.

"I have it," Stellar yelled in triumph.

It only seemed right Stellar would be the one to find the piece of metal that would help them find Darden. The melody continued to play in her head and she needed to believe that Darden was somehow manipulating a crystal's power to gain his freedom.

Stellar handed the metal rod to Frazour. The former vampire ran his index finger along the side of the bar. He then knelt beside the depression and ran the same finger around the opening in the floor. A smile once again graced his face.

"There is an odd edge to this seemingly round rod," Frazour explained. "It just so happens this depression has a similar irregular shape. We just need to see what happens when the two meet."

Frazour placed the rod in the hole, but nothing happened. Cassie let out a loud sigh of disappointment.

"You can't think it would be that easy, Cassie?" Candy said. "Even in movies, you have to move the object to the right or the left."

As if taking a cue from Candy, Frazour tried shifting the bar to the right. When nothing happened, he then tried the other direction. With a loud creak, the stone floor began to move.

"What did I say?" Candy clapped her hands. "Just like in the movies."

A commotion began at the jail's entrance. Chard and Tavlor shot their crystal weapons at whoever was trying to make their way down the stairs. Three additional penal colony dissidents joined Chard and Tavlor while Cassie, Frazour, Candy, and Stellar carefully made their way down the dark passage. Frazour pulled out his sword and the rest of her group readied their own weapons.

The walkway was dark, but Cassie could see light through a small square opening below. There was another door they had to get through to get to the next chamber. Cassie hoped it was unlocked; otherwise, they were screwed. On a positive note, the sound in her head was getting louder. She was getting closer to Darden. She knew it.

Cassie held her breath as Frazour reached for the door's handle. She sighed in relief when she heard metal scrape against rock. They had found the lower chamber and hoped to find Darden and any other crystal telepaths imprisoned there. Every additional soul would be helpful in their fight. She just hoped Darden and the others were in decent shape.

Chapter 18

If she had thought the stench upstairs was bad, there were no words to adequately describe the foulness within the lower chamber. She lifted her jersey and placed it over her nose. Cassie concentrated on breathing through her mouth and not gagging when she accidentally took in the deplorable stink. Her vocabulary was not broad enough to come up with a better term. How could anyone exist down here?

Based on what she had sensed so far, Cassie was terrified about what condition Darden was in. She doubted they would find anyone else alive down here. Jeryl Jarlyn had a lot to answer for.

Unlike the first floor of the prison, this level had cells built into the cave. They would have to meticulously check every cell. There was a single torch lit, but several unused ones lined the walls. Each of them grabbed a torch and used the one already burning to light them.

They traveled together, staying close to take advantage of the light. There was also the possibility their friends above them would not be able to hold off the force attempting to come down to this level. Based on what Cassie saw down here, she could not imagine why they would bother.

The first door they approached opened easily. There was no reason for it to be locked. A body, so badly decayed it was no more than a skeleton, was chained to the wall. That man had once been one of the crystal telepaths who tried to unseat Jeryl Jarlyn. No one had bothered to bury the poor creature after his death. The sight made Cassie's blood boil.

She was certain they would find the same scene with each cell they opened. They were wasting valuable time. Cassie would find her soul mate using the frequency she heard in her head. The melody would lead her right to him.

"Follow me," Cassie said. "After we are victorious, we'll come back and give these poor souls a well-deserved funeral. I know how to find Darden now. You just have to trust me."

Cassie returned to the hall and let the increasing sound of the frequency lead the way. She continued the process as she made her way down corridor after corridor. They had to be beyond the confines of The Palace. Whoever suggested there was another entrance was right. Voices could now be heard within the cells they passed.

"We'll deal with them after we free Darden and win the battle," Candy said behind her. "There is no telling what their crimes were. We now know where everyone who has committed an offense has been sent since they stopped exiling people to the penal world. It's only been a short time, but there are more people than I expected down here."

It was one thing seeing the dead down in this hellhole, but now they knew living souls were here as well. The penal world was paradise compared to the conditions here. But Candy was right, they could not haphazardly release the possible criminals confined in these cells. One of the first things they would do when the battle was over would be to discover why these people were imprisoned down here.

"I'd like to talk to as many of them as I can," Stellar suggested. "Some may be in good enough shape to fight. I would like to free any members of the dissident group I was with."

"Fine," Candy said, "but watch your back."

Cassie came upon a door that was ajar. A light made its way through the exposed crack. She was about to shove the door back and enter, when Frazour placed his arm around her waist and pulled her back. It was clear he wanted to take the lead. Cassie did not want to waste any time arguing the point.

The sound the door made against the stone floor grated on her exposed nerves. Frazour blocked her view, so she was not sure what he saw when he stopped in his tracks. She pushed past him and froze when she saw what had cemented Frazour in place.

Darden was chained to the wall. He was bleeding from various spots and his face was barely recognizable. Barash lay on the ground, his skull split in several spots. It was the same sight her father had walked into when she had killed the crystal telepath over eight years ago. Their coming together had given Darden her mind control capabilities.

Cassie ran to free Darden. He was barely conscious, but somehow sensed she was there, because the frequency in her head fell silent. The power he used to kill Barash was also the beacon that reunited them. Their connection acknowledged she was near and his mind rested.

"Help me!" Cassie shouted.

"I do not see a key," Frazour said, "but the chains are old. It is possible a good yank and at least we will release him from the wall."

The powerful warrior grabbed the chains embedded in the wall and pulled. She could see the strain of his muscles as he successfully detached one of the chains binding Darden. Cassie and Candy positioned themselves to catch Darden when Frazour released his other wrist. She heard a soft moan from him as he collapsed on her left shoulder.

"We are here, Darden," Cassie said through their link. *"Everything is going to be all right. You just rest and gather your strength. We'll get a med-tech to look at your injuries."*

Even though terribly bruised, Darden was a sight for sore eyes. She placed two fingers on his neck to take his pulse. It was weak, but steady.

"Lay him on the ground," Frazour ordered, pulling the last of the restraints from the wall. "I am still partially a vampire, although the sun will no longer kill me. My blood may still have enough healing power to facilitate his body repairing itself quickly."

Cassie nodded her consent. Frazour bit into his wrist and allowed several drops of his precious blood to enter Darden's mouth. She was concerned he had not responded to her through their private channel. Then it dawned on her they had given him ground crystals that would prohibit telepathic communication. Fortunately, it did not inhibit his ability to attack using his telepathic powers.

"Darden, I am here," Cassie said aloud this time. "Frazour, from the Nightshade universe, has given you some of his blood to help you heal." She decided against telling him about the offensive to take over the Troyk government that raged above them. He needed to focus on allowing Frazour's blood to help him heal.

Cassie had silenced the warrior channel link in order to concentrate solely on her soul mate's rescue. She did not want anything distracting her from her primary mission. Once she knew Darden was safe she would join the others in usurping Jeryl Jarlyn.

Not being familiar with vampire blood, Cassie didn't know how quickly Darden might heal. She was unsure how much longer they could remain here without the enemy attacking. Candy was pacing like a wild animal, which was not a good sign.

Darden had been floating after being trapped in his abused human body. He needed to fight to return to his world - Cassie's world - regardless of the pain. He was in a kind of limbo, free from his injured mortal shell. It was similar to how he felt when navigating inter-dimensional portals. It was a feeling that used to frighten him when he was younger. He was pure energy.

Although he fought to leave this tranquil place, something was holding him back. He knew he had killed Barash. For the time being he was safe. Perhaps his body was healing itself, leaving him free to wander this plain. No one knew he was here. Someone would eventually come to see why Barash had not returned. Well, at least Cassie no longer had to worry about that bastard anymore.

Suddenly, he thought he heard Cassie's voice. That was impossible because Cassie was safe in the Troyk penal colony world. Besides, they had laced his water with crushed crystals preventing him from accessing all telepathic pathways.

He tasted something strange, which should not be possible if he was still separated from his body. The taste was metallic and salty, like blood. For some reason, the name Frazour swam in his head. Was that not the name of one of Drake's blood brothers? At one point,

Koel had joked about using the vampires from the Nightshade universe when they made their move against Jeryl Jarlyn.

That single thought brought him back into his broken body. He struggled to open his eyes. Remembering one of his eyes was swollen shut, he concentrated on opening the other one. Unfortunately, he was so disoriented, he could not remember which eye was damaged. He was in terrible shape.

He licked his chapped lips. The taste of blood was still present. Somewhere along the way he must have bitten his lip and caused himself to bleed. After all, he was a bloody mess, what was a little more?

"Darden, I am here," a precious voice said. He would recognize Cassie's voice anywhere. "Frazour, from the Nightshade universe, has given you some of his blood to help you heal."

Darden opened his good eye and caught the sight of Candy Phillips pacing. Though concern was written all over her face, she looked down at him and smiled.

"Welcome back," Candy said.

"What?" Cassie cried. "He's awake?"

His body moved as Cassie shifted and he suppressed a moan, not wanting to alarm her. They must have gotten him down from the wall and were waiting for him to regain consciousness. He struggled to rise, not wanting to appear weak before his soul mate. It did not matter he had been beaten, Darden wanted to appear strong for Cassie's benefit.

"We've run out of time," Candy said. "The best thing to do is find the other exit. We do not want to be trapped in here when the Palace Guard swarms us. Frazour can carry Darden."

Cassie and Frazour helped Darden to his feet. He thought the vampire he once fought beside looked different, but his mind was not clear enough to determine why. Their rescue would fail if they did not leave the cell immediately. He did his best to aid Cassie and Frazour move him toward the exit. Movement made the pain unbearable, but he did not complain.

When Darden saw Barash on the ground, a better escape plan came to him. If he had the ability to destroy Barash's mind, he should be able to open and navigate a portal. He was not sure how he managed to harness the power to kill his adversary, but he imagined opening a portal would require less energy. Starc could aid Shirl in portal travel, so why couldn't Cassie assist him?

"I can open a portal," Darden struggled to say. His voice was rough and scratchy, his throat dry from lack of water.

"You don't have a charged crystal," Candy responded.

"Look at Barash," Darden suggested. "I did not have a crystal and I managed that." He took a breath. Just communicating that amount was difficult. "Cassie can help me. The crystals above us are full of power."

Darden gazed down and saw Cassie lift her face. She was so beautiful, and she was his. He could not count the number of times during his captivity he was afraid he would never see that face again. For eight years, he watched her grow until she was the woman who stood before him now. His soul mate.

"Shirl and Starc can do it," Candy said. "I imagine the same can be true about the two of you. Darden managed to use your abilities, so it's possible you have the ability to be a crystal telepath as well."

Although she looked doubtful, Cassie said, "I'll give it a try. What do I do?"

He imagined Cassie would be concerned about what would happen if he passed out while they were in the wormhole. As soon as they entered the portal, he would give her the frequency that needed to be sustained to get them to the penal world.

"Can you enter my mind, but not through telepathic communication?" Darden asked. "Use the same ability you use when you enter JoAnna's mind. Until those crystals are washed from my system, we can only speak out loud to each other if you are unable to connect with me."

Cassie turned her beautiful blue eyes on him and stared into his. He was mated to one of the most powerful women in existence. She should be able to make up for any weakness on his part.

"*How are you feeling?*" he heard Cassie ask within his mind. It was an incredible feeling having her there.

"*We are connected,*" Darden said with relief. "*Focus on me and transfer some of your power, while I attempt to open a portal. Opening a natural portal is second nature to a crystal telepath, while creating one will require more energy and concentration. Continue to push what you can toward me and I will do all the work.*"

Darden concentrated, but was unable to open a gateway. He knew he had the capacity and ability to do so with Cassie by his side. He went to the place he always did in his mind when he navigated portals. Focus was all that was required to be successful.

"Hurry," Candy warned.

"You are not helping, Candy," Darden groused. *"Focus on me, Cassie. Share with me what you can and I will do the rest."*

Footsteps echoed down the hall when a portal finally opened. It was on the smaller side, but it would be adequate for the five of them. Unfortunately, if none of the others in their party were close by they would have to be left behind. Darden was grateful he had been able to open that portal. There was no telling how long this one would last. They needed to leave now and hope they would be able to navigate once they were within the wormhole.

They entered the event horizon, all of them working to physically support Darden. Once within the center of the portal, Darden mentally reached out to Cassie and found their connection strong, even within the wormhole. The melody for the penal colony played in his mind. He pushed that tone forward, hoping the penal colony's harmonics would open a portal and allow them entrance into that world. Darden also pushed the frequency to Cassie's mind, assuring it would be sustained if he lost consciousness. If the frequency was off by even one Hertz, who knew where they might end up.

Chapter 19

THE TROYK PENAL COLONY WORLD

Cassie once again stepped into the penal world she had recently called home. The settlement was deserted. As planned, the children and all remaining citizens had evacuated the camp in case the invasion did not turn out as they hoped.

She should have reconnected to the warrior link before they left the Troyk universe to hear how the mission was going. No one was expecting a swift, bloodless battle. Their primary goal was to secure The Palace and capture Jeryl Jarlyn. Everything else would take time. Shirl also had to ensure Drake and Jace returned to the Nightshade universe before the sun rose or found a secure, safe, and dark place the two vampires could wait out the day.

"How did it go?" Alex asked. She had come from the direction of the lake, so Cassie had not initially seen her.

Cassie looked over at Darden before responding to Alex. Her soul mate appeared better, but in no way ready to return and join the battle determining the future of the Troyk universe. That was something she, Frazour, and Candy would have to do without him. Stellar had stayed behind to free as many people from the prison as he thought wise. She was not sure how he faired. The Palace Guards had descended on them right before she and Darden opened the portal.

"Why aren't you with the others?" Cassie asked.

"What, and wait for information?" Alex replied. "I don't think so. Tarsea, Shirl, JoAnna, and our friends are still fighting."

"They were working to secure The Palace when we left." Candy provided the information Cassie had been unable to. It had not dawned on her to ask Candy how things faired before they left the Troyk universe. "I need to return. Can you open another portal and take me back?"

Cassie stood there, staring at Candy. She hoped Darden would be in better shape before plotting their return. He was able to open a portal with the power of the crystals within The Palace. Although there was a naturally occurring portal within the settlement, Darden still needed to be able to set the coordinates. Even with Frazour's blood running through his veins repairing his body, Darden was barely able to stand.

"We may have to stay here," Cassie finally admitted. Before Candy could object, Cassie began explaining the delay. "If my dad and our friends fail, we need more than your soul mate and a hand full of former dissidents to protect the children." She hoped throwing Tolfer in there would help pacify Candy. Fortunately, getting Frazour back to the Nightshade universe immediately was not of paramount concern. The transforming elemental would be able to tolerate the sun until Darden was strong enough to get him home.

Candy remained silent, considering Cassie's explanation. The more Cassie thought about it, the better she liked the idea of staying put. They already successfully executed their part of the plan. Three more fighters were not going to make a difference whether the Troyk universe was won or lost, but they would make a difference if there were reprisals.

"Let's get Darden settled and maybe give him a little more of your blood, Frazour," Cassie said.

"Candy and Frazour can do that," Alex said. "I'd like to talk to you, Cassie."

'Oh, boy', Cassie thought. She did not like the look on Alex's face. Cassie didn't know what Alex had to say, but she had a feeling she was not going to like it. Alex turned and walked back toward the lake. Cassie followed her, feeling she had little choice. Candy and Frazour were already on their way to make Darden comfortable.

Alex picked up a flat rock and skipped it across the water. How did a girl who grew up in a desert learn to skip stones? If circumstances were different, she'd have Alex show her how to do it. There was still the contest with Darden to be won.

"When are you going to admit who you truly are?" Alex asked. "How can you stay here when your father, my soul mate, and our friends are all fighting for the future of the Troyk universe?"

"I don't know what you are talking about," Cassie said, although she knew exactly what Alex meant.

"What type of channel opened between us at the orphanage?" Alex inquired. "I know it's not a closed communal channel between close friends. Such things do not exist. When Chartail was able to enter it, I thought it had to do with her being Benko's soul mate. But the more I thought about it, the less sense it made until I factored you into the equation. The warrior channel did not open originally between Benko and Darden, did it? It opened between you and Darden. You just never admitted it. Benko Jarlyn is not the True Ruler, you are!"

Cassie's world shattered. She actually started to believe her own lie, but this girl - one she once wanted to be her sister - knew the truth. Benko was everything a ruler should be. He was brave, idealistic, and a born leader. Cassie was a mess, but how could she deny it?

Measuring her words carefully, Cassie explained. "It's not that simple, Alex. I am not sure what the channel is we share. Chartail's presence in the pathway makes no sense. You don't think I don't wake up every morning wishing the warrior channel first opened between Darden and my father? I don't want to be the True Ruler."

"You are who you are, Cassie," Alex replied. "Didn't you realize the effect you had on people when you were in the Troyk universe? I didn't get to witness it firsthand, but JoAnna and Candy told me about it. You had the ability to calm an agitated crowd. They probably suspected who you really are, but did not have the courage to say anything. How can you stay here when they are fighting for your world?"

"My world?" Cassie countered. "I grew up on Earth, just like you did. Although I knew I had telepathic powers, I fought to hide them. Do you know I killed a man when I was ten? If I am the True Ruler, then something is really screwed up!"

"Did that man attempt to hurt you or your father?" Alex asked.

Cassie had spent years blocking the memory of that day from her mind. At times she almost convinced herself it was all a horrible nightmare. Her untrained power caused the man's brain to swell and his skull cracked like an egg, just like Darden had done to Barash. No one should have that kind of power.

"He came after me," Cassie admitted. "My dad had taught me how to defend myself. I didn't think; I reacted. I focused on following my dad's instructions every time we trained. Until that man attacked me, I had no clue that training would help me kill anyone. You know, when I close my eyes, I often see that man lying there, his skull shattered and brain matter oozing onto the floor."

She never talked about that day, even with her father. Discussing it with Alex brought everything flooding back. Cassie swore she would never use her powers again, but as soon as one of her friends was in danger, she broke her oath. How many horrific things can you do in the name of self-preservation or saving a friend before madness sets in?

"Cassie, I had a similar discussion with Shirl not too long ago," Alex admitted. "A police officer sometimes has to use deadly force to protect the public, just like you must from time to time. Cassie, no one enters a situation intending to kill someone, but tough choices are made when things go wrong. You can let your soul mate, father, or friends die, or you can stop it. All the chatter I heard in the Troyk universe was about how you used your abilities to stop violence. You can do so much good there after everything those people have suffered."

"But I'm not ready to rule," Cassie cried.

"Cassie, you were born to rule," Alex said, "but that does not mean you have to be put in power right away. The people are ready for your father to take Jeryl Jarlyn's place. With time, you will learn what you need to govern the Aster Province and replace Benko one day. No one else needs to know you are the True Ruler."

Darden could not believe what he was hearing. He had left Candy and Frazour behind to find his soul mate. He needed Cassie, not rest. He was still in a tremendous amount of pain, but he had to be with his soul mate. Thoughts of her had gotten him to overcome the fear he, too, would perish in that cell, as did many other crystal telepaths before him. Now, he was learning his soul mate had lied to him all these years.

"When were you going to tell me, Cassie?" Darden demanded.

Cassie swung around and he saw panic reflected in her eyes. How had he not felt her in the warrior channel? They were soul mates; he should have felt her presence in any telepathic channel she was active in.

"How could I admit it to you, when I could not admit it to myself?" Cassie responded. "Do you think I wanted this? I was a refugee from another dimension hiding to save my life and my father's. What would Dad do if he knew the truth? Besides, I didn't know what was happening. The soul mate channel was so much stronger than the warrior pathway. A link opened between the girls and me even before that and I did not know what it was. Frankly, I still don't. I was taught to hide my telepathic gift, unless my life depended on it."

"But why keep it from us once we knew what the warrior channel was?" Darden asked. He just could not understand why Cassie had not confided in him.

"I grew up hearing lovely stories about soul mates and the legendary Warrior Woman," Cassie said. "Dad left the Troyk universe behind. He did not bother to tell me what the True Ruler was. When I realized what the warrior channel was, he was fine being the True Ruler. It was something I never wanted. All I ever desired was you, Darden, not to rule the Troyk universe."

"But why pretend not to have finally entered the channel?" Darden asked.

"You should have had faith in me whether or not I could enter that particular link," Cassie stated. "Besides, it had been years. What excuse could I possibly have if I, all of a sudden, entered a pathway you believed was exclusively yours and my father's until Tarsea finally entered it? The longer I waited, the more difficult it would have been to explain."

Cassie looked so young and innocent. Alex returned to the village to give them much needed privacy. He still felt like crap, but all he wanted to do was make love to the girl he had longed for the last eight years. There was a battle raging in another dimension and they had to leave the safety of this world and aid their friends.

"Your father has a world to conquer," Darden said. "I have been stronger, but I cannot stay here while they risk their lives to liberate my world. The amethyst in your ring is calling to me. It holds enough power to open a portal and allow me to get us home. With you by my side, I have more than enough power to open a temporary portal that will open within The Palace."

"What difference can we possibly make?" Cassie cried.

"You will make all the difference in the world, my love," Darden answered. "Your presence will allow the world to heal faster. I have no idea what telepathic ability you use to bring a crowd together in a peaceful manner, but you do. People are drawn to you. We have yet to determine what will be done with your grandfather. Regardless, the people have to be soothed. We cannot allow infighting among the different factions. Calm will be required to discuss matters and find necessary compromises while we rebuild. Whether or not you choose to rule, that is the gift you bring your people."

"I spent so little time in the Troyk universe," Cassie said. "How can you possibly know that's true?"

"Sweetie, I witnessed it firsthand," Darden answered. "I should not feel anything coming from the communal pathways, but I sensed love brimming from those channels while you were among the people. My telepathic enhancements once we made love must have included having the ability to both feel emotions and communicate through the communal pathways."

"We should head back to camp and get Candy and Frazour," Cassie said. "I have one stipulation before we go."

"Whatever you want, it is yours," Darden replied. He could deny this woman nothing. If he could fill her every wish, he would.

"When this is over and my dad is ruling the Troyk universe, I want to move in with you and start our lives together," Cassie said. "Maybe, one day, I will be willing to be the Prime Ruler, but not for a long time. My dad deserves the title. I may be a woman of legend, but I choose to live my life as I desire. I don't want my birthright to determine what we get out of life, especially if it is something neither of us wants. For eight years, I waited to be with you; and, for the time being, that is all I desire."

His soul mate had the ability to cut herself off from any channel, but he could feel her love and desire through their private link. It had been too many years and he wanted nothing more than to make love to Cassie. Once things stabilized and their relationship was solidified, they would figure out where their future might lead them.

"We have a world to help conquer," Darden said. "Afterwards, we will figure out everything else."

"Oh!" Cassie exclaimed. "I forgot I had these." Cassie reached into a pocket in her tunic and pulled out three small crystals. "I viewed them as ammunition for the gun, not crystals you could use to navigate with."

"Hold on to them," Darden said. "You may need them when we return to the Troyk universe. Your ring is sufficient to generate enough power for me to open a special portal."

Hand-in-hand, the couple walked back to where a portal would take them to meet their destiny. Neither considered anything other than victory. The alternative was too horrible to face. Should Jeryl Jarlyn prevail, he would rip them apart. Darden would become the weapon used to force Cassie's compliance and a political marriage would be arranged. Darden envisioned only one possible outcome — victory. He would fight to his last breath to give Cassie a world where she would be free to love and become whatever she desired.

Chapter 20

THE TROYK UNIVERSE

Darden opened a portal to one of the conference rooms on the third floor of The Palace. He did not want them behind enemy lines when they re-entered the Troyk universe. Cassie immediately entered the warrior channel to discover both how the revolution was unfolding and her father's location. She glanced at Darden and did not like what she saw. Her soul mate was pale and unsteady. How was she going to find a diplomatic way to have him stay behind while she made her way to her father's side?

"We are directly below Jeryl Jarlyn's receiving room," Cassie said. "Can you feel the crystals' power? There may be injured that will have to be evacuated. If Darden stays here, we can bring the injured to him and you can transport them through a portal. My amethyst, coupled with the power from the crystals above us, will allow you to open a portal to the penal world."

Darden's gray lips parted in the beginning of a smile. Frazour's blood was not healing him as quickly as she hoped. "Nice try, Cassie," Darden said. "I am not leaving your side."

"Actually," Candy interceded, "Cassie is right. You look horrible and will endanger her life once we leave this room. Don't bother throwing that 'soul mates need to be together' crap at me. Tolfer is where he can do the most good and so am I. We all have sacrifices to make to liberate this world. Once Jeryl has been unseated then we can be together. I will protect Cassie, as will Frazour."

Frazour extended her soul mate his hand in friendship, a sign of respect for a warrior willing to stay behind and aid the wounded by evacuating them to a safe location. The Nightshade elemental realized Darden knew he was outnumbered and felt too crappy to fight them.

"Promise me you will enter the portal and return to the penal world if it looks like your safety is compromised," Cassie requested. "I need to focus on the people fighting and don't have the luxury to worry about you. You kept my dad and me safe for eight years by keeping our whereabouts a secret from my grandfather. My dad and I slept sounder knowing you would bring Shirl, Candy, JoAnna, and Alex to the Troyk universe if anything happened to us. We all have our roles to play, Darden. No one has done it better than you, my love."

Cassie kissed Darden, perhaps for the last time. There were no guarantees once they left the conference room. It would have been so easy to ask Darden to flee with her and find a world where the two of them could live in peace. But in the long run, Cassie knew she could not turn her back on the Troyk universe and its people. Whether she liked it or not, she was the True Ruler. This was her world and she was more than willing to die liberating it. Not that she would admit that to Darden.

From the somber look on his face, Cassie knew she let that last thought seep through their channel. Destiny was a bitch, but she had been fighting it too long. She had done a lot of growing up in a short period of time. Maybe it was no longer being isolated on Earth or her inability to deal with circumstances in the penal world. Her life had been irrevocably changed when she entered the Troyk universe.

Darden looked at her long and hard. Everything she was thinking made it to her soul mate. His expression pensive, he ran his index finger across her cheek, saying goodbye to the little girl he once knew and welcoming the woman she had become. His mate was meant to rule one day.

"Be safe," Darden said, choking on the words.

She could only imagine the turmoil running through his mind. For once, Darden managed to block his feelings from entering the soul mate channel. It was his way of respecting her decision. Regardless of her words, she knew Darden did not want her to know how terrified he was.

"The Grand Hall has been secured," Candy announced. "We are working to control all the entrances. Your grandfather maintains control of the fourth floor. There is still fighting on the second floor between those Primes that are mind control telepaths and our group. We managed to enter this world in a buffered position."

"Dad, where are you?" Cassie communicated through the warrior channel. She would have preferred a private conversation with him, but Jeryl Jarlyn also had access to their familial link.

"Outside The Prime Ruler's living quarters," her father replied. *"He continues to use the power of the crystals to manipulate the weaker minds of his followers. His guards have him well secured and average citizens are finding their way in to try and stop us. Watch your back."*

There were so many entrances into The Palace, securing the Grand Hall only cut off access to part of the building. Although they had control of more than three-quarters of the first floor, her father was right, they needed to be careful.

"Darden will be on the third floor evacuating anyone who can't make it past the second floor," Cassie shared with her dad her soul mate's role in the current battle. *"Where are the med-techs set up?"*

"Cassie, you will do more good rallying the people in the Grand Hall," Benko Jarlyn told her. *"Reach out to the people outside and reassure them we are working on as peaceful a transition as we can. Tell them the days of mind control are behind them."*

Before she had a chance to say a final goodbye to Darden, a badly injured man was brought into the room. Crystal weapons fired a short laser beam and he was missing part of his arm. Due to the heat of the blast, the wound should have been cauterized on contact. He must have fallen on the wound, opening the scab, causing his arm to bleed.

"We have a med-tech located in the Grand Hall, but I cannot get to him," the Palace Guard who was helping to support the man said. He had abandoned her grandfather and now was loyal to her father. "Can you open a portal to anywhere on the first floor?"

Cassie handed Darden her ring and gave him a quick kiss before he worked to open a portal. Frazour drew his weapon, ready to assist in finding a way to the embattled second floor. It would be interesting to see how a water elemental dealt with laser fire. Between his strength and Candy's foresight, Cassie knew she was in good hands.

Cassie grew up in Scottsdale, Arizona and had never been exposed to a war zone. She wondered what she would encounter as they made their way down the hall. People were shouting ahead, as others from the second floor were making their way to their level. She did not know if they were going to battle armed hostile Prime Representatives and their staff eager to put an end to their little uprising or some of their freedom fighters.

Candy's premonitions were received right before the event. If Cassie was too far away from Candy, there may not be time for her friend to take the appropriate action. Cassie's nerves were getting the best of her and she began to breathe rapidly.

She tried to get some insight within the warrior link, but there were too many conversations to figure out who was where. It was easy to communicate with her father in that link because of their relationship. Singling out a single person advancing on them and identifying them as friend or foe was beyond her ability. If she had been active in the link earlier, she may have already mastered the feat.

A laser blast exploded two feet above her head. It was either a warning shot or someone had really bad aim. Either way she was happy with the results.

"Who are you?" Cassie yelled.

The communal pathways were chaos. Most of Troyk's citizens were probably suffering from headaches and nosebleeds. Cassie doubted they were used to this kind of activity. If anyone had the capability of turning down the volume or exiting the pathways they would be wise to do it. Oral communication seemed the best way forward over short distances.

"We are loyal to The Prime Ruler and the Prime Council," a male voice shouted back.

"Well, then you better head back to the second floor," Candy yelled. "I support the True Ruler. What do you think about that? By the way, I have someone from the Nightshade universe next to me, who is rather thirsty."

Candy turned, smiled, and winked at Cassie. She was not sure if Alex and Candy had discussed their suspicions or if Candy had figured out who she really was on her own. Either way, it was the first time any one of them had mentioned it outside their small circle. Cassie was not sure which statement would better forestall the person they were conversing with. The Nightshade universe was now well known as a parallel dimension of vampires. It was illegal to enter that dimension after the scandal involving Chartail was revealed. Who would dare say anything when a revolution was under way?

"The True Ruler is a legend," the man shouted back. Cassie could hear the doubt in his voice.

"My name is Candy Phillips and people call me the Warrior Woman. The Prime Ruler knows soul mates exist, but has not bothered to share that little fact. I should know, I am one. You wouldn't happen to have a new pathway that recently opened that feels a bit strange?"

Her friend was fishing, but Cassie was all for ending this particular skirmish peacefully. She knew this man might very well support Jeryl Jarlyn, making a fight inevitable. Daring a quick glance at Frazour, Cassie thought he seemed ready for hand-to-hand combat. Although there were still sounds of battles taking place throughout The Palace, things were relatively quiet in the nearby halls.

Three crystal weapons came sliding across the floor in their direction. Cassie took it as the man's surrender and whomever he had with him. Two men and a woman came forward slowly, with their arms lifted in the air.

"We surrender," the older of the two men said. "I am Prime Ione and these two are members of my staff."

Cassie did not recognize the Prime, but she had not met every member. Her grandfather had spent his efforts introducing her to young, eligible men from wealthy, influential families. She did not miss the three of them looking at her in wonder. This was not how Cassie wanted to be viewed by any citizen of Aster Province.

"I'm Cassie Jarlyn," she said and extended her hand. The name now rolled off her tongue. She had finally accepted who she was. "This is Candy Phillips and Frazour from the Nightshade universe.

Thank you for laying down your arms." When she noticed fear replace their awed expressions she added, "Frazour no longer drinks blood. He is my father's ally. He helped rescue Candy from the Troyk penal colony world and is my friend."

"I heard what happened the other day at the gathering place restaurant between you and the armed man," Prime Ione informed her. "I thought you were a very lucky girl, but now I understand what really occurred. You and your father have my support."

It was unlikely they would continue to be so lucky. Cassie still needed to get to the Grand Hall.

"I'm an idiot," Cassie admitted. "Do any of you have any crystals on you?"

Prime Ione turned over a key chain with a beautiful blue topaz and his female assistant gave her a clear quartz pendant. She gathered her bounty and headed back to Darden. He could get them to the Grand Hall in seconds. Cassie had concerned herself with keeping him out of harm's way and had not realized her soul mate was the easiest solution to her problem.

"Thanks," Cassie said. "Ever traveled through a portal before?"

She led them into the conference room where she left Darden. He was sitting in a chair, resting, with his head in his arms. He looked up when they entered and relief washed over his face.

"How about opening another portal to the Grand Hall and joining us?" Cassie asked. "These should help in opening the gateway."

Cassie passed him the crystals she just collected and took his hand. She channeled her power through Darden and a large portal opened. Darden may look awful, but they were both becoming more powerful, Cassie observed, as the portal was larger than usual. Together, they entered the gateway and Cassie could hear Darden's mind manipulate the portal's frequencies. Candy, Frazour, Prime Ione, and his assistants accompanied them.

When they stepped out of the portal into the Grand Hall, Cassie was surprised to see the room teeming with people celebrating a victory that had yet to be won. Her first priority, regardless of her father's orders, was to get Darden to a med-tech. His complexion continued to worsen every time she glanced his way.

Her hand was tugged downward. When Cassie realized why, she started to panic. Darden had collapsed.

Chapter 21

Cassie's world spun out of control. She stood back in horror as Candy called for a med-tech. Frazour bit into his wrist and fed Darden more blood. Her soul mate's face was white as a ghost. Beads of sweat dotted his forehead, and Cassie wasn't sure if that was a good or bad sign. Prime Ione took her into his arms and tried to comfort her. Cassie was not aware she was crying hysterically.

People swarmed around her, wanting to help. All Cassie wanted was space. She could barely breathe. Conversations took place around her, but she couldn't make sense of them. Frantic with worry, Cassie gasped for air.

A hand slapped her face — not hard, but it got her attention. When she focused on the person before her, Cassie recognized her father. She collapsed into his waiting arms. Even though the coup to overthrow the Troyk Prime Council and its Prime Ruler was in full swing, her dad still managed to find her when she needed him.

"Daddy," Cassie cried. "Darden…" She couldn't utter anything else. How could she put into words that her soul mate was perhaps dying. Frazour's blood did not seem to help him at all.

The med-tech was kneeling over Darden with his diagnostic equipment beeping. She tried to read his face to determine if the readings were good or bad. Alex once told her about the time Tarsea had been stabbed and the med-tech had him healthy within minutes. Cassie could only pray the beatings Barash inflicted upon Darden had not damaged any of his organs.

The examination seemed to take an eternity. Darden was still unconscious and his coloring had not improved. Cassie never considered herself a violent person, but she wanted to kill her grandfather. He was responsible for the beatings Darden received, she was sure of it. She could hear her father giving various orders, but he never left her side.

Cassie's eyes never left the med-tech. She willed that he would finish and tell her Darden was going to be all right. It startled her when he got to his feet and approached her.

"There is nothing more I can do," the med-tech said. "He has a couple of broken ribs. Fortunately, they did not puncture his lungs. My concern is with his kidneys. Most of the damage he suffered was to his abdomen. I am afraid whoever inflicted the punishment used more than his fists at some point in time. His abdomen has suffered blunt trauma which in turn damaged his kidneys."

Everything she knew about kidneys rushed into her mind. She knew they filtered blood and produced urine. Although there were two kidneys, people only needed one. It is not uncommon for one person to donate a kidney to another, assuming they met some kind of matching criteria. That was the extent of her knowledge.

"What does that mean?" Cassie asked.

"From the tests I have performed, his kidneys will no longer function properly," the med-tech continued. "I am sorry."

"Wait," Cassie shouted as he walked away. "What about a transplant?"

"Not possible in our dimension. I'm sorry," he said again. "All we can do is make him comfortable."

Cassie stared in disbelief as he walked away. Things could not end this way. She ran over to her soul mate and took his hand. People were going to die today, but she did not think Darden would be one of them. She would make sure her grandfather suffered when her father was the new Prime Ruler. After Darden's death, Cassie would return to Earth, and try to forget the Troyk universe ever existed. String theory was exactly that, a theory. Multiple dimensions did not exist. Her grief would make her believe the lie.

She could feel the link between them weakening. Cassie pushed energy to her soul mate, but it would not heal the damage to his kidneys. With all the power she possessed, she could not save him.

"Now is not the time, Drake," Cassie heard Shirl growl. Her friend truly hated the vampire.

Cassie had not noticed Shirl and Starc's arrival. Of course, Darden's twin brother would want to spend Darden's last minutes with him. She lifted her eyes from Darden's pale face to see Starc take his brother's other hand. They shared a brief glance and Cassie directed her attention back to her dying soul mate.

She watched a shadow pass over Darden's chest as Drake came to kneel beside her. Cassie was not in the mood for the smooth talking Lothario. Couldn't everyone just leave her and Starc in peace as they said goodbye to Darden?

"What would I get, precious, if I save your love's life?" Drake whispered in her ear.

Anger brewed within Cassie. It was bad enough this monster was blackmailing her friends to get access to Alex and her baby. The creature had the unmitigated gall to interrupt her final moments with her soul mate. She had waited eight long years for them to be together, only to have it come to a tragic end; and all because of her grandfather's grandiose ambitions.

"Go taunt someone else, Drake," Cassie could barely keep the anger from her voice. "Frazour already tried to save Darden by feeding him his blood, more than once."

Drake laughed and Cassie looked up at him, horrified. If she had a stake handy, she would have shoved it into the bastard's heart — assuming he even had one. Tears she had been holding back, so she could appear strong, finally started to run down her cheeks.

"That animal is trying to play hero? Darling," Drake drawled, "calling Frazour my blood brother is now a misnomer. He no longer has pure vampire blood since his elemental conversion started. Besides, Frazour is only a little over two thousand years old. I am older than dirt. No blood, including the Creator's, is as powerful as mine."

New hope blossomed in Cassie's heart. "What do you want?"

"Only that the True Ruler kindly intercede so I can visit Alex, and Star when she is finally born," Drake replied.

"I would never force my friend to do anything," Cassie said, "regardless of whatever title or power I may possess."

The vampire looked between Cassie and the dying man on the floor. Cassie would give her very life to save Darden, but there was no way she would force Alex or her daughter into a relationship with the creature beside her. Granted, he and Alex had developed an unusual friendship, but there was no guarantee that would continue.

"Then how about one soul mate for another…" Drake continued, "consider how you feel right now, when Darden is so near death. I would go through the same pain if I lost Star. When she reached out to me telepathically, my life changed forever. All I demand of anyone now is either the right to see her or a promise to give their life for hers."

"You have yourself a deal," Cassie said. She did not have to consider her answer once Drake mentioned the soul mate bond. From what she had witnessed, every decision Drake made was done with Alex's daughter, Star, in mind.

Drake bit into his wrist and placed it against Darden's lips. She willed Darden to drink the crimson elixir that would save his life. He kept feeding Darden until a little rose color finally graced Darden's cheeks. Drake withdrew his wrist and Cassie saw it heal before her eyes. When her glance returned to Darden's face, he was no longer pale.

Their friends had used their bodies as shields to keep the Troyk citizens from watching what occurred between Drake and Darden. Her soul mate's recovery would be considered a miracle or that the med-tech's instruments had somehow malfunctioned. No more would a mind control telepath interfere with anyone's recollection of what occurred today.

When Darden's eyelids began to flutter, Cassie cried out in delight. She wanted to throw herself on Darden, but took into account his healing body. The last thing Cassie wanted to do was re-injure his abdomen or kidneys before the vampire's blood had finished its magic. She was not sure if the blood would heal bones, too, and Darden still had broken ribs near his lungs to consider.

Finally, she got to bask on the sight of his beautiful blue eyes. They were sharp and clear. He gave her a questioning look, which she answered with a smile.

"What happened?" a bewildered Darden asked.

"A miracle," she whispered, giving him a chaste, kiss on the lips. Darden did not have to know at this moment he had vampire blood circulating through his system. "Can you get up?"

"Let me try," Darden answered. He must have remembered how much pain he was in when he collapsed. She noted his surprise when he rose without grimacing in pain. "The med-tech did a wonderful job."

"He certainly did," Cassie answered with a covert wink at Drake.

Her soul mate was whole and standing next to her. Thanks to Drake's blood, he was healthy once again. She owed the vampire a tremendous debt.

A commotion on the top floor of The Palace grabbed her attention. It appeared her father and his men were mounting another attack against the small army protecting her grandfather. Cassie determined it was time to put an end to this revolution and confront the man who was responsible for her soul mate almost dying. Jeryl Jarlyn was going to answer for everything he had done to her people.

Chapter 22

Darden saw the determined look on Cassie's face and knew he would be unable to stop his soul mate from seeking vengeance. She had risked her life to save him, so he was in no position to suggest others finish the battle. Besides, he knew how powerful she was. He had a small taste of that power when he stopped Barash.

He felt unbelievably strong and knew it was not the med-tech that was responsible. There was still the telltale taste of blood in his mouth. Frazour's blood did little to heal his body, so he knew it was Drake who saved his life. The sun would be rising in two hours, so they needed a final surge to bring down Jeryl Jarlyn once and for all.

"We storm the fourth floor living area," Darden said. "If we throw everything we have left at that one location, we will topple the Prime Ruler."

"Not a bad idea, cousin," Koel shared through the warrior link. *"I am still on the second floor. We secured the Prime Council chamber and will not attempt any other aggressive moves. Once Jeryl Jarlyn is in our control we can begin negotiations. I will have the rest of my men deliver JoAnna to you and aid in the effort. Together, Cassie and JoAnna's abilities should be able to counteract Jeryl's superior mind control."*

"He has barricaded himself in a room filled with crystals," Shirl said "We need to destroy as many of them as we can. The larger the stone, the more power it generates. A shattered stone will temporarily be worthless. Jeryl used me and inadvertently gave me the power to destroy him. If I have to, I will open a portal and use its power to end this war once and for all."

The crystal telepath spoke with confidence, seemingly unafraid. Darden's brother, Starc, often worried how Shirl handled her unspeakable power. It appeared she finally made peace with her new powers and would not hesitate to call upon all her gifts.

"We take the fourth floor then," Tarsea concluded. "The women will be placed in the middle of the force. Drake, you will make sure nothing happens to Benko. Frazour, Candy, and Jace will protect Cassie. All other assignments will continue as before. Do what you have to in order to stop any resistance we come across. Our fight will soon be over."

They moved as a unit up the stairs. Their first problem would be getting beyond the second floor. With Koel succeeding in containing the opposition already within the Prime Chamber, they should only encounter minimal resistance.

As they walked up the stairs, his eyes scanned the floors above them. His friends and family, as well as the Nightshade contingent, rallied for this last strike. Supporters turned their backs to them, protecting their ascent. Candy announced through the communal pathway that anyone facing them would be considered a threat and eliminated. Darden heard Cassie share the hope that Benko's return would bring an end to mind control against the people of Aster Province. Once again, he could sense feelings of joy and contentment from the communal pathways.

Four laser blasts sounded and Afton sent a fireball in the direction of a man pointing a crystal weapon in their direction. The man burst into flames before he could pull the trigger again. Darden had heard tales of the incredible powers Afton acquired while transforming into a fire elemental, but took them with a grain of salt. Now he knew those stories were frighteningly true.

Three of the men surrounding their party engaged the other aggressors, overpowering them with ease. All four of the men who fired upon them were dead before they had the chance to do it again. Fortunately, none of their group was hurt. The unfortunate men were amateurs and had no clue what they were doing. They would hopefully be her grandfather's last victims. Cassie breathed a sigh of relief.

Their forces increased as they joined the freedom fighters embroiled in the conflict on the second floor. Flanked by Frazour and Jace, Cassie walked a short distance ahead of Darden. Candy was beside him, directly behind Cassie. Strategically, she was in the best position to push Cassie down if a direct threat was imminent.

His soul mate was so focused on capturing her grandfather he could not sense any fear coming from her. Cassie saw Jeryl Jarlyn's treatment of him as the final straw. Whatever tender feelings she once held for her grandfather were gone. If Jeryl Jarlyn thought Cassie would show him any mercy, he was sadly mistaken. Cassie gave her grandfather the benefit of the doubt when she first entered this universe and made her own decision about Jeryl Jarlyn's merits.

Cassie continued to use her power to bring people together and sway some of the opposition to their side. Darden heard her actively communicate in all the communal pathways, no longer afraid of who she was. By the time they reached the fourth floor, only the true zealots attempted to protect the Prime Ruler.

"Give it up, my friends," Karlon Flonder yelled from the front of their force. They had now made it to the landing outside the private residence. The intelligence officer was well acquainted with many of the Palace Guard. "Why sacrifice your lives for the Prime Ruler when the True Ruler is present? Can you not feel her in the communal pathways?"

Benko and Cassie continued to talk to the Troyk people through the communal links. Jeryl Jarlyn was silent. Cassie was using her power to support her father. The volume of voices within the warrior link became unbearable due to the sheer number of people with access to the channel, and communication through that pathway was now impossible. He only heard Koel's earlier conversation clearly because of their blood relationship.

"You have until the count of ten to surrender and move forward," Tarsea yelled. "Lay down your weapons and get out of our way. If you still insist on remaining loyal and martyring yourself for Jeryl Jarlyn, I cannot stop you. I hope you all heard about the man who burst into flames. Give up now or that will be your fate. I will count to ten. When I am done, anyone who has not surrendered will be killed by a fire bomb shot down the hallway."

Tarsea started counting slowly, his voice echoing menacingly in the outer hall. Darden only saw two men walk forward and lay their weapons down. He sincerely hoped Afton could control the blast and was not going to burn The Palace to the ground. The beautiful structure was erected long before the mind control government took power and would hopefully stand long after its downfall.

When Tarsea got to ten, Afton produced her second fireball. It traveled down the hall, incinerating everything in its path and vanishing when it reached the end of the far wall. The fire only burned what was within that space and nothing else was even singed. They would never know whether the casualties were human or other objects — only ash lay where everything else once stood,

"That was so cool," Candy commented.

The rest of the group stood in silent awe, digesting what they just witnessed. Most of them had never seen any power manifest itself outside the body. Clearly, there were greater powers in the universe than their telepathic abilities.

"Now what?" Cassie whispered.

There was only one thing left to do. Cassie took a deep breath, regally raised her head, and squared her shoulders. Darden's connection to her was so strong he could feel Cassie's fear. It was time to face Jeryl Jarlyn and he was not sure if Cassie was truly ready.

Each step Cassie took up the marble stairwell brought her closer to her destiny. Now, staring at the demolished hall leading to her grandfather's living quarters, she couldn't seem to move. Fortunately, no one else had started down the hall.

It was not concern over how many men would be protecting her grandfather or how many of Benko's followers would be lost during the final assault that kept her glued in place. Once her father took over the government, her life would change. It would be almost impossible to hide who she truly was. She had lied to everyone and only Alex, Candy, and Karlon had ever guessed the truth. Even her soul mate had been clueless until he overheard her discussion with Alex.

Cassie's feet moved forward, as if walking in a dream. Frazour and the beautiful Jace walked beside her. As before, Candy and Darden followed. The rest of their group lagged behind. She could not sense where her father was in the troupe.

When she reached the door to her grandfather's meeting room, she opened it and walked in. Afton's fireball had not done any damage to the entryway. She was surprised to see her grandfather alone in the room. His face and neck were covered with blood. There was a wide crimson ring where his life force had dripped down and was absorbed in his shirt. The fact he wore white only magnified the amount of blood he had lost.

An odd sound came from Jace, reacting to the blood before him. It would have been so easy to release the vampire and have him feed, condemning Jeryl Jarlyn to the very fate he once meant Chartail to suffer. She figured her father's soul mate was somewhere behind her and may have been thinking the same.

"Is Benko among you?" her grandfather asked. His voice was weak, but she was not going to lower her guard.

"I am," her dad replied.

Her father stepped out from the crowd with Drake at his side. The vampire's quick reflexes would counter any attack her grandfather may have planned for his son. Jeryl Jarlyn did not look capable of mounting a telepathic attack against anyone.

To her surprise, her grandmother quickly made her way to stand beside her son. It seemed oddly appropriate that mother and son would confront the man who separated them.

Jeryl Jarlyn basked in the sight of the man his son became. If he recognized Elyn, he showed no sign of it. Her grandfather did not seem aware of the crowd that had entered the room and fanned out behind them. Their weapons were drawn to stop any aggressive act of the man who was about to lose his status as the Prime Ruler.

"I waited years for your return," Jeryl Jarlyn said. "If you had come home, I would have forgiven and pardoned you. Why did you stay away so long? How could you have denied me my granddaughter?"

"You know I never believed in controlling the minds of others," Benko replied. "When you started sending people to the Nightshade universe to die terrible deaths for your own gain and exiling not only criminals, but dissidents, to life off-world, I could no longer stomach being a part of your world. I just heard about the cells on the lower level and what you did to crystal telepaths who broke your laws or disagreed with your government."

"And did you find paradise, son?" her grandfather asked.

"No," Benko replied. "I lost all my friends to a world where the telepathic brain is destroyed by the pollutants in the air. You were well aware of that, though, were you not? Even if we had left Gingko Terra before Jenka Thork died, we would not have returned here. At least my friends would have lived to raise their daughters."

"And you blame me for that?" Jeryl Jarlyn asked.

"No, they followed me," Benko hung his head. "I am responsible for their deaths. If I had to do it over again, I would have found some other way to stop you that did not result in anyone else dying. But I cannot change the past." Her father slowly raised his head, narrowing his eyes, and glared at his father. "The future, on the other hand is a different story."

"Do you feel what is happening in the communal pathways?" her grandfather asked in wonder, ignoring his son's veiled threat.

"One should not feel anything emanating from the channels, but I do," Benko replied.

"Shortly after you left, I found an ancient text. Many of our legends were based upon it," Jeryl Jarlyn said. "I remember reading many of those stories to you when you were a boy. The text foresaw the return of the seeds from the Troyk universe. The first was a young woman who could read minds and blend into the background; a perfect chameleon. There were no stories about that particular woman, other than the beginning of tales about soul mates. I searched for my soul mate, but never found her."

Cassie knew Alex was the chameleon the story spoke of — the first soul mate of legend. She would have to find the text Jeryl referred to and share it with her friend - the one she always wanted to be her sister.

"The second story was of a mated female crystal telepath who could harness the power of the portal," Jeryl Jarlyn continued. "Can you guess what the third story was about?"

"The Warrior Woman," Candy answered.

"Yes," her grandfather replied. "You can imagine my surprise when Shirl and Candy came back to this world. I had my suspicions about Tarsea's Alexia, but did not know for certain until JoAnna came home, a powerful mind control telepath." The old man smiled. "It has been so many years, I have forgotten everything the prediction had to say about JoAnna. It was the fifth woman that drew most of my attention. Cassie, do you know what it said you are?"

She imagined Karlon's earlier words were playing in people's minds. It was not long before the answer bombarded the communal pathways. *The True Ruler*. Cassie remained silent.

"So, you see, my boy," Jeryl Jarlyn said, "it was your destiny to leave this world. And years later, the five women of legend would return to The Troyk universe. Only by your leaving, would the True Ruler return. It was my responsibility to shepherd the population until the True Ruler arrived and then teach her how the use the gifts given to her by The Supreme Being."

Cassie could stay silent no longer. Her grandfather was wrong. Not about who she was, but about how she should rule.

"If you believe those old fables, I guess part of what you said is true," Cassie said. "The five of us have special talents that can be interpreted to agree with the stories, but I grew up in a different world and was raised by a good man. I cannot deny the existence of the warrior link or that it opened as soon as I touched Darden."

Cassie looked around the room and continued, "Destiny shouldn't be manipulated. People should have the freedom to make their own decisions about how they are going to live and who is going to rule over them; and that's assuming, they even want a Prime or True Ruler." Cassie paused for effect. "There was a sixth woman, wasn't there?"

Her grandfather looked surprised. He had interpreted the stories he read and tailored them for his own devices. Weaker women would have succumbed to Jeryl Jarlyn's manipulation. Cassie needed to know what the sixth woman of legend was destined to be.

"I assume the sixth child was miscarried by one of Benko's followers on Gingko Terra," her grandfather informed her. "The sixth woman would suffer and be subjected to violence. She would rise from her circumstances and bring about the Golden Age of the Troyk universe. Her role otherwise would be unimportant because she bore no significant telepathic power."

"*Holy crap*," she heard Candy say in their pathway.

"You know who he is referring to," Shirl said.

Cassie pressed her lips together to suppress the smile that threatened to creep across her face. Fate was a strange bedfellow.

"Come on forward, Miss Golden Age," Cassie pushed through their closed link shared by the six women of legend. Now Chartail's presence in the pathway that opened all those years ago in the orphanage made sense.

When she extended her arm behind her, a warm soft hand took ahold of hers. Five women walked forward, while the sixth was protected in the Troyk penal colony world.

"You speak of your God-given duty to manipulate your people because of the telepathic power you have, Grandfather," Cassie said, "yet it is someone with common telepathic powers who will bring about the greatest period this dimension will ever experience. I find that rather ironic. And you were wrong about one thing. Another daughter of the Troyk universe did leave this dimension and returned. Chartail was destined to fail in her plot to assassinate you. Otherwise, she would not have left this world and suffered the atrocities in the Nightshade universe. You know, I love a happy ending. Do you know what happened to her? She ended up meeting her soul mate in the penal colony." Cassie put a hand on Chartail's shoulder. "Meet your son's soul mate, Grandfather."

Jeryl Jarlyn looked at Chartail in horror. His bloodied face became redder, if that was even possible. He placed both hands on two of the giant crystals next to him.

"No!" he screamed.

The crystals glowed and light flashed, temporarily blinding her. It was as if time stood still as the light approached them. Her grandfather had used the crystals' power to create a lethal laser beam, meant to destroy the women of legend.

Chapter 23

Cassie watched in horror as a wall of energy came toward her. She did not know how else to describe it. She could not move. A body knocked her sideways and shoved her to the floor. She quickly turned her head to see if the crystalline beams were still coming toward her and if she was out of the way. Above her head another burst of energy pushed forward to meet what her grandfather had created.

The second energy field held back the first. It looked like a portal coming into contact with another event horizon. Cassie cautiously lifted her head and peered behind her. Shirl and Starc held hands beside an open portal. Somehow, Shirl had harnessed the portal's power and sent its energy to fend off Jeryl Jarlyn's attack.

The two forces continued to push against each other and Cassie could see both were losing mass. Candy had taken her to the floor and still covered most of her body. She knew enough about the Warrior Woman's talents to stay put until Candy released her. Darden had crawled to lie beside her. He did not have the lightning fast reflexes Candy possessed.

"It is all right to get up now," she heard her father say.

Cassie looked in the direction of his voice and saw Benko kneeling over his father's body. Cassie struggled to stand and was relieved when Darden offered her his hand. With a gentle pull, she stood beside her soul mate. Together they walked toward her father and grandfather. Cassie was not sure if Jeryl Jarlyn still lived. The powerful energy surge he produced may have killed him.

Jeryl Jarlyn raised his feeble hand toward his son. Her father took it, the first physical contact the two had in over twenty years. Cassie knew this would all end with her grandfather's death, but had not faced what that truly meant. Fortunately, her grandfather was not destined to die at either of their hands. His abuse of crystals ultimately killed him. From here on out, she would have a new respect for the rocks that fed most of their telepathic powers and would take great care while handling them.

"My son," Jeryl struggled to say. Her grandfather was fading fast.

"Rest, Father," Benko said. He did not give his father false hope he would survive.

Her grandfather was hemorrhaging from his ears and nose. It was a blessing his eyes were clear, so he could see his son one more time before he died. Cassie did not rush to his side. This time belonged to Benko.

"Cassandra is the True Ruler," Jeryl said. "She can…"

Jeryl Jarlyn never finished his sentence. His lungs gasped for several more breaths and then he died, with the son he loved, holding his hand. Tears, she was uncertain her grandfather deserved rolled down her cheeks.

"JoAnna, send across the communal channels that Jeryl Jarlyn is dead," her father ordered. Benko now looked at her. "What do you want to do, Cassie?"

She had asked herself that question so many times. By now, she should have an answer, but she didn't. All evidence pointed to the fact that she was the True Ruler of this dimension. But she did not want it. She was not ready.

"Assemble the Primes that are loyal and declare yourself The Prime Ruler," Cassie told her father. "You are your father's heir, not me. Daddy, you are a folk hero in this dimension. They need you to heal the wrongs perpetrated by your father and his cronies. The True Ruler is a legendary character. Maybe one day I will be ready to rule, but it is not yet my time. I have a lot to learn and growing up to do."

Cassie had seen her father's face bear many expressions over the years. This was the first time she saw pride. He was proud of her. Her dad was kneeling next to his dead father, but rose and took her into his arms.

"You and Darden need to stay here for the time being until things stabilize," her father said. "We will start sorting everything out in the morning. Chartail, Solfa, JoAnna, Koel, and Tarsea will make up my transition team. Solfa, it will be up to you to figure out how to fix the mess my father created in The Palace's lowest level."

"What are you going to do, Daddy?" Cassie asked.

"I am going to start talking to the people," Benko said. "Not through communal channels, although there is no getting around that. Face-to-face discussions are what our people need. Mind control is a thing of the past. We have talented telepaths and need to find ways their gifts can enhance society, not limit it."

"I am happy for your victory," Drake said. "But I fear the sun will be rising soon and it is time we return to the Nightshade universe."

Benko released Cassie and made his way over to the powerful vampire. "I am again in your debt."

"And I am sure you know what my demands continue to be," Drake said. "We can once again open negotiations between our worlds."

"We are in desperate need of blood," Lorenz said. "Naturally, we will not enter the same type of agreement your father had with Yorik regarding how that blood is obtained. My soul mate Afton is dedicated to changing the way our world runs. We will be setting up more settlements, similar to my keep, where humans and vampires live in harmony. Would it be possible to get donated packets of blood? I will gladly trade them for the crystals your father so desired from our world."

"Isn't it time you left the Nightshade universe?" Shirl asked as she approached the blond vampire. "You and Afton are welcome in this world. You could even return to Earth. Anywhere must be better than that bleak dimension."

"Afton will not budge until all my brothers have mated and the Nightshade universe is a haven for human and vampire alike," Lorenz said. "Believe me, I have tried."

"Shirl," Benko said. "Return our friends to the Nightshade universe and bring Alex home from the penal colony. Tell our friends there we plan to bring them all home, but need to stabilize things here first. I imagine there are some of our freedom fighters who want to be reunited with loved ones in this world, so hurry back."

Cassie watched Shirl opened a portal and their allies entered behind her. She figured Shirl would be returning with Alex soon, but she was too eager to be alone with Darden to wait. She could catch up with her old friend tomorrow and tell her what transpired here today.

Before Cassie could escape with Darden, two Palace Guards entered the greeting room and an elderly couple followed. Cassie did not know who the couple was, but she knew they were important. The four approached Benko and had a quiet exchange.

"Cassie," her father called out, "come here before you leave."

Darden escorted her to Benko's side and she waited to be introduced to the elderly couple.

"I would like to introduce you to Prime Addum Feabigger and his wife, Sacha," her father said. "They were arrested as soon as your grandfather knew you had entered the Troyk universe. When Stellar started releasing the prisoners from below, the Prime and Sacha were set free. They are your mother's parents."

Cassie stood frozen in place, staring at her maternal grandparents. Her father never spoke of her mother and only gave cursory answers when Cassie inquired about her. Obviously, Jeryl Jarlyn feared what they might tell her, so he had her mother's parents arrested before she had a chance to meet them.

"Our daughter disappeared so many years ago," Prime Feabigger said. "We had no idea she escaped our dimension with Benko. She was barely out of school and we did not like the people she was hanging out with. Cathey, our daughter, was not a mind control telepath, but we are. After all these years, we figured she had been captured, used a false identity, and was sent to the penal world. I am embarrassed to say, we washed our hands of her so many years ago. When Prime Adholm petitioned to see his daughter in the penal world, we never bothered to explore the possibility Cathey was there."

Her grandmother stood crying, but did not say a word. Cassie was drawn to the woman. She went over and hugged her grandmother. The woman shook, she wept so violently.

"Don't cry, Grandma," Cassie said. "We will get to know each other and you can tell me all about Cathey. I have no memory of her, so I am counting on you to provide me a mental picture of who she was."

Cassie nodded to Prime Feabigger. She was not yet ready to allow another grandfather into her life, especially one who had lost his daughter without a fight. Benko would have made inquiries and fought for her, unlike the old man who stood before her. Perhaps tomorrow she would be in a more forgiving mood. Jeryl Jarlyn's body was still within a glance of where her father stood.

She applied pressure to Darden's hand, signaling she wanted to go. Right now, all she wanted was to be alone with him. Cassie silenced any pathways that she found distracting, which were all but the link she shared solely with Darden. She needed rest and her soul mate.

They left the greeting room as more people entered to meet with her father. There would be a short period of chaos while power shifted from the mind control telepathic government to her father's vision for the future. She knew she had a role to play in that transition, but not tonight. Her current plans had nothing to do with ruling people, but focused only on a single individual.

Drake's blood still surged through his system. He had never felt so alive and energized. Cassie, on the other hand looked ready to collapse from exhaustion. His needs were of little concern when it came to the well being of the precious young woman next to him.

They decided to stay in The Palace instead of heading to his apartment or the Childers's residence. The idea of a bed a couple yards away from the greeting room was too much of an opportunity to pass up.

"How does a nice hot shower sound to you?" Darden asked. She was filthy and needed to bathe before he tucked her in for the night.

"Only if you take it with me," Cassie said as she wrapped her arms around his neck. She kissed him gently and they headed for the bathroom within her quarters.

"We need to burn these clothes, baby," Darden said with a laugh. "I was beaten to a pulp, so how did your jersey end up in worse shape than mine?"

"I'm not sure," Cassie said while looking at the filthy, disheveled woman in the mirror. "At first, all I could think of was saving you and then defeating Jeryl Jarlyn, regardless of what it took. When I thought I was going to lose you, my world shattered. I never want to feel that way again. You are my everything."

He cupped her face in his hands. She was beautiful, even with her face covered with smudges of heaven knew what. When he was imprisoned, all he saw when he closed his eyes was her face. He no longer saw the ten-year-old girl, but the grown woman before him.

"Let me take care of you, baby," Darden said. "I love you so much, it hurts." He was being true to the promise he made to tell Cassie how much he loved and adored her.

Darden pulled the ruined tunic over her head. She wore a transparent bra that gave her support, but did not hide the beauty of her breasts. He knelt and pulled her leggings to the floor. When Cassie stepped out of the pool of fabric at her feet, she wore nothing but a barely visible pair of panties that matched the bra he had been admiring. Her eyes never left him as he removed his clothing. Cassie did not move or attempt to remove her undergarments. She was leaving that privilege to him.

He wrapped his arms around Cassie and unhooked her bra while his mouth captured her lips. She had the sweetest taste. A flavor uniquely hers. He had kissed a lot of girls before he met Cassie, but none ever brought him as much pleasure. His fingers hooked under the elastic band of her panties and pushed them down past her hips. The panties joined the rest of her clothing on the floor.

Together, they entered the stall. He turned on the shower and sheltered Cassie from the cold water until it heated. His lips never left hers. He could feel her fatigue, but her excitement pushed it aside. The last thing Cassie wanted was to take a relaxing shower and go to sleep. She wanted to celebrate their victory and being alive. Countless emotions travelled through their connection.

When the water temperature was just right, he shifted their positions and let the soothing stream hit her exposed back. He reached for the shampoo and clumsily poured some in his hand. He didn't want to release Cassie for a single moment. With his free hand, he lathered the lavender scented shampoo throughout her hair.

Cassie tipped her head back to rinse the soap from her tresses. Her beautiful neck was exposed and Darden ran his tongue up her carotid artery. For an instant, he wondered if Drake's blood was influencing his behavior. He immediately dismissed that thought. His desire was to drive deeply within his soul mate, not drink her blood. Nor did he need Drake's ability to put a woman in a trance and take advantage of her. He needed no supernatural powers with this woman. His woman.

There was a sponge in the shower, but he did not use it. He wanted to feel every inch of her body as he cleansed the evidence of battle from her skin. Adorable sounds of pleasure escaped her as he massaged her flesh. Her mouth sought his and Darden was more than willing to kiss her with all the passion he held for her.

He could feel how much today's activities weakened Cassie. Darden needed to towel her off and get her into bed. There he would love the woman he waited eight years to be with. So far, their love-making had been urgent and out of control. Today, he was going to savor the experience, taking her slowly and methodically. He intended to discover how to bring pleasure to his beautiful mate.

Darden wrapped Cassie in a warm towel and used a second one to clumsily dry her long hair. He lifted her onto the counter of the vanity while he tended to her. She closed her eyes as he massaged her head through the ultra-soft absorbent material. When he was satisfied he had removed most of the moisture, he tossed the wet towel aside. Gently, he ran his fingers through her hair, working out the few tangles that existed.

His hands left her head and wiped the drops of water resting on her shoulders and upper back. Her skin was silk. Where he was muscle hard, Cassie was so soft and fragile. He thought of everything they had been through today and how close they came to losing each other. He would never again lose an opportunity to love the woman the Supreme Being made specifically for him.

He lifted Cassie into his arms, allowing the towel to slip from her body and fall onto the floor. With great care, Darden placed Cassie on the bed. Someone had entered their room and turned down the sheets. In the future, he was going to have to lock the door, but tonight he was grateful for the intrusion.

"You are still wet," Cassie observed.

"I know," he replied, "but I am going to get wetter before I am done loving you. Odds are, we are going to have to take another shower before we are finished."

Cassie's lips shifted into a sexy little smile. "That sounds good to me," she said. "You realize my father will probably be staying across the hall."

Darden laughed, something he feared he would never do again during his captivity. Cassie, his brother, and their friends had rescued him and freed this realm from the mind control government. It was something he only dreamed about, like lying next to Cassie in their bed.

"Your father has Chartail sharing his bed," Darden said. "They will be making too much noise of their own to hear any cries of passion coming from this room. Your father knows what we are and can no longer keep us from being together. The damage has been done, as he may say. The power everyone feared turned out to be a unifying ability, not anything destructive. I couldn't imagine anything evil ever coming from you."

His soul mate stared into his eyes as if trying to determine what he said was true. All she had to do was reach into their channel and all his feelings would be revealed. Life was too precious to hold anything back.

He knew the moment her mind touched his and understood he was truthful because her arms and legs wrapped around his body. Cassie lifted her head and plastered her lips to his. Darden deepened the kiss, bringing her head down onto the pillow. His hands ran up and down her torso, memorizing every curve. She had lost some weight since leaving Gingko Terra and he needed to make sure she ate more so she would not lose her delicious figure. Men liked something other than boney flesh to hold on to.

As he continued to kiss Cassie, he ignored how hard he was. This was about loving Cassie, not relieving his driving need. It was about love, not sex. He owed Cassie that.

Darden released her lips and planted kisses down her chin and neck. He let them drift to her ear and ran his tongue along the outer shell. She caught her breath and moaned. The fingers of one hand tangled in his hair, holding him in place. Her delicate shivers made it obvious she enjoyed what he was doing.

"Do you like it slow, baby?" Darden whispered before he again used his tongue to caress the sensitive spot he had discovered.

When she went to grab his engorged shaft, he caught her wrist and gently held it against the mattress. If she touched him, he would lose all control. He did not want to deprive her of anything, but this time he had no choice. It was best to otherwise occupy her mind.

He let his hand drift to her glistening folds, already wet and prepared for him. First one finger entered her, then another. Like what his tongue was doing to her ear, his fingers moved slowly within her. Brushing by, but not touching her clit. He wanted to build a slow fire within her.

He brought his lips back to hers, wanting to taste her again. When Darden was held prisoner, he could almost taste her when he dreamt of Cassie. Now he could not get his fill of the unique flavor that was his soul mate's alone.

"I want you inside me," Cassie cried as his fingers quickened the pace.

She would have to wait a little longer, as he still had yet to reacquaint himself with her delectable breasts. Cassie wrapped her free arm around his neck when he attempted to move his head to her chest. His soul mate had other ideas. He had to rethink his strategy.

Darden removed his fingers and place the crest of his staff against her feminine core. Instead of entering her with a powerful thrust, he gently broached her glistening folds in a slow, graceful entry. He released her hand and lifted his head a couple of inches above her face. Cassie did nothing to stop him and their eyes met. For once, he wanted to watch her expressions as he inched into her core.

Her breathing changed slightly, as she stretched to accommodate his size. Sweat began to accumulate on her nose and he lowered his head to lick the moisture from her skin. Cassie brought up her legs to wrap around his hips, bringing him deeper inside her. Her muscles contracted around him and he ground his teeth to keep from shouting out with joy. It felt so damn good!

Now that he was fully seated inside her, Darden withdrew and drove back into her core. With each withdrawal and re-entry, he increased the speed of his thrusts. Cassie met his rhythm with each change in his tempo. They made beautiful music together.

He knew she was on the edge of an orgasm. This time he was not going to deny either of them the rapture possible when soul mates came together. He entered her mind through their telepathic channel so he could feel her climax both physically and telepathically. Her breathing now matched his own. They had come together to be one. Darden needed to hold on a little longer, waiting for her to fracture.

When Cassie cried out her passion, Darden released his seed in her body. Holding her closely, he imagined a child who resembled Cassie. Today they had secured the future for their children and generations to come. There was still so much to do, but right now they would rejoice in each other. He was not ready to lose his mate to the demands of the Troyk people.

Chapter 24

It had been two weeks since her grandfather's death. She and Darden had conceded to Benko and Chartail's request to stay in The Palace with them. Since Chartail was the sixth woman of legend, Cassie felt she needed to make a real effort to get to know Chartail as a person and stop dwelling on the fact she was sleeping with her father.

They redecorated the greeting room with warm colors and now dubbed it The Palace's Common Room. Leenea was called upon to help it resemble the room in their home where family and friends gathered. They intended to do their best to turn the fourth floor into a home. A place fit to raise their children and have intimate celebrations among their extended family.

Benko's first act as Prime Ruler was to call for new elections. The Prime Council would now be elected without any of the mind control telepaths influencing people's decisions. Although a new crop of candidates came forward, a number of Prime Representatives who were mind control telepaths ran for office. They believed they could work with a transitional government without using their powers to influence others. Benko placed himself on the ballot to give the Troyk people the freedom to choose another leader. Her father would run unopposed.

The six women of legend gathered in The Palace's Common Room to plan the first official royal ball during Benko's reign. Mated couples started coming out of the woodwork after the announcement admitting soul mates were real. Their soul mates were present, figuring it was their duty to make sure the male participants of the ball were represented.

"Oh my God!" Alex exclaimed. "The baby just kicked."

Tarsea moved to kneel by his soul mate and placed his hand on her abdomen. He closed his eyes and concentrated on feeling his daughter move within Alex's womb. Cassie could not wait until Darden did the same when her time finally came. When she glanced at Darden, Cassie noted he was staring at her. She wondered if he had the same thought while watching the two.

"It's your imagination," Candy said. "The earliest the book said you could feel the baby move is thirteen weeks."

Candy had Darden go back to Gingko Terra and bring back every baby book he could get his hands on as soon as she found out she was pregnant, too. The two Childers brothers sure proved to be virile. Since Darden was mated to a mind control telepath, he no longer got headaches when he traveled to Gingko Terra. He continued to make trips to her former world to gather as much of the gingko biloba herb as possible and pick up items she and the girls could not find in the Troyk universe.

"I was the first to come through the portal," Alex said. "It must have been at least thirteen weeks since I've been with Tarsea."

"Nope," Candy replied. "Shirl arrived shortly after you disappeared, while for me it was two weeks. I've lost track of time, but it has not been three months, Alex."

"Actually," Cassie interceded, "as of tomorrow, it has been twelve weeks since Alex was dragged through the portal. And who knows what a telepathic child is capable of doing. Star has already made her presence known through the feelings she pushes to Alex. I think we should use these books as more of a guideline, not as absolute fact in some cases."

"I cannot believe all our lives changed in such a short period of time," Shirl said. As usual, Starc was by her side.

The crystal telepath's mother's amethyst was once again around her neck. Cassie knew how much that stone meant to Shirl, so she had searched Jeryl Jarlyn's office for the necklace after his death. She would never forget the look of pure joy in Shirl's eyes when it was returned to her. Shirl also wore a number of crystals; the birthday presents Cassie had given her over the years.

Shirl had taken many of the crystals that were housed in this room. The rest of her grandfather's collection was moved to Crystal Telepathic Headquarters. Both Cassie and Benko wanted them out of their home.

"Koel and I are going to visit my father in Gingko Terra after the ball," JoAnna said.

"I miss watching the thunderstorms coming in across the Gulf of Mexico," Koel said. "Since Darden can now come and go without adverse effects, Cassie, we would love you both to join us."

Cassie was sad that Shirl, Candy, and Alex could not return to Earth without suffering severe headaches the polluted air caused. They left no ties in that world. Until they entered the Troyk universe, they only had each other. Now they had soul mates and a world to help heal.

"One day Darden and I will join you," Cassie said. "There is too much to do here for the time being."

Cassie met with groups daily, trying to bring people together. She was going to prove her grandfather wrong. It would be possible to get things done without sacrificing other important programs.

"I would love to see Benko's home in Scottsdale," Chartail said. "We will need some time to relax and recharge when things have stabilized."

"What plans do you have to bring about the Troyk Universe's Golden Age, Chartail?" Tolfer asked. "If you need any assistance or recommendations, I am happy to help."

"Thank you, Tolfer," Chartail said. "I was thinking about approaching you in regards to a pre-school curriculum focused on telepathic training for toddlers and teaching the instructors. Our children should not have to suffer as their telepathic channels open."

Chartail worked as hard in the last two weeks as she had in the Troyk penal world. Koel had set up a plan to evacuate people from the Troyk prison world. There were people throughout that world they wanted to welcome home, in addition to all the other dimensions Tarsea and other Gatherers found dissidents hiding. Tarsea organized efforts to find homes for the refugees.

The Prime Council also had to deal with the prison below The Palace and the people who were mistreated there. Although Benko had a long list of items the council had to handle, her father joined them for breakfast and dinner each day. He refused to sacrifice his family life while rebuilding the world he left twenty-two years ago.

Darden moved from the spot he stood chatting with his twin. He knelt before her and took her hand. When Cassie looked around her, all the men in the room knelt before their soul mates. She directed her attention back to Darden, knowing what was coming next.

"Will you marry me?" Darden asked her.

The same question echoed through the room, as each man asked their legendary woman the same question. She listened as each of her friends and Chartail replied they would marry their mates. Darden patiently waited for her response.

"Why don't you ask me again in our room," Cassie said as she rose. "Continue without us. Darden and I need privacy."

She could feel how nervous Darden was through their channel. Cassie did not want an audience when she accepted her mate's proposal. As soon as the door to their room was closed, Cassie removed her tunic. She would answer Darden's question when they reach their rapture together. Darden rewarded her with a smile as he started to undress. Maybe they would skip their first dinner with her family this evening, after all.

The End

'Nightshade'

NIGHTSHADE SAGA SERIES: BOOK ONE

Prologue

THE NIGHTSHADE UNIVERSE

He was older than dirt, Drake thought after the lovely blonde who stood before him asked his age. How do you explain the unexplainable? Drake's existence defied nature.

This was one of the rare occasions he wished he was something other than what he was. His kind was a blight on any world they inhabited. A mistake, never intended to exist in this or any other universe.

At the beginning of time, as worlds fractured across dimensions, a division went terribly wrong. A sentient energy was forged rather than coming to life organically. The oddity traveled between worlds, leaving holes of negative matter in its wake. These frequency pathways between universes were never intended to exist.

As the energy mass traveled, it drew on the life-force of living particles. When it came across man, it claimed its first victim as a shell to occupy.

After settling into the primitive brain and physiology, it evolved from draining a being's life-force to drinking the fluid carrying the elements needed to regenerate the fragile biological cells, allowing the body to physically continue.

Thus, the first vampire came to be.

Drake had been one of the first men the vampire converted. For eons Drake traveled with this creature, living off the blood of others. Over time they converted worthy victims to join their family. Since women had the ability to reproduce, they only changed the male of the species. As a sense of ennui set in, more of the sacrificed were changed into vampires. The newly made helped to relieve the boredom of immortality.

The vampires grew weary of being intergalactic nomads. Eventually they settled in the Nightshade universe. Satisfied within their own world, the knowledge to manipulate matter to travel between universes was lost. Thus, only the original retained the ability.

There had been so many world divisions since his making, Drake had no idea which world had been his birthplace. It was best not to think along those lines. The ones he left behind had long been in their graves. Their progeny would no longer have known he ever existed. His life was now tied to his creator. The entity seemed content to stay in the Nightshade universe, while Drake had nowhere else to go.

The numerous portals leading to the Nightshade universe provided enough unfortunate beings pulled into their world to offer ample sustenance. Blood was plentiful in those early days. The maker was comfortable living off the unlimited supply of blood, until a woman came through one of the portals and life as they knew it changed.

She had a type of power over his creator Drake had never witnessed before. Her presence seemed to relieve the constant hunger the entity suffered. The master referred to her as his soul mate.

Through their bonding, the master thought he would transform into whatever nature had originally planned. They would venture off together, sometimes disappearing for weeks. Finally, one day the master left through a portal with the woman, never to be seen or heard from again.

After his departure, various legends related to their destined pairing began to be told. Over time, most vampires chose to ignore and ultimately forgot those stories. However, in Drake's darkest times, the thought of one day finding his own soul mate made him persevere.

Over several millennia the numerous portals started to close, until only three were active in the Nightshade universe. The vampire population had become so large, and the blood sources so scarce, most were shadows of what they once were.

Now blood frenzied creatures, they slowly wasted away. No amount of blood could regenerate those beings back into what they once were. Only the vampires who had been created by the master, had been spared the horrible thirst. Their bodies were as they were when they were first transformed. Drake held on to what little humanity he had left, waiting for his soul mate to become reality. Through her, Drake could finally transform from the parasite he was.

The woman in front of him was someone else's soul mate. She had the ability to navigate portals using her telepathic abilities and a crystal. The woman, Shirl, had entered their world and was now being held captive. Drake took the opportunity to offer his protection, capitalizing on the opportunity to spend time with the beauty. He had abused his role as a guest within the Venture Hive, to possess the woman for whatever time he could have with her.

Drake manipulated the telepathic bond that tied Shirl to her soul mate. Until he was forced to give her up, he would hold on to her with every fiber of his being. She was as close as he had ever come to finding his own soul mate.

What little happiness he currently had would be cut short when the daughter of the Venture Hive's master was exchanged for Shirl. Everything would be lost if Afton returned to the Nightshade universe.

Enjoy the first chapter of the YA Sci-fi adventure

'Selected'

ZARATAN TRILOGY: BOOK ONE

THE INVASION

Chapter 1

Barrow, Alaska was gone in a blink of an eye. The small town north of the Arctic Circle had disappeared. Although there was no rubble or nuclear fallout, the United States pointed their finger at the Russians. When the same thing happened to an isolated settlement in Siberia, both governments looked to the heavens.

With the world in turmoil, everything in Kara Howard's life turned upside down. She had thought her parents invincible. For the first time in her life, she saw fear in their eyes. They became engrossed in their respective jobs as a means to replace abject fear with a more familiar anxiety. When home together, the family was glued to the television, expecting all their questions to be answered. Cable and network news filled their programming by reporting the same stories, but with slightly different slants to keep their viewership.

She and her brother, Kyle, attended school as usual, but their classrooms were half full. Parents were removing their children to spend what little time they had left together. Classes were combined since many of the teachers did not report to work. Everyone tried to create a sense of normalcy in a world on the brink of unknown destruction. They failed miserably.

When a third city was destroyed in China, a satellite captured a beam of light coming from deep space. Its origin was unknown, but it was proof Earth was being invaded by aliens. People around Kara were so wrapped up in their own uncertain fates, they did not mourn the Chinese citizens who no longer existed.

A week had come and gone since the attack on Barrow. As far as she knew, the aliens had not contacted any government. Kara joined her father on the couch, his gaze never leaving the television screen. Father and daughter would spend another night sitting together, while he surfed every news channel in search of some explanation for the alien's actions.

He wrapped his arm around Kara. "How are you holding up, baby?" She was the youngest and fourteen, but her father still used the endearment. There was comfort in the name and the way he said it.

"I'm scared, Daddy. Why haven't they told us what they want?" Kara thought it was silly to keep a brave front at this point. The world was panicking, so why shouldn't she?

"I wish I knew."

It must have cost her father a lot to admit not being able to answer her question. She had always gone to him for explanations when she could not find answers on her own. Her father had always been the one she ran to and confided in. There was nothing her father did not know until this point. Regardless, he was still her hero.

They sat in silence as, channel after channel, none of the news anchors could answer her simple question. Heads of state addressed their nations with no concrete explanation given. Radio signals were broadcast into space so the aggressors would know we were aware of their presence and what they had done.

Her mother returned home from work each evening, then locked herself in her bedroom and cried. Kara could not understand how she functioned at work only to return to her family an emotional wreck. Shouldn't she make more of an effort to support her family, rather than the strangers at work? Her father often tried to lure her out of their room, but all he ended up doing was starting an argument. As far as Kara was concerned, her mother should have stayed at work.

Kyle, unable to handle the friction at home, stayed out with his friends most of the time. She had no idea what they did when they were together and Kara figured she didn't want to know. What good were rules and regulations at this point?

On the tenth day, a message was broadcast to the citizens of Earth. Kara was home watching television when the message came through. She had stopped attending school. It seemed senseless to show up for class when only a handful of students and teachers were present. Her parents didn't seem to care either way.

The aliens had hijacked the world's communication networks to share their message with Earth's population. A man with a slight violet tint to his skin appeared. In the background were symbols Kara did not recognize. The set looked odd, like they may be three dimensional, but her flat television did not adequately display the alien cyphers.

One of the images resembled a bolt of lightning on a purple background. The other contained various stripes crossing what appeared to be a planet or a moon. Earth's technology did not seem to adequately handle the telecast. The being stared into the camera and Kara leaned forward in her chair to get closer to the screen.

He appeared to be human, except for his light purple skin. The alien had light brown hair and the camera was too far away to make out the color of his eyes. Even his ears appeared normal.

When he first spoke, all she heard was gibberish; and Kara felt stupid that she had expected him to speak English. A translation finally came through in a tinny monotone, a computer obviously translating his words to the innumerable languages of the Earth's diverse population.

Kara was alone when she learned her possible fate. The visitors wanted human children between the ages of twelve and fifteen. Sixteen-year-old Kyle was safe.

In two days, every child who met the age requirement was required to report to their schools. Children who were home schooled were to attend their local public school. For every child not in attendance, the city they lived in would be destroyed. The aliens had chosen isolated towns to demonstrate their power. This time, they would destroy a city regardless of its population.

She lived in a suburb of Chicago. Just one absent child would dictate the fate of the whole city and the aliens had already proven what they were capable of doing.

Kara's stomach roiled with the news. She ran to the bathroom and threw up the lunch she had eaten an hour earlier. Her hands shook as she turned on the water to brush her teeth. The child that stared back at her from the mirror was white as a ghost.

She fell to the bathroom rug. Curled up like a baby, she cried until she had no tears left. It was hours later when her father finally found her.

Kara awoke the next morning to a deserted house. It was possibly her last day on Earth and she had been abandoned. Tired of feeling sorry for herself, Kara decided to spend the day at her favorite place.

She pulled her bicycle from the garage and peddled to the beach. Rather than taking the steep driveway down to the water, Kara parked her bike in the south parking lot and walked down to the beach. It was a cold and windy day, so she was surprised she was not the only person to seek refuge on the shores of Lake Michigan. The sand was crowded with families spending what little time they had left with their young teenagers.

A feeling of isolation engulfed Kara. She took off her shoes and walked along the shoreline. The water was frigid, but that did not hinder the feeling of peace spreading through her soul. It was why she came here. The beach always made her feel better. Kara wondered, *'If I am one of the selected, will the distant planet have a similar place?'*

She looked up, gazing at the bright sun. There was not a cloud in the sky. No large spaceship was hovering over Chicago like in *Independence Day.* Although she searched the heavens, there was no evidence of the alien presence everyone knew was lurking overhead.

The waves roared to shore. Even Lake Michigan echoed the turmoil of the world's population. Kara sat just past where the water broke onto the flat sandy beach. She closed her eyes and let the sound embrace her. Kara was making a memory. Wherever fate led her, she could always return here in her mind.

"Kara?" A familiar voice broke her concentration.

She turned to see Matt Sparks standing beside her. Normally, she would have been thrilled to see the boy she had a crush on for as long as she could remember. Today, he was just a reminder of all she had to lose.

Matt lived two doors down. He was the blond haired, blue eyed boy of every girl's dream. He was tall and lean, and not too skinny like a lot of boys his age. Kara went to the JV football games to support her neighbor, who was the team's quarterback.

"Hi, Matt," Kara said.

He sat beside her. Together they watched the waves rhythmically pound the sand before their feet. She wondered what was going through Matt's mind. He was fifteen and shared her uncertain fate.

"Are you nervous about tomorrow?" Matt asked. His voice had an unusual tremor to it.

Perhaps he was seeking comfort. Kara knew his parents were going through a bitter divorce. The Sparks' public verbal sparring matches were legendary on the block. Matt was a pawn in his parents' legal battle. He was alone today, like she was.

The odds were she would never see him again. Why not be honest? "I am scared to death I will be chosen. I've been ordinary my whole life. Knowing my luck, tomorrow I will be extra-ordinary."

Matt laughed, a glorious sound. She made another memory. He had the perfect smile and her heart skipped a beat. Matt was not hers to lose, but she felt the loss just the same.

"Special K," Matt said, "wherever you are or whatever you do, it will be special." She loved the name he dubbed her when she was five. "Our parents really suck!"

It was her turn to laugh and she did so until tears ran down her face. The Fates had gifted her with a perfect day after all. She leaned back on her elbows and tilted her head back, her long brown hair pooling onto the sandy beach. The sun's warmth beat on her face, further enhancing her uplifted mood.

"A part of me *wants* to be selected," Matt admitted. "The Earth is so limiting now we know space travel is possible. We will always live in fear of them returning. There has been no discussion about sharing technology. They are here to take, not give."

Kara turned her head to look at Matt. She had not thought of the benefits of being taken, only the disadvantages. Would life on Earth for those left behind go back to normal when the aliens departed?

"I haven't looked at it that way," Kara said. "My thoughts were limited to being forced to leave my friends and family. They destroyed three towns and murdered thousands of people."

"Whose side do you want to be on, Kara?" Matt asked. "How many millions have died in our wars, were victims of genocide, or died from starvation? The way I look at it, they could have shown their strength choosing to destroy Mexico City, Tokyo, or Mumbai."

Kara sighed and fell back on the sand. The sun heated the pulverized shells, their warmth felt great against her back. This discussion was getting too serious. She wanted to laugh with Matt, not dwell on their bleak reality.

He lay next to her. How she wished he would take her hand. Their fates would be sealed tomorrow. Would she ever lie on the shores of Lake Michigan again?

About the Author

When Evelyn Lederman retired from her career as an insurance executive, she cheerfully anticipated the freedom to finally spend as much time reading as she'd always wanted. The twist in her story came when as-yet unwritten characters started cropping up in her thoughts, asking her to tell their stories. Now, she spends her days in Florida on the beach… with her laptop.

She writes adult paranormal romance The Worlds Apart and Nightshade Saga series. In addition, Evelyn also has the first of her Young Adult series, 'Selected', also published. It is the first book in the Zaratan Trilogy series.

Contact her at evelynlauthor@gmail.com and visit her website at www.EvelynLederman.com